Thugs Cry

Lock Down Publications
Presents
Thugs Cry
A Novel by *CA$H*

Thugs Cry

Lock Down Publications
P.O. Box 1482
Pine Lake, Ga 30072-1482

Copyright 2012 by CA$H Thugs Cry

First Edition 2012
Printed in the United States of America

This is a work of fiction. Names, characters, places, and incidents either are products of the author's imagination or are used fictitiously. Any similarity to actual events or locales or persons, living or dead, is entirely coincidental.

Lock Down Publications
Email: ldp.cash@gmail.com
Facebook: Cassius Alexander
Like our page on Facebook: Lock Down Publications @
www.facebook.com/lockdownpublications.ldp
Amazon: http://www.amazon.com/Ca$h
Cover design and layout by: **SoSo**
Book interior design by: **Shawn Walker**
Edited by: **Shawn Walker**

Acknowledgments

As always, I must acknowledge my mother whose love never buckles no matter the trials or tribulations. Ma, you epitomize love.

To my sisters, brothers, nieces and nephews, and all other family, our blood is a mighty one.

A special shout out goes to the following: My niece Wanda, thanx for being my conduit to many things. I can't ever quantify how much you have helped me. I love you.

Lil sis, Lisa Williams Locklear, I am very proud of your accomplishments. Who would have thought that your little bitty self would become principal of a school? Of course, I would have because I always knew that you would be whatever you designed for yourself. Love you.

Ebony, keep elevating the bar for the family.

To all the women who have passed through my life for a reason or a season during my long incarceration, which is now in its 22nd year, at times I could not appreciate you because it can be all about survival in here. If I've left a bad taste in any of your mouths I apologize. If you left a bad taste in mine I probably deserved it.

To all my children, my love is forever.

To Fred, the son who found me after twenty years, I can't even express how it feels to have you in my life. Love you man. Last but neva least, I acknowledge all of my label mates at Wahida Clark Publishing. This is an independent joint but I have not abandoned the team. A special holla for Nene Capri, author of that heat titled *The Pussy Trap*. Keep trappin, ma'am. To my typist, Ms. Tammi Eggleston, my cover designer, SoSo, my editor, Tobias A. Fox, my loyal home girl, the West Coast Diva and fine author, Aleta Williams, thank you for holding a brother down.

To all my fans and close supporters, my success is yours. If you are new to my work, be sure to check out my other novels: ***Trust No Man, Trust No Man 2: Disloyalty is Unforgivable,***

Trust No Man 3: Like Father, Like Son, Bonded by Blood, Shorty Got A Thug, A Dirty South Love, Trust No Bitch, Trust No Bitch 2: Deadly Silence, Trust No Bitch 3: Deadly Alliance, Til My Caskets Drops, and the sequel to this book, Thugs Cry 2.

Ca$h

Prelude

Niggaz think they know but they don't. They see the money, cars jewels, and the baddass hos, and they conclude that this gangsta shit is sweet. But they don't see all of the other shit that a *G* has to endure as he rises from peon to Don status. They don't realize he suffers as much pain as he dishes out. They only see the hood fame and the fortune. The platinum smile.

Well, let me tell y'all some grown man shit. You ready? Here it is: Thugs Cry!

Let the saga begin...

Raheem

Me and my dude, CJ, started out at the bottom like most niggaz that fuck with the game. We had the typical ambition, which was to clock enough duckets to make it out of the hood, nah mean? Little Bricks, a housing project in Newark, New Jersey, is where we were born, bred, and bled. We both wanted out of Little Bricks badder than a muhfucka. Not just for ourselves but for our fams as well.

CJ was more gully than me, but we both would let them thangs pop off. I was just a nigga that liked academics, got my high school diploma, and wanted a college degree. But don't be fooled by my scholastics prowess. I was on that street shit hard, too.

The streets is like a shady ass chick with a sick sex game. You know the ho ain't no good but you just can't walk away. That's the hood for ya? The shit is as addictive as crack. So at the end of the day, it wasn't even about getting out of the hood, the struggle was to get the hood out of us.

We both did our thing, and one thing I can say is that no matter what came at us, we never turned on each other. Love was love, even when everybody and their mama had the screw face.

7

When I went away, CJ hooked up with my girl, Tamika. But yo, I never stressed over it 'cause I knew my nigga wasn't tryna do me dirty, him and Tamika was just meant to be.

Besides, in spite of her drug addiction and all, the shorty that was really meant to be my wifey was Kayundra. 'Cause see shorty persevered. She made it from the crack house all the way to R&B diva, but then…

Anyway, I'ma let that story tell it herself. All I'm saying is that we all wanted out of Little Bricks, but it was hard as hell to get that hood shit out of us.

I'ma get back at y'all.

One.

CJ

Sup? Yeah, I'm CJ. Maybe you heard of me, maybe you haven't. Don't matter, yo. Before this story is over best believe you gon' recognize my name. I put it down with the best of 'em. Went from rocks to blocks, had The Bricks on smash, killin' everything and anybody that got in my way, or any fool who violated my peeps.

I love my fam, I love my girl, I love my dawg, and I love the streets. Fuck with any one of 'em and you could get it! Of course, Newark niggaz ain't pussy so they fucked with all of the above—and they paid the price yo. Word!

I ain't about a lot of talk, though. Just ride with me peoples, while I make it do what it do. Oh, get ya black suits and dresses ready 'cause it won't be long before you're gonna find yaself at some muhfuckaz' funeral as we go on this journey.

ONE

The first thing Cam'ron *CJ* Jeffries saw when he opened his eyes was an army of goddamn cockroaches attacking the half-eaten Checker's burger that he left on the dresser last night. The burger sat next to his Glock .40 and his roll of old dead white men.

"Damn, yo!" CJ cussed as he rolled out of bed, knocking about ten fat ass roaches across the room. The rest scattered like niggaz when the popo came around.

The only thing CJ hated more than roaches were snitches. He rested in Little Bricks with his Mom Dukes and his little brother and sister, and in the projects, the roaches were just like the residents—they refused to move out.

CJ checked his Movado and saw that it was already 9:00A.M. *Time to go get on my grind. Today is the first of the month, Mother's Day in the hood. Muhfuckaz gon' be clucking like mad, yo. Yep, I need to hit the block ASAP.*

He flipped through his bank but couldn't tell if any was missing. He knew that his Mom Dukes, who was on that shit real bad, could creep a nigga'z shirt off of his back without awakening him. Well, if she had touched him up last night, it couldn't have been for much.

CJ stepped into a pair of Roca Wear baggy jeans, pulled on a crisp white T-shirt that hung down to his knees, and slid his feet into a fresh new pair of construction Timbs. Even while grinding, he stayed looking fly. Chicks said that he looked like the football player Reggie Bush.

He hit the bathroom to handle his morning hygiene, then went back to his bedroom to get his work from his stash spot. He retrieved his work, which was a quarter bird bagged up in half oz's for certain clientele and stones for the fiends. He grabbed his strap and tucked it in his waist. Niggaz knew that CJ went hard for his so most drama avoided him. Still, Newark niggaz were the grimiest so he stayed strapped 24/7. By the age of nineteen, he had already put two niggaz in the ground.

As he headed down the hallway, he heard moans and slurping come from inside his Mom Dukes' bedroom. Because the door was cracked, he stopped and peeped inside. The fuck if his Mom Dukes wasn't on her knees giving head to a nigga named Red.

CJ's face screwed up, he warned Red about playing his mom's like that, giving her crack to suck dick and shit.

I oughta blaze this nigga right now! Thought CJ as his hand went to his waist. *Nah, I'ma just lay until I catch this fool slippin'.*

He fought back the urge to spazz out as he quietly pulled the bedroom door closed so that his little brother, Eric, and his lil' sister, Brianna, wouldn't wake up and walk up on that foul shit.

I'ma get at that ass, though, 'cause I told him 'bout handling my Mom Dukes like dat!

Out on the block, CJ tried to push his anger aside and concentrate on his grind. He had a line of fiends to serve and he had to keep one eye out for popo.

"Can I get eight for fiddy?" asked Fat Benny, a fiend who didn't lose any weight despite smoking like a chimney.

"You killin' my hustle, yo!" complained CJ, breaking him off nevertheless. "What you need, Joyce?" he asked the next customer in line.

Joyce held up the same number of fingers as the number of teeth she had in her mouth. CJ handed her two rocks and pocketed her twenty dollars.

"Thanks, baby," she said, having the nerve to try to switch her iddy biddy ass as she rushed off to go get high. All CJ could do was chuckle. Joyce's little booty was comical. She was so small he could sneeze and blow her ass all the way to Trenton.

"I need four," the next girl in line said. When CJ looked at her, she dropped her head and bounced from foot to foot 'cause she knew he recognized her from back in tha day. "Hook me up. I got you."

"You got me? What dat mean?"

"You know—whateva."

10

"Nah, ma. I'm grinding not trickin'," he checked her, shaking his head in disgust as the girl walked away cussin'. CJ couldn't believe how quick crack had broken Kayundra down. He guessed that she hadn't been smoking more than a year but already she was busted the fuck up.

Damn, my nigga, Rah, would be surprised to see how bad this ho is looking.

CJ's man, Raheem, dipped to ATL on a partial scholarship to Morehouse. Raheem and Kayundra used to kick it from kindergarten until age fifteen when Raheem and CJ got sent to juvie for dumping on some niggaz that they got into it with at the skating rink on Route 22. By the time they came home, eighteen months later, Kayundra's and Raheem's teeny love thing was over.

Back then Kayundra was thick to death. She was a cutie with mad booty, as they say. Now crack had her sweatpants sagging like a G, CJ observed just before Kayundra disappeared into the building across the street.

CJ was still buggin' off of Kayundra when his girl, Tamika, pulled up in his three-year-old black Q45 with the chrome rims. She was bumpin' Remy Ma as the whip came to a stop at the curb, the summer sun bouncing off the $4,500 paint job.

"Hey, daddy," said Tamika, getting out of the Q45 rockin' a yellow Prada tennis skirt, a white and yellow baby tee, and white Prada sandals.

The shine on her fingers, wrists, and around her neck spoke volumes about CJ's hustle. Though he was still a one bird nigga, he stayed breaking it down, flippin' it, and re-upping on the regular.

Tamika put CJ in the mind of that porn chick Pinky, phat ass and all, but Tamika was much cuter in the face.

"Wassup, ma?" CJ greeted her with a quick kiss, tasting her watermelon lip gloss.

"I need salon money," she held out her hand.

"You just got your hair done, yo."

"Uh-huh, and you just messed it up the other night, need I remind you," she said, sticking out her tongue and showing him her diamond tongue ring.

"Nah ma. I'm broke," he teased.

Tamika touched the lump in his pocket. "Tsk!" she sucked her teeth.

"Here you go, hold this," he said, handing her the strap off his waist. Now if a nigga roll up sideways, you bust that ass, a'ight?"

"Okay boo," purred Tamika, aiming the strap up and down the block, feeling like a bad girl, while CJ counted out two stacks.

CJ didn't mind lacing Tamika. He reasoned that he was the one who spoiled her in the first place. Before they hooked up, Tamika had a job and had enrolled in nursing school, but CJ deaded all of that. "That's why I grind ma, so you don't have to do shit but look beautiful for me," he'd told her.

At first Tamika wasn't feelin' that, but CJ was persuasive, and the glamorous ghetto lifestyle that he subjected her to was intoxicating. Now, less than a year later, she was a certified mall rat and a hustla'z wifey.

The twist was that Tamika used to kick it with CJ's boy Raheem. She and Rah had kicked it strong before he bounced to ATL to go to school. They had broken up before Rah went away because Tamika was too needy to do the long distance thing.

CJ kinda felt shady about hooking up with his man's ex, but Tamika was so not trippin' it.

After Tamika bounced to the mall CJ stayed out grinding until the sun fell asleep, and dusk's dark enveloped the projects. Earlier, a fiend had tried to creep CJ's stash while he was serving; CJ caught him with his hand in the hole on the side of the building where he hid his shit, and split the fool's head to the white meat.

Otherwise, today has been drama free, he thought as the hood darkened a bit more and he bopped toward home, strap down at his side, already locked and loaded just in case some fool tried to jump out at him on that ski mask bullshit.

Oh yes! Looka here! A sinister grin came across CJ's face and his pulse quickened. He could not fuckin' believe his good luck. Fuck if it wasn't that nigga Red coming toward him. CJ's mind flashed back to his Mom Dukes on her knees sucking Red's dick. The image played like a DVD stuck on replay.

"Peace, yo," Red spoke when they passed one another, but he paid no attention to the banger down by CJ's side.

"Peace," CJ quickly scanned the area to see if anyone else was in the cut where they passed through.

Seeing no potential witnesses about, he spun around. Now he was behind Red, quiet as a panther on the prowl. The sound of CJ stepping on a broken bottle caused Red to jerk his head around.

Boc! Boc! Boc!

Red's face disintegrated.

Boc! Boc! CJ squeezed off two exclamations to Red's chest before the body hit the ground.

When CJ got home, he was sweatin' like a thief about to be polygraphed.

Tamika, who was there waiting for him, met CJ in the living room and showed him the air brushed design on her French manicure. Then she went to hug him.

"Eww!!" she exclaimed, stepping back. "Why are you so sweaty?"

"I just got chased by popo." He lied.

Miss Wanda, his Mom Dukes said, "Didn't I ask yo ass not to bring no guns in my muthafuckin' house CJ?"

He followed her eyes down to his side and realized that he was still gripping heat.

Damn, I'm slippin, he thought tucking the strap in his waist.

"I love you too ma," he said, sarcastically.

"See, that's what the fuck I be talkin' about. You let what the fuck I say go in one ear and out the goddamn other. Fuck you think? You can do what the fuck you want up in this bitch?"

CJ was used to his Mom Dukes' foul mouth; the whole projects knew that Miss Wanda held the crown when it came to cussin'.

"Yo black ass gonna end up dead or in prison. Why couldn't you get out these streets and go to college like Raheem?"

"I'm in school ma," he said.

"Huh?"

"The school of hard knocks."

"I oughta slap you in yo goddamn face!" she said, throwing a dish towel at him. "Raheem got some damn sense in his head, but you..." she went on and on, comparing him to Rah.

"Now what if I compared you to Big Ma?" who was Raheem's grandmother, he asked.

"Say what?"

It would've served her right, he thought. If he had told her that even if he had wanted to go to college, she would had smoked up the tuition. But he caught his tongue; life was already giving his Mom Dukes hell, he wasn't gonna pile on more.

"Nothin' ma. Sup, lil' soldier," he touched fists with Eric, who was sitting in front of the TV in the living room, caught up in his Xbox. Eric was twelve, watching and learning.

"I'm good, nigga. Sup?"

"Where's Brianna?"

"In her room on the phone, like you ain't know."

Brianna was just nine years old, but she talked on the cell phone as if she was a teenager. CJ bought her the phone for her ninth birthday.

"Anyway," CJ's Mom Dukes said as he and Tamika headed back to his bedroom. "You and Miss Ghetto Booty should be ashamed of y'all selves, creepin' around behind your boy's back. With friends like y'all, Raheem sho' don't need no muthafuckin' enemies." She laughed then said, "Fuck if you ain't just like your trifling ass daddy."

CJ closed his bedroom door on his Mom Dukes' insults. He didn't even know who his daddy was, and didn't give a fuck.

14

He grabbed a coupla 'fits and his stash; then him and Tamika bounced. He saw the police lights flashing up the block where he had left Red slumped, so he let Tamika drive just in case popo was pulling muhfuckaz over.

"Where are we going?" she asked.

"Drive out to Elizabeth, we gon' get a room and chill for a few days ma. Just me and you."

Tamika liked the sound of that.

CJ came out of the bathroom freshly showered, wearing nothing but boxers. He fired up a blunt and sat down on the bed where Tamika sat with pillows propped up behind her. Her back was against the headboard. She changed into a pair of skin toned boy shorts and a baby tee. She was counting the last stack of trap CJ had made today.

CJ started rubbing her pretty feet.

"Mmmmm, don't start nothing you don't want to finish," she cautioned.

"Who? Me?"

"No. You," she said.

"Trust, shorty, I'ma handle mines," boasted CJ, sucking on her toes.

"You talk a lot of shit dude," Tamika teased.

"Don't I always back it up?"

"Always, baby," she purred, feeling his hand moving up her leg.

"Yo, keep it one hunnid ma, do you still got feelings for my boy?" CJ asked.

"How're you gonna ask me a question like that and rub my feet at the same time? CJ, you are so fuckin' up the mood."

"Nah, I'm serious, yo." His hand went under her shorts and he rubbed her bare pussy this time.

"Can we not talk about that? Dayum, a bitch tryna get fucked."

CJ loved when she talked gully like that. It got his dick hard as a hammer.

15

"I'm just saying, Rah supposed to be coming home for spring break, you ain't gon' see him and catch feelings all over again, are you?"

"No! And I'm about to slap the shit out of you if you don't shut the fuck up and give me some of that goodness."

"What? This?" CJ held up the blunt that was in his free hand.

"Don't play!"

CJ stopped touching her pussy, took one more pull from the blunt and then put it out in the ashtray by the bed.

"You ready for this?" he asked as he pulled out and shook all nine inches at her.

She crawled to the edge of the bed like a minx and cooed to the thick pleasure in his hand. "Hey you. Mama missed you."

Tamika took hold of CJ's half erect dick and kissed the head as she stroked it up and down with her hand. Then she took the bulbous head into the cavern of her warm mouth and slurped it like a lollipop. CJ stood on his toes and grabbed the back of her head and pushed deeper into her throat.

"Don't tease a nigga, shorty" he said, swelling to full erection when he heard Tamika making those slurping noises.

Her tongue ring slid up and down the underside of CJ's rock hard dick as she bobbed up and down on the pole. Tamika had CJ making fuck faces already and she was only warming up. She plopped the dick out of her mouth and dropped his boxers to his ankles then cupped his balls. CJ had balls like plums. Tamika licked those bad boys while stroking his dick.

"Put it back in your mouth ma," instructed CJ. His desire was instantly fulfilled.

Tamika's neck game was sick because she straight up loved to please her dude. Sometimes, when she was really into sucking CJ's dick she could have a mini orgasm just watching the effect her skills had on him. She knew that was some narcissistic shit but CJ loved it.

"You gon' cum for me Daddy?" she murmured around a mouthful of dick.

16

"Fuck—yeah," grunted CJ, feeling himself about to bust.

"C'mon, give it to me," urged Tamika. Seconds later she got what she asked for.

She swallowed the come then licked the dick clean. She removed her shorts and baby tee then laid back on the bed and spread her thighs, crooking a finger at CJ.

Ca$h

TWO

Raheem looked around his studio apartment one last time before getting ready to walk out the door. The black Italian leather couch sat in front of the 54-inch plasma, on top of a Persian rug. The rest of the apartment was dipped too. The king-sized motionless waterbed that sat back and to the left of the couch and big screen had cost five stacks alone.

The studio apartment was on Peachtree Road, a comfortable distance from Morehouse, where he went to school. Though he was a full-time student with no job, the reason Rah could afford such luxury is that he was living a double life. An A-student by day, who had just made the Dean's list, and a hustla by night.

Rah had only been in ATL nine months, yet the city was blessing him well. Soon after touching down in the Dirty South he had bumped into some New York kids that were bubbling in ATL. Whatever type of drugs a nigga wanted, those kids had it on deck, from weed and coke to X and meth. Rah wasn't tryna fuck with no coke or meth, but mad muhfuckaz at school smoked the goodness and popped X, so he fucked with the New York connect on those two. Not that he had come down South with hustlin' in the game plan but hustlin' was in his blood. Besides, tryna survive on a student's allowance and living on campus wasn't an option, it would've suffocated his swag.

Rah had intended to hustle just enough to keep his bills paid and his weight up. But he soon found out that tryna hustle a little was like telling a chick to just let him put the head of his dick in the pussy. Once a nigga'z dick got wet, he was going all the way in.

Rah grabbed the Gucci garment bag out of the closet and slung it over his shoulder. The rest of the gear he was taking back home with him while on spring break was already in the back of his Tahoe. He was locking up his $1,200 a month apartment when his next door neighbor Stephanie happened to be returning home.

"Sup, Steph?" he spoke.

"Hello, Raheem. Where are we going?" she asked, noticing the bag across his shoulder.

"I'm going up top to kick it with my peeps for spring break."

"Oh. I bet they'll be glad to see you. You're from Newark, New Jersey right?"

"None other."

"Enjoy and be safe, and tell that CJ I said hello," she giggled.

Stephanie O'Neil was a sophomore engineering student at Georgia Tech. She was one of those little rich white chicks that loved everything black, from food to music to fashion, and probably black dick too, Rah guessed, judging from that Coco-like ass of hers. White boys wasn't putting it down like that.

Steph was cool, Rah liked that they could hold a deep conversation on various subjects and learn a little something about each other's world. She loved to hear him talk about The Bricks, and she humored him with stories about her lily white upbringing in Maine. She thought that he looked like Mystikal, with his Hershey brown complexion, braids, and six-one, one hundred ninety pound build. He told her that she looked like Jessica Simpson with mad booty.

On the way to his whip, Rah saw Hakeem washing his Lexus Coupe with the factory rims.

"Good morning Raheem," Hakeem called out, sounding like a white boy trapped in black skin. Rah hated muhfuckaz like Hakeem, brothers who thought that being born black was a curse. He gave Hakeem a curt nod and kept it moving.

As soon as Rah pulled out of the apartment complex, his cell vibrated on his hip.

"Yo."

"What it do, shawdy? A nigga need some fuckin' with," said his dude DaQuan who was from ATL's notorious Zone Three. Rah supplied DaQuan with that purp and that X.

"Son, I told you I'm going back home for a minute, I'll fuck witchu when I get back."

"Oh, damn! I forgot, shawdy. A'ight, hit a nigga up when you come back shawdy."

"A'ight." Rah chuckled before ending the call. He was still getting used to being called "shorty," though ATL niggaz southern recant made it sound like "shawdy." They didn't give a fuck if you were six or sixty-six, dude or chick, they called you shawdy.

Rah thought back to when he first touched down in ATL, after he had cut into his connect Don from Brooklyn. Rah was rolling with Don and his mans and 'em to the strip club The New Nikki's.

Rah was in VIP with Don, Grip, and Flatbush. All three were New York niggaz who was putting it down in ATL. Don was the HNIC but they were all getting cake and the strippers in the club knew it. As soon as they were seated in their booth, several chicks came over to entertain them. Before long, big asses and phat coochies were poppin', and those New York boys were making it rain and poppin' bottles. Rah didn't fuck with intoxicants and his bank wasn't official enough to be trickin', so he just sat back and checked out pussy for free.

After the night was over, Grip and Flatbush left the club with two thick stripper hos, headed to the mo-mo to blow those hos backs out. Rah and Don rolled out in Don's burgundy Escalade to the Waffle House on Stewart Ave.

Inside the Waffle House, while they ate blueberry waffles, scrambled eggs, grits and beef sausages, Don dropped jewels to Rah on hustlin' in The Dirty. "You gotta keep niggaz out of ya BI 'cause these dudes play that snitch shit like it's all good, yo. And they sick with the jack game, word."

Rah was nodding his head, soaking up the wisdom.

They finished eating, chopped it up a little while longer then bounced. On the way to the whip a nigga with a mouthfull of gold spoke to Rah, "What it do shawdy?"

"My name ain't no fuckin shorty!" Rah snapped.

"Yo, chill," cautioned Don, who'd overhead his mans agitated reply even though he was talking on his cell.

21

"Whatever, shawdy," dude said in response to Rah and pushed on to his car.

As soon as Don pushed the button on his remote and unlocked the doors on the Escalade, Rah reached under the passenger seat and grabbed the burner he had put there before they went inside the strip club. He was up on Gold Teeth just as dude was opening the door of his '64 Chevy Impala.

"Yo shawdy, what da deal is?" asked Gold Teeth, throwing his hands up in a gesture that meant that he didn't want any trouble.

"Shorty" is a little kid or a bitch, I told you my name ain't no fuckin' shorty!" Rah spat. "Now break yaself, nigga!" he barked, slapping the dude with his chrome.

Dude emptied his pockets.

"Come off of that chain, too!" He was rockin' a nice Jesus piece, which he surrendered with a scowl on his face.

Rah snatched the chain out of his hand, patted his waist to make sure that he wasn't strapped, and out the corner of his eye caught Don coming up to his side, gripping his own strap.

"Run, pussy!" commanded Rah.

Dude was about to take off running in the opposite direction when Don let loose. Boc! Boc! Boc! Two up top and one to the chest, Gold Teeth's body smacked the pavement, bloodied and twisted.

As they dipped away from the scene, Don explained, "You don't sleep on these country niggaz yo. Or they'll send you back to The Bricks with a tag on ya toe. Real talk, these ATL dudes are trained to go, they nice with that gun smoke. That's why I went ahead and finished what you started. Ain't no telling, dude might've caught you with ya pants down one day, nah mean?"

"I feel you." Rah nodded his understanding.

"Now you owe me son. One of these ATL cats owe me a grip and don't wanna pay. I'ma need you to get at him. I'ma get Flatbush to point the kid out to you, he be hangin' out on Wesley Chapel, can you handle it?"

"I got you dawg," Rah said though he hadn't ever got a body. He wetted a nigga back up the way with CJ before, but the dude hadn't died. Still, Rah knew that he wasn't afraid to put in work.

"That's what's up," Don reached over to give him a pound, acting hella calm after just getting a body. "But yo, you can't spazz out on these cats for calling you 'shawdy', that's just their flava," he laughed.

Two weeks later, Rah handled his business for Don.

Recalling it now, Rah could only smirk at the way he had flipped over being called "shawdy." Since then, Don had told him, "Nigga, you the most gangsta muhfucka to ever make a goddamn Dean's list."

Rah laughed at the memory of Don's comment as he pushed Lord Tariq's CD in the deck and hit the interstate. It was going to be a long drive to Newark but the Tahoe rode lovely. He couldn't wait to see the look on his dawg CJ's face when he pulled up on him in the SUV sitting on chrome. He had left The Bricks in sneakers, now he was returning stuntin', just nine months later.

Rah had heard from his peeps that CJ and Tamika were hooked up now. Everybody and their mama felt that it was some shady shit, but Rah didn't see it that way. For one, CJ had never stepped to Tamika while her and Rah were kickin' it. Two, he had always sensed that Tamika was drawn to CJ's go-all-out swag. He also knew that CJ had mad love for him and would lay his life on the line any day to prove it. It was no sweat that CJ had not told him that Tamika was now his boo. Rah figured that CJ was the type of dude that would prefer to tell him face-to-face.

It's all love with me and my nigga, Rah thought as the Tahoe reached ninety miles per hour.

By the time he reached Newark and pulled up in front of his grandmother's, Big Ma's, building it was damn near midnight the next day. Rah got out of the Tahoe with his fitted pulled

23

down low, carrying the Gucci garment bag and a suitcase. He chirped the alarm and walked toward the front door of the building. Suddenly, he was accosted by a fiend that looked like a skeleton with big bulging eyes about to pop out of her head.

"Sup, man? I'll suck your dick for five, take you around the world for ten, I got the tightest pussy ya dick has ever been in." The fiend made her pitch as she reached out and grabbed his crotch.

Rah smacked her hand away and stared into her face horrified.

"C'mon, man, just ten fuckin' dollars and I'll fuck and suck you so good. C'mon man."

"Kayundra! What the fuck happened to you yo?" Rah shouted in disgust.

"I'm good, baby. I'm tryna make you feel good too," she replied, not recognizing him in the darkness. Rah sat down his luggage and removed his fitted. Then he grabbed her face with both hands and grilled her.

"Ma, this is *Raheem* you're talking to!"

Kayundra's eyes got even bigger as she recognized his face and his voice. Rah, the only dude that she had ever loved. She was so embarrassed; Kayundra snatched away from him and ran off.

Rah couldn't believe what he had just seen. "Not baby girl!" he uttered in total disbelief. He couldn't move, he was so distraught. The sight of Kayundra reminded him why he didn't sell crack. Even when he used to be out on the block with CJ, Rah adamantly refused to sell rocks to females. He hated to see what crack did to women because it reminded him of what it had done to his moms before she was killed.

Coming out of his trance, Rah retrieved his luggage from the ground and headed inside the building up to the sixth floor where Big Ma stayed. He heard the echo of gunshots ring out in the night and knew for certain that he was back home in The Bricks.

His was still able to use his key so he unlocked the door and let himself in.

24

"Big Ma! LaKeesha, I'm home," he called out.

Seconds later, Big Ma wobbled out of her bedroom wearing the same frazzled housecoat she had worn for years.

"My baby!" she cried, pulling Raheem into her ample bosom. Her head barely came to his chest. Rah kissed her on her cherubic cheek; he loved Big Ma to no end. His mother was Big Ma's only child. After she was killed Big Ma took Raheem and his sister, LaKeesha, in and raised them both. Raheem was eight at the time of his mother's death eleven years ago. LaKeesha was only five at the time.

"I missed you, baby!" Big Ma cried, still hugging him tightly.

"I missed you, too, beautiful," he said.

"Hey, Rah. Why y'all making so much noise? What time is it?" asked LaKeesha, coming out from her bedroom, rubbing sleep from her eyes.

Rah looked at his sixteen year old sister and his mouth hit the floor! LaKeesha's pregnant belly stuck out like a beach ball. He looked from her to Big Ma.

"I asked her not to tell you," volunteered LaKeesha.

"We didn't wanna worry you at school," Big Ma cosigned.

"Don't be disappointed. I'm good," said LaKeesha.

"Are you still in school?" Rah asked.

"I'ma go back in the fall."

Rah sighed, he had kept a close eye on LaKeesha when he was at home; had tried to protect her from the potholes of their environment. *Now look,* he thought.

He asked who is the baby's daddy.

"Dawoo," said LaKeesha.

"From down the hill?"

"Uh-huh."

"Didn't I hear something about him catching a body in New York? He up on the Island, ain't he?" Rah asked.

"Yeah," replied LaKeesha.

Rah dropped his head; disappointment choked off any response he might've had.

Ca$h

THREE

It was early Saturday and Tamika was out doing her usual weekend thing, tearing the mall up. She was inside the Prada boutique tryna find something cute to wear out tonight. Tamika and her girl Star were going to a new club that had opened in East Orange. Star was twenty-two but Tamika was only nineteen, not even old enough to get into the club because the minimum age limit was twenty-one. But bouncers and doormen never turned away a chick with an ass like hers. CJ, who was under aged too, had already promised to meet them at the club. CJ never got carded at any club, he would just slide the dude on the door some grip and bop right on in.

Tamika had on a peach colored zip-up jumpsuit, the kind that was like shorts not pants. Her smooth caramel thighs were like a very young Chaka Khan's. The zipper of the Dior jumpsuit was zipped down so that it revealed mad cleavage. Niggaz had been clocking her since she walked into the mall and bitches had been hatin'. Tamika loved both.

Not that she entertained another nigga'z holla, she was too sprung over CJ to do that. Although he wasn't a boss yet, Tamika believed that it was his destiny, and she planned to ride with him all the way. She loved his arrogance, even his flashes of jealousy. Shit, she loved everything about CJ. He was kinda sexy, kinda dangerous, kinda mean, the kinda nigga that other hos want to be all up in his face. That's why she tried to keep his face in her coochie so much that the next bitch would smell it on his breath.

Tamika found just the outfit that she was looking for; a sexy tube dress with the stomach cut out to show her flat tummy and navel ring, and a portion of her lower back. It was so short and sexy it would show all of her thighs.

Wait 'til y'all envious hos see me rockin' this! She thought as she prepared to drop down $700 for it. The Prada purse that she found to match it cost $500, and the stilettos cost another $675. CJ had only given her two stacks so that ended her shopping for the day. Tamika wasn't mad, she was gonna be too damn cute tonight.

As she left out of the boutique her cell chirped, but both hands were full so she let the call go to voice mail until she got to the food court and sat down.

She checked the voice mail, heard CJ talking shit, and then called him back.

"Sup?"

"Hey, boo."

"Fuck you ain't answer your phone?"

"Because my arms were loaded with bags."

"Don't let me find out!"

"The only thing you're going to find out is that you got me sprung."

"You done shopping?"

"I'm out of money," she sang.

"Don't trip it, ma. I'ma bless you real well in a coupla weeks. You know I love to see you looking like a diva."

"I am a diva, thank you."

"Fa sho yo. Anyway, how did you get to the mall? You need me to come swoop you up?"

"Nope, I borrowed my mother's car."

"A'ight."

"Where you at?" asked Tamika.

"Me and Rah kickin' it. He came home late last night."

"Oh. Well, did you tell him?"

"Tell him what?"

"Duh. About us."

"Yeah, it's all gravy. You wanna come hang out with us?" offered CJ.

"I don't think so. And y'all niggaz better not be discussing me, comparing no damn notes. I'm serious CJ. Don't make me catch a case," said Tamika as she turned her nose up at some fool that had just walked by tryna holla with a *psst!*

Thugs Cry

"Hold on, CJ" she said 'cause ol' boy had the nerve to stop and *"psst!"* her again. "Excuse me, but I'm tryna talk to my man. You're being very rude."

"Fuck your man, shorty. He can't do what I'll do." He stuck out his tongue and made it move like an S.

"Eww!" Tamika shrieked and the fool pushed on. "Okay baby, I'm back."

"Yo, who da fuck was that?"

"Nobody, just some clown ass nigga."

Yo, Mika, keep talking to that nigga 'til I get there. I'ma smash that pussy!" CJ spazzed.

"He's already gone," said Tamika, laughing.

"Nigga better be out," said CJ, calming down. "Anyway, I'ma meet you at the club tonight. Be looking good for me. Okay, ma?"

"I do that 24/7, 365, don't I?"

"Fa sho."

"CJ, if you get to the club before I do, don't let me walk in and catch no trick all up in your face or I swear, I'm going to jail tonight."

"Come on, ma. Go 'head with all that."

"Okay, you and Rah bet not get into any trouble. Muah!"

CJ, who was riding shotgun in Rah's Tahoe, looked over at his man. Rah had a smirk on his face as he hit Central Avenue headed to Micky D's.

"What yo?" asked CJ, firing up a blunt of some kush that Rah had brought back home with him for CJ to sample.

"Yo, you and Tamika made for each other. Word, son." He touched fist with his brotha from anotha.

"Yeah, fam, baby girl is my heartbeat. Like I said earlier, because of what y'all had, if it was just a fuck thing I never would've got at her. But yo, shorty all up in here." CJ tapped his chest with his fist.

"I wish y'all well, fam. That's on everything."

"Yo, you gotta send me like ten pounds of this shit! This that fiyah, sho nuff!" Exclaimed CJ looking at the blunt. "Ay yo, I still can't believe how you putting it down in ATL. You come back pushin' this fly joint, pockets heavy. Dayum, Georgia must be a Peach fa real."

"It's poppin', but a hustla can make it do what it do, wherever."

"That's what's up," said CJ as they pulled into Mickey D's drive-thru and ordered up a load of shit.

While they waited for their huge order to be filled, Rah told CJ about the night he had spazzed on dude for calling him 'shawdy'. CJ was cracking up.

Leaning against the door and grabbing his nuts, he said, "Hol' up! You jacked him for his chain?"

"Yep, and threw that shit in a dumpster."

"You wild as fuck, yo! But did the right thing to toss that joint. Yo, what part of Brooklyn that nigga Don from?"

"Marcy."

"Word?"

"Yep, and son is official. I fucks with him hard. But I'm still doing my thing in school, gon' probably major in journalism. Get that degree and come back and elevate the hood," said Rah as their food was being passed to him through the window.

Nigga, The Bricks gon' be The Bricks long after our black asses are gone. Ain't no elevating shit," said CJ, dipping two McNuggets into some hot mustard sauce as Rah drove off, biting into a chicken sandwich.

"Yeah, you probably right," Rah conceded.

"You know I'm right. Niggaz ain't tryna hear that cornball shit, we after the money, hos, and shine. Nah mean?"

Rah turned on the radio and some station was playing an old school jam by Minnie Riperton. CJ didn't even know who Minnie was, but Rah did because Big Ma had her old albums.

The song on the radio was one of Rah's favorites because Kayundra had sang it in a talent show in the ninth grade and won

First Prize, dedicating the song to him before she had brought the gymnasium down. Teachers said afterwards that only a few singers in the world could hit Minnie Riperton's notes, and Kayundra was one of them.

"Yo, nigga, don't fuck wit' dat," Rah slapped CJ's hand away from the dial when he tried to change station. Minnie was taking Rah down memory lane.

When the song went off, Rah was quiet.

CJ turned on the CD player and Young Jeezy was rapping about coming up from the bottom to the top. Rah was feelin' Jeezy, but hearing Minnie Riperton's song had him stuck.

"Man, what da fuck happened to Kayundra?" he asked CJ then replayed last night's scare for him.

"Baby girl on that glass dick yo. Ain't no help for her; she's gone."

"In less than a year?"

"Shit, shorty was clucking on the low before you left."

"Word?"

"Like Pookie in *New Jack City*," CJ cracked.

"That shit ain't funny yo. Baby girl used to be my boo. Dayum, I hate to see her fucked up like that," sighed Rah.

"Look!" CJ pointed out the window toward the sky. Rah tried to look, thinking a helicopter might be hovering.

"Up in the sky! It's a bird—it's a plane! No! Coming to a crackhead's rescue…it's Supa Nigga!" CJ screamed.

Rah spit food all over the windshield. They were both laughing so hard, Rah had to pull over before he fucked around and wrecked. CJ had tears running down his face.

"You stupid, yo," said Rah after he stopped laughing.

"On the real though, I know you son, you used to love shorty. Watch, you gonna try to save her."

Tamika was cussin' Star ass out for calling at the last minute with some shit that her car wouldn't start. She told Star that she needed to upgrade.

"Bitch, what kind of car you got?" asked Star.

"Uh," Tamika stuttered.

"Yeah, that's what I thought."

"Dayum, mama is gone for the night with her car, and I am looking too damn cute to miss the club tonight. Call one of your tricks to give us a ride," suggested Tamika.

"Them niggaz ain't acting right," sighed Star.

"Ho, how you got a name like *'Star'* and can't even get us a ride to the club? If you're busted up ass is a *star* I'm the Queen of the Nile," cracked Tamika laughing at her own joke.

"Whateva, bitch. Why can't you call CJ?"

"Because he hates it when I call him with last minute shit."

"So?"

"So, I'm not calling him."

"A'ight, we can catch a cab"

"*A cab?* Gurrrl, I am not catching no cab to no damn club! That's tacky."

"Call it whatever you like. See ya, bitch."

Tamika quickly checked her mental Rolodex for a nigga she could play for a ride. "Malcolm," she said out loud and dialed his number.

Malcolm was an older square dude who Star used to fuck with. Star had stopped kicking it with him because his dick game was weak. She didn't care what else a nigga brought to the table, if his dick game was wack, she bounced. It was all about the orgasms with her.

After Star kicked Malcolm to the curb, he had started checking for Tamika. What made him think that she would want Star's sloppy seconds; Tamika had yet to figure out. But she hollered at Malcolm just enough to get a few dollars out of him once in a while, and a favor or two. Of course, she wasn't letting him *hit* it. CJ would snap her neck! Hell, she would snap her own fuckin' neck.

"You only call when you need a favor," complained Malcolm. But Tamika knew how to handle his weak ass.

"Neva mind." She hung up on him and then started counting to herself. "One—two—three," Her phone chirped. She answered on the second ring.

"Gimme a sec' to throw something on then I'll come through," Malcolm said.

"Okay and could you give me a little money to party with?"

"I got you."

"Thank you, boo."

"It's all good. I'ma hang out at the club with you and Star for a minute. I ain't doing shit else."

"That's cool, but CJ is rolling through later," she warned him so he wouldn't be all up her ass at the club. Malcolm feared CJ more than he feared the wrath of God.

When they finally pulled up, Tamika scanned the parking lot for CJ's whip just in case he had beaten her to the club. She relaxed when she didn't see his Q45 in the lot.

She entered the club ahead of Malcolm so that word wouldn't get back to CJ that she had fell up in there with a nigga. Some jealous bitch would love to pour salt on her.

Star was already there, seated in a booth with a jacked up ass nigga whose breath smelled like booty. She was covering her nose with her hand, like *hint hint,* as dude tried to lay down his mack, but playa was determined. Star felt like she had been rescued from a sewer when she saw Tamika walk up with Malcolm a few steps behind.

"Hey, chick." Star stood up and hugged Tamika.

"Hey, Miss Thang," said Tamika.

"Gurl, this nigga'z breath is terminal," Star whispered to the side of her face.

Tamika had to swallow fast to keep from busting out in laughter. "Don't you look cute," she lied. Star had on a halter dress that was so last year.

"You do too."

Dude felt neglected so he bounced.

"Thank God!" exhaled Star.

"I thought he was your next baby's daddy," joked Tamika as she slid into the booth.

"Puhleeze! That nigga clothes fit tighter than mine." They laughed and gave each other a high five.

"Hey, Malcolm," said Star, finally acknowledging him.

"What's good, Star?"

"You know same ol', same ol'."

"Malcolm would you go get us something to drink?" asked Tamika, batting her hazels at him.

"What would you like?"

"A strawberry daiquiri."

"Make that two, boo," Star chimed back in.

Malcolm was straight gravy.

"Have you seen CJ and Rah?" Tamika asked, looking around the crowded club. Damn, she could not see shit. *Too many niggaz up in here!*

"Nope, you know your man ain't coming without making a *grand entrance.*"

"Don't hate, ho."

"Puhleeze, bitch, ain't nobody hatin' on your little baller."

Hmmpf! Nobody but your trick ass. Ho, I know you want to do CJ, but you got too many babies' daddies for my man to fuck with you, and you're too loose with the kitty cat. Plus, I'll catch a case.

"Rah is back?" asked Star.

"Uh-huh."

"How he lookin'? Still mouthwatering?"

"I don't know how he's looking. I haven't seen him yet. CJ was rollin' with him when I talked to him earlier. I'm guessing Rah will come to the club with CJ." Anyway, he's only been gone eight or nine months. He probably looks the same."

"Delicious then," said Star.

"Bitch, you just a ho."

"Pot calling the kettle black. Hello!"

"Whateva, trick"

"CJ done told Rah the deal?" whispered Star.

"Yeah and stop whispering. You must be on some X?"

"Hell no, but I'ma be on some D tonight. Got to search the crowd for the nigga with the biggest dick print. But dayum, all these niggaz saggin'!"

"Hey, cuz," waved Tamika's cousin Nee Nee, walking by in a banging Versace pant suit.

"Hey!" Tamika waved back. "I can't stand that jump off," she muttered to Star.

"Oooh, bitch, ya man and his boy just walked in the door," said Star. She stood up and started waving like she was flagging down a cab. "CJ! Rah! Over here!"

"Bitch, will you sit your bama ass down," Tamika laughed as she watched her boo and her ex get intercepted by two thirsty looking hos.

"I'm going to jail," she said, giving CJ two minutes before she was going to show her ass. CJ beat the clock by a few seconds

Rah and CJ walked up.

"Sup, ma? How long y'all been here?" asked CJ. He bent down and tongued Tamika.

"Mmmm! Not long."

"What it do, Star? Who babysittin' those bad ass kids of yours? Let me find out you put them to bed then dipped off to the club."

"Hey, CJ," she spoke back. She didn't find his joke funny, but she didn't try to clown him back. CJ could flip like a light switch. "What's good Raheem? How do you like college in ATL?" she asked in a much sweeter tone then the one she spoke to CJ.

Tamika rolled her eyes.

"I'm lovin' it, yo. How you ma?" Rah replied.

"I'm good, need a thug in my life though."

Not this one, Rah thought.

"I hear dat," he said. "Tamika, how you?"

Tamika responded by lifting her hand an inch off the table and wiggling her fingers as a gesture of "hello."

Then she looked up and saw Malcolm returning with their drinks. She kicked Star's foot.

"I'll be right back," Star said suddenly and slid out of the booth.

"Ain't that one of ya girl's tricks?" CJ nodded in the direction of Malcolm.

"Yep, who ain't," replied Tamika wearing a poker face.

CJ sat down and put his arm around Tamika, while Rah slid in on the other side. Tamika felt a little funny having her nigga on one side and her ex on the other. But this was her chance to really show CJ that it was all about him. She turned his chin toward her and licked his face, real seductively. Then she tongued him down.

Rah wasn't stressing. He just kicked back like a real playa and bopped his head to the wild ass Lil Jon joint that was beating hard throughout the club. That crunk shit had reached The Bricks.

Honeys were doing their thing on the dance floor. All was needed were a coupla poles and Rah would've thought he was at a strip club. Star returned with the daiquiris for her and Tamika, having sent Malcolm home. Before long, Star was on the dance floor, backing that thang up and dropping it low.

CJ saw a few dudes that he needed to holla at, so he told Tamika he would be back in a few.

"How long?" she pouted.

"What, I'm on a time clock?"

"Just hurry back CJ, and don't be all up in no bitch's face 'cause that is *not* business. I know how y'all niggaz do."

"Fuck you talking 'bout, yo?"

"I'm just warning you boo. My mama ain't raise no fool. You're fine, a money getter, and bitches can see that you don't mind splurging on ya girl. A slick bitch will try to slide you her digits or have her boy to pass them on to you. If I slip, you'll end up fuckin' her. Y'all niggaz dicks don't have a conscience."

"*Y'all niggaz?*"

"Well *yours*. Just hurry back, okay?"

36

"Whateva." He stood up after giving her a quick kiss. "Ain't no chick up in here I want but you. Stand up and let me see it twerp."

She stood up and modeled the outfit for him.

"You bangin', ma."

"Thank you, daddy," she purred.

CJ tongued her down again.

"I love you," she told him.

"I love you, too," he said. Then to Rah, "Yo, fam, I'm finna go holla at my dude, keep an eye on wifey for me."

"I got you," said Rah, who up until he heard CJ call his name had not been paying any attention to anyone but the honeys on the dance floor.

When CJ bounced, Tamika decided that now was a good time for her to visit the ladies room. She did not want to be left alone with Rah. Guilt was eating her ass up.

"Excuse me," she stood up to leave. Rah put his hand on her arm.

"Hol' up. I wanna holla at you," he said politely.

"About what?"

"Me and CJ already talked. Besides, Big Ma and LaKeesha had already—"

"Let me interrupt you, Rah. Long story short: it is what it is," said Tamika and walked off.

Rah was left wondering, *Dayum! How baby girl gon' catch a 'tude with me, like I did her dirty? If I smoked, I'd have to puff one to the sky on dat.*

He watched Tamika saunter off, her dress so short and tight it rode up her ass as she walked, and she had to hold it down. *If you walk around with your butt hangin' out, it's only a matter of time before some boy is gonna grab it,* he recalled Big Ma warning LaKeesha when she wore skimpy outfits.

"Tamika is wearing the fuck outta that dress though," Rah admitted to himself. "But yo, what's with the 'tude? Straight up, I ain't mad. Like Jigga said, *jealousy is a weak emotion.*"

Rah tossed Tamika out of his mind and was hollering at a cutie who had just pulled up at the booth.

"Hey, Raheem. How have you been?" she smiled at him.

"Yo, who you?"

"Tasha Montgomery."

"From?"

"From Mrs. Darwin's eighth grade English class," she finished for him. Rah couldn't believe his eyes. The last time he had seen Tasha Montgomery she wore braces on her teeth, thick eyeglasses, and was a tomboy with no booty. Now baby was thick in all the right places and was pleasing to the eye.

"Dayum, ma! You done got right yo," he praised.

"Thank you. Uh, are you and that girl, Kayundra, still together? I know that was a long time ago but—"

"Nah, I go to Morehouse in ATL now. I'm just home on spring break," he said.

"Oh. Well, you were always one of those intelligent thugs," she smiled.

Rah never considered himself a thug. He just made it do what it do, but he let Tasha's comment stand.

"Where you been, besides in some nigga'z dream?" he asked.

"Nice. I like that. My family moved to D.C. I'm visiting a cousin. Say, wasn't that CJ over here a minute ago?"

"Yeah, that was my guy. Sup? You tryna holla at him?" Rah asked, correctly reading the interest in her tone.

"I would like to," Tasha was saying but Rah had averted his attention to Tamika returning from the ladies room.

Tamika sashayed past a cluster of dudes holding bottles of bubbly up, tilting them down, and pouring champagne down into chick's mouths. He saw Tamika wave the offer off. Then he saw one of the dudes grab a handful of her ass as she passed by him.

"Oh shit!" Rah said just as Tamika slapped fire from ol' boy.

Bam! Dude punched Tamika dead smack in the face, knocking her on her ass!

Rah left Tasha standing there. He ran up to dude and hit him squarely with a two piece combination that dropped him to one knee. *Whop!* An uppercut put him on his back.

Crack! Somebody smashed Rah over the head with a champagne bottle. *Whop!* A punch to the jaw further dazed him.

Star screamed from the dance floor. The dude she was dancing with was from Little Bricks also; he peeped the ruckus and ran over to help Rah and Tamika. Star was now jumping up and down screaming for CJ. Once CJ ran over and saw that Rah was involved he put two niggaz on their asses instantly.

"CJ!" Tamika cried out.

CJ saw Tamika on the floor with her mouth busted and he went ballistic up in there! When the crowd saw that CJ was involved every Little Bricks nigga in the club started swinging on niggaz. The shit got ugly quickly 'cause the dudes they were into it with were from Orange Projects and those niggaz weren't pussy.

The DJ was on the mic asking niggaz to chill, but he shut the fuck up and ducked after champagne bottles started whizzing by his head.

Club security couldn't restore order. The spot quickly turned into an all-out brawl. Newark's finest were called and ran up in there thirty deep, dressed in riot gear.

Popo started snatching cats up at random, putting ghetto bracelets on them and loading them up in paddy wagons to go to jail. Niggaz with warrants on them was tryna hide, jump through windows, whatever to avoid arrest. CJ, Rah, Tamika, and Star were safely whisked outside by a bouncer who was from their hood.

Outside they watched popo load dudes and chicks into paddy wagons. Those that weren't being arrested shouted insults at the boys in blue. Tamika saw the dude that had grabbed her ass being put inside a police van.

"There that nigga go, CJ!" she pointed.

"Yo, drive my car home. I'm going to jail," said CJ, passing his car keys to his girl.

Before anyone could stop him, CJ ran over to where the dude was being put into the van handcuffed. CJ hauled back and knocked dude the fuck out!

"Bitch nigga! That's what you get for puttin' ya hands on mine," he spat and kicked the dude in the face right before the startled cops grabbed him and slammed him on the ground, face first.

"Oh hell to the muthafuckin' nah!" yelled Tamika. She tossed Star CJ's car keys and handed Star her purse, then she ran over and jumped on the cop's back who had slammed CJ on his face.

"Punk muthafucka!" she wailed, punching him in the back of his head.

He dumped Tamika over his shoulder onto the ground and cuffed her up.

"You ain't have to do the sistah like that!" yelled someone out the crowd.

"Y'all bitch ass cops stay on some Rodney King bullshit. We'll burn this bitch down!"

Rah realized that he needed to keep his head so that he wouldn't get arrested next. It took Star's pleading to keep him cool because he wanted to ride for his man.

"No Rah, we gon' have to bond them out of jail," Star pleaded.

They heard mad sirens getting closer so they decided to bounce. In the mad rush to leave before more of Newark's finest arrived, Rah lost Star, who was in CJ's whip. He figured that she would know to meet up with him in the projects.

Rah was about a mile from the crib when a black Suburban pulled close beside him at a traffic light.

"Dayum!" He wasn't strapped, he had left his bangers in ATL, not expecting to encounter any drama while home visiting.

Rah pulled off, running the red light, but the Suburban was still side by side with him. He stepped on the gas. So did the driver of the whip in pursuit.

The passenger window of the Suburban came even with Rah, and the window eased down.

Boc! Boc! Boc! Boc!

Rah's body jerked and fire exploded in his left shoulder and in his neck.

Boc! Boc!

He couldn't breathe.

His life flashed before his eyes in a blink of time.

Then he lost control of the steering wheel and the Tahoe smashed into the side of a building.

Boc!

The shooter inside the Suburban squeezed off one final round before the vehicle raced away.

Ca$h

FOUR

"A'ight. It's about to pop off in the streets! You bitch niggaz want bloodshed, I'ma show y'all not to fuck wit' mines! Y'all on some rah rah shit? I'm wit' it. Y'all blazed my man—bodies gon' drop fa dat!" CJ spewed to the walls of his bedroom while slipping on his Timbs.

Star and Tamika's mother had posted CJ's and Tamika's bails earlier that morning. CJ had just found out that Rah was in ICU, clinging to his young life.

He mashed out and went to the hospital to check on his man. Big Ma and LaKeesha were sitting in the Intensive Care Unit's waiting area. When Big Ma saw him she turned her head away in contempt. There had been a time when Big Ma treated CJ like a son, but that time had come and gone. The final straw had been when CJ hooked up with Tamika.

"It's not your fault about Rah," LaKeesha whispered. "You know how Big Ma is quick to judge."

CJ nodded.

When he was allowed in to see Rah, CJ shed a tear for his dawg. Rah's head was bandaged and swollen like a pumpkin. Tubes ran from seemingly every part of his body and plugged into machines. He was in a coma but at least he wasn't flat lined, thought CJ, pulling for Rah to come through.

"Them niggaz gonna bleed soon," he whispered into Rah's ear.

CJ had been watching and plotting for the past week. Tonight it was going down.

The rain pelted hard against his bedroom windows as he strapped up for ghetto retribution. First, he pulled on a pair of black fighter pilot pants, then a black T-shirt and a black hoodie. He stepped into a pair of black jump boots, and pulled on black leather driving gloves. Next, CJ opened the duffle bag that sat at his feet when he plopped down on the bed. He pulled out a choppa and a banana clip, and two boxes of AK-47 shells.

Tamika, CJ's Mom Dukes, and his lil' sister, Brianna, stood in the doorway watching him. CJ paid them no mind; he was methodically pushing shells into the banana clip. Once the clip was full he locked and loaded the choppa, put it inside the duffle bag and swung it over his shoulder.

"No, CJ, please don't go and do nothing crazy!" cried Tamika.

"Man, I'm not tryna hear that shit!" he snarled.

"You wanna end up in prison for life?" his Mom Dukes asked, hoping to dissuade him.

"If that's the price I gotta pay to avenge what them niggaz did to Rah—*it is what it is.*"

"Don't you care about me?" cried Tamika.

"I care about Rah, too."

"If you go out and kill someone, how is that helping Raheem? He still gon' be in ICU," Mom Dukes interjected through her tears.

"Niggaz gonna know, if they touch my dawg I'ma touch back—*hard!*"

"He shouldna jumped in the fight, he just made things worse!" said Tamika, making CJ hot. He sat down the duffle bag and grabbed her roughly by the face with two hands, pulling her face within inches of his.

"Fuck you mean? He was tryna help yo' ungrateful ass! What da fuck did Rah ever do to you? Huh?" CJ gritted then pushed her away.

Tamika fell across the bed sobbing.

"Don't you go blaming her, she can go to the club butt ass naked and that still don't give a muthafucka the right to touch her!" Mom Dukes defended Tamika.

CJ knew that his Mom Dukes was right and he hated to see his shorty crying, but there was nothing no one could say to stop him from unleashing that choppa on Orange niggaz tonight. "I hear you ma, but it ain't even about that. You and Tamika can save y'all breath, niggaz finna feel my heat. And if my nigga dies, I'ma turn Orange Projects into Iraq," he vowed, grabbing the duffle bag and heading out the bedroom.

His Mom Dukes and Brianna blocked the doorway. Tamika was hanging on to his leg, begging him not to go. CJ shook Tamika off of him and forced his way past the two human barricades. He encountered Eric in the hallway.

"Rah is good peoples yo. Can I ride with you on this?" Eric asked in a serious tone that defied his age.

"Nah, lil' souljah, sit this one out."

"A'ight, be safe, man. And come back home."

The rain continued to pour down from the night's sky. The wipers on the fiend's hooptie that CJ had rented were a little faulty, but CJ could not be deterred from his mission; he just hoped Tavaras and Nas was out grinding in the rain.

CJ had heard on the ghetto wire that Tavaras was the nigga who had dumped on Rah. Tavaras's man, Nasir, owned the Suburban that had been seen by Star following Rah from the club. CJ had peeped the cut in Orange Projects from where Tavaras and Nasir hustled.

Not much was moving in the projects due to the streaming rain, but CJ saw two or three niggaz up in the cut as he drove by. He stopped up the street and got out, choppa down at his side. With his back pressed against the building, CJ was moving in silence as he crept closer to his prey.

Now in murdering range for the choppa, and ducked down behind a car, CJ yelled to the four people he saw posted up in the cut. "Y'all niggaz know Raheem?"

"We don't know nobody! Fuck is you?" Tavaras yelled back as he watched his man, Juice, serve a female fiend.

CJ popped up like a jack-in-the-box.

"I'm my brotha'z keepa!"

The choppa spat in murderous rapidity.

There was no time for the prey to react. A slug took a whole side of the chick's face off. She dropped like a Raggedy Ann doll, twisted. Nasir went down next as a hole appeared in his chest, then a gaping hole appeared in his back when the large AK-47 shell exited his body.

That left Tavaras and another dude who had been involved in the fracas at the club a week ago. Tavaras looked down at his man, Nasir, while reaching in his waist for his strap and trying to get his legs to move. But he was temporarily paralyzed by fear.

CJ ran toward them in a crouch, squeezing off revenge from his hip.

Boc! Boc! Boc! Boc!

Tavaras caught two to the body and fell dead with his strap in his hand. The last dude, Sedric, had his strap out. He fired back at CJ while tryna run for his life. His .380 sounded like a cap gun compared to the choppa.

CJ sloshed through mud chasing him.

Nigga, you ain't gettin' away.

Boc! Boc! Boc!

End of chase.

Eric opened the door to let CJ in before he could even knock or use his key. CJ's lil' brother had been looking out of the front window repeatedly until he saw CJ come home safely.

"Sup, yo?" he asked.

"Everything's gravy," CJ assured him.

When CJ entered his bedroom and flipped on the light switch, Tamika was sitting on the edge of the bed crying softly into her hands. She looked up from his muddy boots to his sweat drenched face.

CJ looked into her puffy eyes.

"What did you do CJ?" she asked.

"Hollered at them pussies for Rah," he confessed.

"CJ, what does that mean?" she sniffled.

"It means what it *means*, now let it rest at that." CJ said forcefully. "Stop crying and be a souljah for a nigga. I'ma need you to put the choppa up for me, not at ya Mom Dukes' crib. What about ya cousins, Nee Nee or her sister, Danyelle?"

"Let's give it to Star," Tamika suggested.

"A'ight, shorty, let's roll."

46

Thugs Cry

Tamika stood up ready to do what had to be done to protect her man. Denying him wasn't an option. Her love made her willing to catch a case for him.

"Where my Mom Dukes?" CJ asked.

"Gone in the streets." They both knew what that meant.

"Is Brianna in her bedroom?"

"Yep."

CJ went into his lil' sister's room; she was in bed crying. He sat down on her bed and kissed away her tears.

"Shorty, you gotta be tough, okay?"

"Okay," she sniffled and smiled.

"Shit ain't gon' always be happy Bri. That's just keepin' it real with you. But you don't have to worry about your big bruh. I can take care of myself and all of y'all too. A'ight?"

Brianna nodded.

"One day I'ma move us all away from here. Would you like that?"

"Will I still be able to come visit my friends?" she asked.

"Yeah, pretty girl."

"Okay, we can move then."

"A'ight, gimme a kiss."

Muah!

Before bouncing, CJ gave Eric money for groceries in case their Mom Dukes stayed out getting high for a couple of days. Eric would hold the crib down and make sure Brianna went to school each day, even if he skipped school himself. The Bricks turned boys into men at an early age.

Like CJ, Eric and Brianna didn't know either of their fathers. That's why CJ stepped up and always made sure that his younger siblings were a'ight. His attitude was—*I'm the man of the house; it's always been that way. I'ma grind, slang, and flip until me and my whole fam is good. I'll lay my life on the line fa mines! Nah, ain't none of us got no pops—Mom Dukes is on drugs...but we still gon' be a'ight, I'ma see to it!*

CJ had Tamika to stash the choppa at Star's crib. Then he returned the hooptie to the fiend he'd rented it from. He dropped

47

some work on the block then him and Tamika copped a room at a motel in South Orange where they laid low for a minute.

They went to the hospital to check on Rah three days later. He was still in a light coma but doctors expected him to come out of it soon. Rah had caught a slug in the shoulder. Another bullet had ricocheted off the car door, entered through the side of his neck and lodged in his throat. He also had head injuries sustained from when his Tahoe wrecked.

CJ spoke to LaKeesha and Big Ma, who sat at the hospital with Rah for hours every day. LaKeesha spoke back, but Big Ma would not.

Big Ma looked at Tamika like she wanted to hit her upside the head with the Bible she clutched while rocking back and forth in the plastic seat outside of ICU.

"Hi, La, wassup?" said Tamika, ignoring Big Ma's undisguised animosity.

LaKeesha was tripping too. She rolled her eyes.

No this bitch didn't! Tamika thought. *They acting like I shot Rah! I'm the same bitch this hot-in-the-ass ho used to affectionately call her big sister. Now, she wanna act sideways toward me? Pregnant bitch ain't never liked me no way!*

Tamika gave LaKeesha her ass to kiss and followed CJ into ICU.

"Sup, yo? Nigga, you gotta open your eyes and prove to everybody that niggaz like us are built to last. I don't know why you tryna front, I believe you just like having muhfuckaz worried about you." CJ chuckled, talking to Rah. "Fa real, fam, I know you gon' pull through. I'm not even stressing about that. Tamika right here with me, we both praying for you kid. One." He tapped his chest.

"Hey, Rah. I just wanna tell you that I'm sorry for how I acted toward you that night. Get well, okay?" said Tamika. She bent down and planted a kiss on his cheek and a tear slid down her face; she truly felt bad and her remorse made CJ feel better because Rah was his peeps.

Four bodies means heat, so CJ continued to lay low for another week then he had to get back on his grind. The block accepted him back without change. The coupla dudes that he had hit off with some work, so that he would still have some grip coming in while he was laid low, paid him what they owed. There were whispers that CJ had wet those niggaz over in Orange Projects so nobody on the block in Little Bricks was gonna test his G. Common sense told them that they could get it too.

CJ was back in his usual spot grinding. He looked up and saw his Mom Dukes approaching.

"CJ, I need to holla at you," she said as she walked up.

"Let me handle this first!" he said, agitated because she was distracting him. He needed to really be on point because of that thing he had done. Besides, he had told her a thousand times not to come on the block looking for him.

CJ served the two fiends that were waiting to cop, while Miss Wanda waited impatiently with her arms folded across her chest.

"Sup?" asked CJ after he had handled his business.

"I need three hundred dollars to pay the utilities bill," claimed his Mom Dukes.

Before CJ could respond Kayundra walked up.

"What you need, yo?" he asked, thinking that she wanted to cop.

"Nothing. I came to ask if Raheem is getting better. I heard about what happened."

"Fuck you inquiring about my nigga for? You wanna cop or not?"

Kayundra shook her head.

"Kick rocks, then!"

"Dang, you don't have to clown me," sighed Kayundra who didn't look geeked up today.

"Bitch, you is a fuckin' clown! Push on!" barked CJ.

"Chile, he's at University Hospital if you wanna go visit him," interjected Miss Wanda.

"Thank you," said Kayundra and walked off up the block to get a ride to the hospital.

"You gon' gimme the money?" CJ's Mom Dukes asked.

"Three hundred dollars? Dayum!" he replied suspiciously.

"*Yeah, three hundred dollars!* Unless yo' ugly ass wanna be in the dark with no water to wash ya ass!"

"Nah, ma, you tryna run game. I can see it in your face."

"I am not!"

"Give me the bill, I'll have Tamika go pay it," CJ offered her a compromise.

"I don't need yo' little ghetto booty hood rat handling my muthafuckin' business for me! What, you think I can't handle it my goddamn self? Who the fuck you think has been handling it all of these fuckin' years?"

"Nah, I'm not going for it, you tryna get high. That's why you spazzin' out." CJ peeped game.

"I tell you what muthafucka! Come and get ya shit out of my goddamn house! And yo' ugly ass gold digging, dick suckin' bitch bet' not ever step foot in my shit again."

"Here, ma" said CJ, tired of hearing her go ballistic. He gave her a hundred dollars, knowing where it would go. She snatched it out of his hand and stormed away.

CJ always felt conflicted when he gave his Mom Dukes money because he knew she would spend on crack. He knew that he was helping support her habit and that bothered him. But he would rather do that than worry about her being out in the streets sucking dick for a rock. One thing he told himself that he would never do is give her some crack.

CJ watched his Mom Dukes walk up and cop from a grinder up the block. That's when he noticed a detective's car coming around the corner.

"Popo!" he yelled and the block cleared.

FIVE

Tamika knew that CJ had murked those four people in Orange. She had seen a report of the murders on the news one day when CJ had left the room to go get them something to eat. Just knowing that her nigga went that hard for his made her desire him that much more. Her only worry was that he might get arrested. Like Erykah Badu said, *What we gon' do when they come for you?* she thought as she shaved her legs.

She got out of the tub, rubbed herself down with body oil then threw on Apple Bottom low cut jeans, a Baby Phat halter and a cute pair of Baby Phat sneakers. Twenty minutes later, she was walking down to CJ's crib to get his whip. CJ was out grinding but he had left the car keys with Eric.

"Miss Wanda, you better not let CJ catch you doing that in here!" said Tamika, with her nose turned up when she saw CJ's Mom Dukes in the kitchen hitting the pipe. *Dayum! She ain't got no shame!*

Normally any type of smart talk would've gotten Tamika cussed the fuck out by CJ's Mom Dukes who did not discriminate. But at the present Miss Wanda was occupied with her lover, the crack pipe.

"Miss Wanda, you too through!" hurled Tamika on her way back out.

"Hi, Malcolm," said Tamika as she slid into his car and shut the door. She had met up with him outside the mall after he called to let her know that he had gotten his income tax return and would share it with her if she was willing to "act right."

"What's good, stranger? Where have you been?"

"Oh, I ended up going to jail that night after you left the club. Then lately, CJ been trippin'."

"Right. Well, you miss me?" he asked, massaging her neck.

"You know I did."

"Can I get a kiss?" She had to think about that. *Shit! Oh well.*

She touched lips with him so fast Malcolm wasn't sure that it actually happened.

"Damn, can a brotha get some tongue?"

"Un-uh, I have an abscess." She lied.

"So."

"No Malcolm, it's infected. Eww!"

"A'ight, but ain't nothing wrong with this," he said, rubbing her thigh.

"Of course not, let's go inside the mall. I gotta pee."

When Tamika came out of the bathroom, Malcolm was all ready to go from store to store with her as she shopped for whatever she could buy with the one thousand dollars he had told her he would spend on her. With Tamika's mean designer habit, one stack might only buy one outfit, at one store. There was no way that Tamika was going to have Malcolm sporting her through the mall and risk being seen by some hater who might run tell CJ.

"Uh—Malcolm—Boo, you can't be by my side while I shop. Somebody might see us together and call CJ and neither one of us wants that," she explained.

"I guess you're right. Okay, I'ma go grab myself a couple pairs of slacks and a nice pair of shoes. Why don't we meet back outside where we parked in an hour?" Malcolm suggested.

"Malcolm, no girl worth the clothes on her back can shop in an hour."

"Jeez. Well, just how long might it take you?"

"I'll call you on your cell when I'm done," she answered without really responding to the question. Malcolm went for it though because Tamika had promised to let him hit it today. Just thinking about running up in all that booty had Malcolm walking with his hand in his pocket tryna hide the fact that he was on bone.

Malcolm slid the stack to Tamika and she bolted off.

Two and a half hours later, Tamika hit Malcolm up to tell him that she was done shopping. "Where are you?" she asked.

"In the car. I was just checking my Facebook on my cell phone, waiting on your call. Man, it took you a long time to shop," he said with a laugh.

"Sorry."

"No, babe, it's okay. As long as you enjoyed yourself."

"I did. See you in a sec' okay? Bye."

Tamika put her phone in her purse and headed to the car. She had picked up some things from Vicky Secret; sexy stuff that Malcolm would never get to see her in. His grip just wasn't long enough for her to even consider letting him sample the goodies. If a small money nigga had the only dick on earth, Tamika thought she would rather start dyking than fuck with a petty bank dude.

Tamika smiled as she walked out of the mall, not at her thoughts about niggaz with short grip but at the cold-hearted humor she found in having used some of Malcolm's nine to five money to buy her hustling nigga a pair of True Religion jeans, which she disguised inside of a large Vicky Secret's bag.

I ain't shit! she smirked.

Tamika rode with Malcolm to some little Italian restaurant about fifteen minutes from the mall. The plan was to enjoy a nice meal then go back to Malcolm's place.

They were seated at a small, cozy booth. Wine and bread sticks were served as an appetizer. Malcolm ordered spaghetti and meatballs, and a Caesar salad. Tamika had baked ziti, a garden salad, and a side of chicken strips with spicy sauce.

While they were waiting for dessert Tamika put her head down on the table.

"Oh, my god! I think I'm about to be sick."

"What's wrong?" asked Malcolm, genuinely concerned.

"I feel like I might lose my food. Malcolm, could you ask the waiter to bring me a fresh glass of water, please?"

"Of course, babe." Malcolm darted off to find a waiter. He didn't need anything to spoil what they had planned for the rest of the night.

53

The water didn't seem to do Tamika any good. Malcolm and a concerned waiter fussed over her as she dry heaved. Then Tamika jumped up and ran to the ladies room with a hand over her mouth.

Inside the bathroom she looked in the mirror and giggled. Malcolm had said that she would have to "act right" to get that stack. Well, she wasn't "acting right" but she damn sho was hella acting. And the stack had already been spent. She laughed at the thought.

Malcolm knew that he wasn't hitting that pussy even before Tamika returned to the table and stated, "I'ma have to take a rain check on what we had planned, my stomach is too tore up. I'll never come here to eat again."

When Tamika told Star how she had played Malcolm, they laughed like crazy at the fool's stupidity. But Tamika's mother advised, "It's not good to play with a man's feelings. There's blood on some men's money. More than that, when a man feels used, he becomes very unpredictable."

"Aww, ma, Malcolm's scary butt ain't gonna do nothing but fall for my next trick."

"I don't like it, Tamika."

"She's hard headed," intoned Star. The three of them were sitting in the living room of Tamika's Mom Dukes apartment in Little Bricks.

"She better listen or she'll mess around and some man will end up hurting her," warned Miss Jerkins as she got up to go to her room.

"Okay, mommie, I'ma stop with the games," Tamika called out to her.

"You need to or I'ma tell CJ," she called back.

"You wouldn't dare!"

"Don't be so sure hooker."

"Girl, you a trip," Star said to Tamika as she fired up a blunt.

"Don't hate, ho."

"Tssk! Ooh, let me tell you about this fine ass nigga I met. His name is Diamond Rick—"

"Hol' up right there! Sounds like a pimp's name to me. Don't tell me you 'bout to be a *real* ho!" cracked Tamika.

"Shut up bitch and listen. It's not always about *you*," said Star, passing her the blunt to keep her quiet long enough to get a word in.

"Okay, give me the short version 'cause you tend to be a little long winded sometimes," replied Tamika, laughing.

"Whateva. Anyway, the nigga is all of that! And he has the swag of a major baller, not on the street level either."

As Star went on, Tamika half-listened while thinking. *This ho just tried to dis my man on the sly with that street level comment. A'ight, I'ma let her have that but she's probably blowing this Diamond Rick clown up to be more than he is. Because if he really is all of that, why would he want to take on this chicken and her Bay Bay kids?*

Tamika was saved when Star's cell chirped and it turned out to be Diamond Rick calling.

"Well, I'll holla boo. Mr. Fine himself wants me to come spend some time with him." She hugged Tamika and broke for the door.

"You know the game, bitch. A nigga is usually the opposite of his nickname. Remember that broke ass nigga you met at Chuck E Cheese with your bad ass kids? What was his name?"

"Millionaire!" recalled Star.

"Exactly." They cracked up.

"Bye, ho" said Star.

Tamika woke up early and went down to CJ's crib. She stirred him awake with a tongue in his ear.

"What time is it?" he growled.

"Dayum! Who let you in?"

"Eric," replied Tamika, pulling off her jeans.

"Is that why you came waking me up? You want some dick?"

"Yep."

"You's a lie," he laughed. "You just wanted to make sure I came home last night."

"Sho did! Uh-huh, 'bout to smell your balls too."

"Smell 'em. Put 'em in ya mouth while you're down there."

"Nigga, you ain't said nothing but a word," replied Tamika, licking his balls after they had passed the creep test.

Later, they went by the hospital to check on Rah's condition. When they arrived they were both shocked to find Kayundra at Rah's bedside tenderly stroking his hand singing *Back Down Memory Lane* in a low, sweet tone. She stopped singing when she realized that CJ and Tamika were standing there.

"What you doing here?" asked CJ in a harsh tone.

"I've been coming here every day for the past week and a half."

"Don't be molesting my nigga," CJ knocked Kayundra's hand off of Rah. "And if you keep up that shit, tryna sing to him he might not ever open his eyes. Who would wanna wake up to you?"

Tamika covered a snicker with her hand.

"Leave that girl alone. Apparently her singing to him is doing some good, he has come out of the coma," said Big Ma who had just waddled up.

"You lying! Oops, my bad Big Ma. When did that happen?" asked CJ, smiling sheepishly.

"Yesterday. Praise God."

"See!" added Kayundra, wanting to stick her tongue out at CJ and Tamika.

"Can he hear us?" Tamika asked.

"Well, loud as you're talking I'm certain he can, but he's medicated and asleep right now," explained Big Ma.

"He'll probably be awake in about two hours," Kayundra repeated what the ICU nurse had told her.

CJ and Tamika waited out in the lobby for Rah to awake. CJ's connect called to tell him that he was on deck. CJ was ready to get those two birds he said that he needed, but he was so excited about the news regarding Rah that he wouldn't leave the hospital. He had to see his man with his eyes open.

When CJ stepped outside again, this time to call Tricia, his secret jump off, Tamika called Star and gossiped about Kayundra being at the hospital.

"Crack fiend Kayundra?" asked Star.

"The one and only!"

"Dayum! Well, Rah and her was together since before they had hair on their privates, until you stole him from her, right?"

"Whateva! I didn't steal Rah from her. Anyway, I'ma call you back, I'm not supposed to be on a cell phone near ICU. Fuck around and flat line somebody," she joked.

Bitch, you sick. Bye." Star hung up.

"He's awake, but he's groggy and very weak," Kayundra came out to the waiting area to inform them. CJ bolted to his man's bedside.

Rah's eyes were open, though glassy, but it was all good.

"Welcome back, fam," said CJ, grinning from ear to ear. "Word, I love you, dawg."

Rah wasn't able to respond besides allowing the recognition to flash in his eyes. But it was all good. The nurses only allowed them fifteen minutes with him because according to the nurse, Rah needed to rest so that he could begin to regain his strength.

CJ left the hospital in a festive mood. Outside, he picked Tamika up and spun her around, screaming. "My nigga done bounced back on these clowns!"

The next day, out on the block, CJ was whistling as he served fiends and other customers. He stayed on his grind for hours, thinking about his man and wondering where the hell Tamika was. It was seven o'clock, he hadn't heard from her since ten that morning when she came down the hill to get his car keys.

On cue, Tamika pulled up. She parked and got out of the whip with a box of hot wings.

"Hey, daddy, I brought you something to eat."

CJ ignored her and served a fiend that had just walked up in the hallway of the apartments where CJ pumped.

"Where yo ass been?" he asked after the clucker bounced.

"My ass has been with me."

"Don't get pimp smacked," CJ snapped, not finding her response funny.

"Whateva, CJ! You like my new hair style." She spun around slowly, showing him her long bob.

"It's a'ight. Go home and wait for me," CJ grumbled.

"How long you gon' be out grinding?"

"Probably all of my fuckin' life, yo. The way yo ass like to spend ducats."

Wow! Where did that come from? Tamika wondered.

"What's wrong, baby?" she asked.

"Ain't shit wrong, just do what I asked you."

"Excuse the fuck out of me!" she snapped and stormed back outside and got in the car.

"Yo, gimme those wings before you bounce," CJ demanded as he followed on her heels.

"Okay. Here muthafucka! Tamika threw the bag of hot wings out the window onto the ground, and peeled off.

Five minutes later, her Mom Dukes was asking, "Who is that bangin' on my door like they're the police?"

"Probably CJ," said Tamika, going to answer the door.

"Either 5-0 after that ass or he's hot at you," her Mom Dukes guessed.

"The second one," Tamika said over her shoulder as she snatched the door open. "Boy, don't be bangin' on my mama's door like that!"

"Girl, you gon' make me catch a domestic charge!" CJ was finna spazz out on her until he saw her Mom Dukes.

"You the one who started it CJ," Tamika whined.

"I'm sorry, ma." He kissed Tamika. "Sup Ms. Jerkins?"

"Hi, CJ." I found some of that *stuff* in Tamika's room. I don't know how many times I have asked you and this hard-headed daughter of mine not to bring your drugs in here. I don't care about the money but the drugs will get my ass put out and I don't do homeless."

"My bad," apologized CJ.

"Dang, ma! I don't have *no* privacy. I wish you would stay out of my room rambling," whined Tamika.

"Chile puhleeze," replied her Mom Dukes as she watched Tamika lead CJ to her bedroom by the hand, giddy as a two-year-old at the circus.

Not much later, Tamika came into the kitchen in a long T-shirt. Her Mom Dukes was in there smoking a cigarette and frying some chicken. "Got yourself a minute man, huh?" she joked.

"Ma, shut up!" laughed Tamika, pushing her.

"I timed y'all," her Mom Dukes said, looking at the Cartier on her wrist.

"You did *not*! Anyway, it was the best minute ever. Don't hate."

It was dusk dark when CJ and Tamika pulled in front of his building. They got out of the car, took a few steps and were blinded by flood lights.

"Police! Freeze! Put your hands in the sky! Now get on your knees and put your hands behind your head. One hand at a time!" CJ wanted to run for it but a dozen cops had them surrounded, guns drawn, aimed to kill.

Tamika heard the click of the cuffs being put on her man. A female officer patted her down then turned her loose.

"Cam'ron Jeffries, you are under arrest in connection with four counts of murder. You have the right to remain silent. You..."

CJ was lucky that he had mistakenly left his Glock at Tamika's, he realized as a cop continued to read him his Miranda rights. He had murked Red with the Glock.

Whew! He exhaled.

"...if you can't afford an attorney the state will appoint—"

"Yeah, yeah, yeah! Yady, yady, whooptie, whoop!" CJ mocked.

Miss Wanda came flying through the throng of onlookers that had quickly gathered.

"What the fuck are y'all doing to my muthafuckin' son?" she screamed, looking like a wild woman.

"Ma'am, are you Wanda Jeffries?" asked one of the detectives on the scene.

"Wanda *Marie* Jeffries! Yeah, that's muthafuckin' right! Now, you need to tell me why the fuck y'all are lockin' up my son!"

"He's being arrested for four counts of murder."

"What? Murder? My baby ain't never hurt a muthafucka in his life. We're God fearing people," she said, sounding crazy because her foul mouth contradicted her. But she was lying to try to save her son from going to jail. Some in the crowd snickered, but they all could respect that.

While Miss Wanda was out there giving the cops hell, Eric was on point. He was inside the bathroom flushing weed and coke, tossing his Mom Dukes crack pipes out the window, assisted by Brianna.

"Ma'am, we also have a search warrant for your apartment," the detective was saying to Miss Wanda.

"Uh, no the hell you don't! Y'all bastards got me fucked up. Try searching my shit. I'll spit in one of y'all's muthafuckin' face! Watch and see!"

Meanwhile, Tamika stood there crying as CJ was being put in the back of the police car.

"Don't cry shorty. Love is love," CJ called out to her. But the tears poured.

The lyrics drummed so loud in her mind, it was like Badu was inside of her head singing. *What you gon' do when they come for you...*

When the police car took her man away, Tamika fainted.

SIX

CJ had been in jail for almost two months. His bond was a million dollars so he wasn't going anywhere. All he could do was sit tight and wait for the DA to play his cards. CJ had already gotten Tamika to pay thirty stacks to a hard-hitting lawyer as a retainer. That was half of his trap, and he would have to cough up the other half along with his whip if he had to go to trial. There's no price too high for a nigga'z freedom, so CJ wasn't sweating the attorney fees.

Tamika had gotten the choppa from Star and disposed of it the way CJ had instructed her to. She had paid the lawyer from his stash and was holding down the rest, checking on his peoples and the whole nine, up until a coupla weeks ago. Since then, she hadn't visited him and she would no longer accept his calls. That's the shit that had him stressin'.

Tricia, his jump off, was trooping as best as she could for him. That was all and well but he knew that he was fucked in the game if wifey had gone sour on him.

In jail, CJ was keeping to himself; he knew the play, somebody might try to slide up to him and get him to reveal something that they could run and tell and turn State against him. He wasn't going down like that. Speaking of which.

"Say, son, them Orange Project niggaz hit ya man up, huh?" asked a fool who had just come on the tier yesterday.

"I don't know what you speaking on yo," CJ tried to cut him short.

"Nah. I heard what happened and—"

"Yo, black, fall back a'ight."

"Damn, son, it ain't like that. I was just—

Whop! Whop! Whop! A three punch combination silenced the fool and sent him to medical to get the gash over his eye stitched up. CJ wasn't playing with those niggaz on the pod, he viewed every last one of them as potential rats.

He was on the phone with Tricia when a guard came to inform him that he had a visit. CJ thought, *Finally this bitch done got back on her square.* Assuming that it was Tamika.

When he stepped into the visitation booth and saw Rah on the other side of the glass, CJ was all smiles.

"Dayum yo! How you be fam?" He saw that Rah's neck was heavily bandaged and underneath both eyes were still slightly discolored.

"I'm making it, fam. How you?"

"I'm maintainin'! Yo, fam, why you sound like a frog?" CJ chuckled.

"A bullet damaged my throat, vocal cords, and some other shit," Rah tried to explain.

"Fuck dat, you alive and gettin' around. That's all that matters yo." CJ said, speaking through a small screened hole.

"Word. Yo, Kayundra said hello."

CJ looked to the ceiling. "Dawg, don't let me find out you hittin' dat. Dayum!"

"Go easy on her, fam. She's gettin' herself back right. Anyway, she drove me down here to see you."

"On what, a stolen bicycle?" asked CJ being sarcastic.

Rah shot him a look.

"A'ight, son. Whateva," CJ continued.

"Fa real though, we in a rental. She had to drive 'cause I can't yet."

"I hear you. Just get well nigga. You ain't gotta come down here, I'm good. You know how ya boy do it."

"Only death could keep me from checkin' on you dawg. You know how it is with you and me," said Rah. "Yo, what you need me to do for you?"

"Just get well fam. Oh, there is one thing I need you to handle."

"Name it and it's done."

"Go by Tamika's and tell her that I said to get her ass down here ASAP!"

62

Two days later, Tamika showed up. Rah had delivered CJ's message. She was looking as fly as usual but CJ was too hot to appreciate her looks today.

"I wish I could get to yo shady ass! I would stomp a mud hole in that ass!" was the first words out of CJ's mouth.

"Nah, baby boy, you need to save that for that weave-wearing bitch that's been creeping down here to see you," Tamika shot back.

"Fuck you talking 'bout, shorty?"

"Nigga, don't play yaself. You busted! And you don't even have the little jump off in check 'cause if you did, she would've lied for ya ass!"

"What you talkin' about Mika?" CJ needed to know before he 'fessed up.

"*Tricia*, muthafucka! Yeah. I bumped into her down here two weeks ago. Asked the ho straight up who she was down here to see and the bitch had the nerve to say, *our man!*"

CJ couldn't say shit.

"I'm sorry, yo," he finally said.

"Trust, you are gonna be if you don't handle your business. You better make that ho come to my door and apologize for disrespecting me. Then you better cut the bitch off. Holla at me when you do playa," said Tamika then she bounced.

Tamika was at home listening to Star go on and on about Diamond Rick's diamond dick game. They were smoking a blunt just kicking it.

Knock! Knock! Knock!

Tamika went to the door and looked out the peep hole. Star's nosy butt was right on her heels. Tamika saw who it was, opened the door and stood there with her arms folded across her chest.

"I came to apologize for disrespecting you. I will never do that again, ever. CJ loves you and does not want me. I'll fall back," said Tricia.

"Make sure that you do," Tamika closed the door in her face.

Star cracked up.

Now that wifey was back on board CJ wasn't stressing shit. He knew that the DA couldn't have shit on him. Just the other day they had him in the interrogation room tryna run the good cop/bad cop routine. CJ just laughed at them and told both cops to eat a dick. It was the third time they had tried to come at him with some bullshit to get him to confess. CJ would die and go to hell before he would admit to four murders.

Bright and early the next morning a guard came to tell CJ to pack up his belongings.

"Sup? Where I'm going?" CJ asked.

"Home. All charges against you have been dropped."

CJ played it cool but inside he wanted to dance, shout, and do the Holy Ghost.

Rah asked Kayundra, "What made you start using drugs?"

"A man," she answered succinctly.

"Who?" he delved further. "And why would a dude wanna get his girl hooked on drugs?" He could not see that with bifocals.

"Remember Red who lived a few buildings down?" replied Kayundra in a tone filled with shame and regret.

"Used to hustle with that old head dude, Shep, who caught a bid for killin' some dude at the bodega up the street?"

"Yeah, that's the Red," she confirmed.

"I thought he hustled. I didn't know that he got high too."

"I didn't either when I first started kicking it with him."

"That nigga like thirty-five, what you see in him?" asked Rah.

"Okay. I'm not trying to lay a guilt trip on you but here's the truth: When we broke up while you were in juvie I was still in love with you. I always believed that we would get back together because up until then you had been my only boyfriend. You know that."

Rah nodded.

"Then you came home all mad at me because I had been talking to a few boys. But honestly, I hadn't had sex with no one else. You wasn't trying to hear that. Then you got with Tamika and that right there crushed me. So I was like, you know what, I don't need no man for like two whole years. Then Red started checking for me and since he was much older than me knew how to run his game. I fell for him. I can't lie. He had me open."

"Did he?" Rah chuckled.

"For a minute. Still, I would always think about you. Then I heard that you had gone off to school and it hurt me because you didn't even tell me goodbye," Kayundra said, her eyes watering and her voice breaking up.

"I apologize, fa real."

"It's okay." Kayundra tried to smile. "Anyway, long story short: I caught Red getting high two or three times. He told me that it was something he only did occasionally to get away from the stress." She laughed at the lunacy of it.

"I wasn't buying it and he knew that I was about to stop dealing with him, so he tricked me into drugs as a way to hold on to me," she concluded, crying in shame.

Rah held her as Big Ma waddled by on her way to her room.

"It's a'ight shorty." Rah comforted Kayundra. He asked where Red was at now.

"He's dead. Somebody killed him shortly before you came home."

"Good fa that nigga. Was y'all still together?"

"Nope. By then my habit was way out of control. You saw how bad I was that night. Red was the rare smoker who never let crack take him all the way down. My problem was, besides being stupid, I don't do anything halfway. I go all out."

"I wanna see you go all out getting ya sparkle back," Rah told her.

"I am," she promised. *I want you back, too,* she thought but was afraid to say.

Tamika was so bored she wanted to scream. Malcolm had called asking her out to lunch but she nixed that. She hadn't accepted anything from him since her Mom Dukes warned her about playing with nigga'z emotions. She was about to call her big cuz, Danyelle, and see what was up with her when she heard someone knocking on the door.

"Mama, get the door!"

"Okay, you don't have to scream."

A minute later, her Mom Duke came to her bedroom and said, "Tamika, someone is here to see you."

"Why are you being all dramatic, Mama? It can't be nobody but Star's tired behind," figured Tamika, getting out of bed and going out into the living room and getting the best surprise ever. CJ was standing there with a blunt in his mouth and a bottle of Remy in his hand.

Tamika screamed then ran and jumped in his arms, raining kisses all over his face.

SEVEN

CJ chilled for a week, figuring that popo would be watching him hard since he had escaped from their grasp. The streets told him Cujo, a dirty ass white detective, had been rolling through the projects hard ever since he touched back down.

CJ knew how Cujo got down. He would plant drugs on a nigga, go to court, and give false testimony, even murk cats, rumor had it. CJ was not tryna run into that dirty ass cracker and get set up. But he had to get back on his grind. He had wifey and fam to provide for and his trap was leaking.

Niggaz surrendered his old spot on the block and CJ got back on his grind, though he was being extra alert. The first two days that he was back out there getting it up, he was paranoid as fuck. By the third day it was back to normal. He stayed out hustling until three in the morning. CJ was tired as a dog when he walked into his building. That's how he got caught slipping.

Two hooded men snatched him up, threw his ass inside a van, and drove off.

A half hour later, he was pulled out of the van and forced inside a dark basement at gunpoint. His abductors had already taken his strap that was tucked in his waist.

CJ didn't know what the fuck was going on, but he knew that the niggaz with the bangers pressed to the back of his head and the middle of his back probably wasn't anyone out to avenge their Orange Projects' homies. Nah, that type of revenge would've come in a quick burst of bullets. Street niggaz didn't take hostages, they bodied ya ass and mashed out.

In the darkened basement, they pushed him down into a chair.

"Fuck is you, muhfuckaz?" he asked.

"Shut ya face before I shoot you in it," one of them barked.

A garbled voice belonging to neither of his two abductors said, "We know you killed those four boys over in East Orange, but we probably won't be able to prove it. But we know the spot you hustle from, we know where you live, and where your girlfriend lives. If you don't cooperate with us we are going to nail you for something, even if we have to plant some kilos on you. Understand?"

"I understand I have the right to an attorney." CJ said, not with the bullshit.

"Oh, yeah?"

Pow! CJ's ears rung from the noise of the gun, fired inches from his head.

"My boys won't purposely miss the next time. Now listen up. We'll allow you to sell all the drugs you want and no one will bother you. We'll stop investigating those four murders if you'll help us bring down a rogue cop."

"Man, get me the fuck out of here yo."

"You wanna go back to jail? We're the ones who got you out. If you don't cooperate you're going back. Four murder charges CJ. Four!"

"Like I said, get me the fuck outta here."

"So you'll rather go back to jail? What do you care about a cop? A white one at that. Cujo, we want him."

CJ, like everyone else in the hood, hated Cujo. But he hated snitches even worse.

"Tell ya mama to set him up."

"Oh, he's a tough guy. He can do a bid. But what about your mama? Can she do a bid? Can that pretty lady of yours do a bid?"

"We're all built to last," spat CJ defiantly. He didn't give a fuck about Cujo but snitchin' was snitchin'. It was death before dishonor with CJ. Unlike most niggaz, he didn't just say that shit, he lived it.

They continued tryna break him with threats and offers. But you can't turn a real nigga into a bitch. If they flip, it was in them all along. CJ wouldn't flip so after a while they gave up.

A lamp came on in the basement and Cujo stood up from a couch holding the voice distortion device he'd been speaking into. He smiled and said to the two cops who had abducted CJ, "I think we've found our man."

"Fuck you mean, cracker?" gritted CJ.

Cujo laughed.

"This cracker is about to help you become the next Akbar Pray."

Every hustla, young or old, in Newark had heard of the street legendary Akbar Pray. His legend was synonymous with hustlaz like Nicky Barnes, Frank Lucas, and such made men who at one time had the game on smash from coast to coast.

Cujo fired up a cigar and said, "Just hear me out CJ. I think you'll find our offer impossible to refuse."

Rah had recovered from his near fatal injuries, well enough to return to school. Summer classes were due to begin and he needed to attend in order to make up for having missed the spring quarter. He also needed to get back to ATL and get his hustle back on.

He looked around the living room and saw the only people that mattered to him in this world, the people that he would miss; the ones who were motivation for him to get that degree. They were all present, fawning over LaKeesha's newborn baby boy, whom she named after his father, who was still locked up in New York on the island.

Big Ma, whom Rah loved and wanted to make proud, was anxious for him to go back to school. "Newark and these projects is bad news," she had explained her anxiety the other day.

Rah thought he had her fooled but Big Ma had seen it all, she was hard to hoodwink. She knew that he was into something down in Atlanta, she just didn't know what. The night that Rah was shot he'd had $5,000 on him. The hospital had turned the money over to Big Ma while Rah was in a coma.

When Rah was well enough, Big Ma asked him, "Where did you get all this money from?" returning it back to him.

"Oh, that belongs to CJ."

"Raheem, look me in the eye and tell me that you are not down in Atlanta selling drugs or involved in anything else illegal," she demanded.

"Nah Big Ma. I ain't doing nothing like that. I told you this money belongs to CJ." Rah lied, though it tore him up to do so to her face. He felt like a fake.

Big Ma hadn't been fooled; she'd seen the lie in his eyes. Rah's conscience made him a terrible liar.

I'ma make it up to you, Big Ma, he thought now as he watched her rock back and forth in her favorite chair.

His attention shifted to LaKeesha. Rah was concerned about her. Since being home he had peeped that she was no longer focused on her goals, her focus was on niggaz, particularly her baby's daddy. *"That's all good, but don't give up on your dreams,"* he had recently told her, but he didn't think the advice had registered. He needed to set a good example for LaKeesha, who had just handed the baby to Kayundra.

"Hey, little bitty baby," cooed Kayundra, rubbing her nose against the baby's tummy. "You going to grow up to be handsome, sweet, and smart like your Uncle Raheem, aren't you?"

Rah couldn't help but smile when he looked at Kayundra. It was truly amazing how much better she was looking now that she was no longer using drugs. She had wanted to give them up months ago but couldn't find the motivation. It was not until she saw the horrified look on Rah's face the day she accosted him, begging to trick off with him for ten dollars, did she decide to do a one-eighty.

"Oh, she claiming to be off of drugs?" CJ had asked skeptically the other day.

"Yeah, but she admits to slippin' back once," Rah said.

"C'mon, fam, I know you ain't buying that lie. Fiends can't just quit like that!" he'd said, snapping his finger for emphasis. *"One of those bullets must've hit your head yo. But if you like it, I love it. Word."*

"All I'm saying is that I wanna believe her and I will until I see otherwise. Look at her dawg, she's been by my side damn near 24/7. She's getting her weight back and that sparkle I used to see in her eyes." Rah defended her, but CJ wasn't buying it.

"That sparkle you see is that flame she put to that rock when she's cluckin'." CJ couldn't stop himself from cracking.

As Rah studied Kayundra now, he really believed that she was going to be all right. Tomorrow she was checking herself into drug rehab. She wanted to go through the ninety day program to further her chances of avoiding a relapse.

While Rah saw so much in Kayundra, such as love, hope, and a sweet disposition, CJ viewed her as a crack fiend. He was grilling her like mad. *This bitch frontin', she's still a clucker.* CJ told himself.

Unable to stomach Kayundra any longer, CJ asked Rah to take a ride with him. "I need to holla about some graveyard-serious shit," he emphasized without letting the others overhear him.

"A'ight."

CJ recounted the shit that happened with Cujo to Rah as they rode around chopping it up. He didn't leave out a single detail; he knew that Rah would never betray him by repeating what they discussed to anyone.

"So they was just testing ya gangsta, huh?" asked Rah once CJ concluded the story.

"Yep. That's why I always say, snitches get found dead, real niggaz get blessed."

"What kinda deal you got with them?"

"They hit me with work on consignment as much as I can handle at fifteen a bird, protect me from arrest, smash all serious competition, and eliminate anybody I got beef with."

"That's wild, yo. Those muhfuckaz can get away with it too; they got a license to kill."

"Yep, it's called a badge," understood CJ.

"What about the feds? How Cujo get around them?"

"Shit, fam, one of the niggaz that snatched me up is feds. You know Cujo ain't really the HCIC so I figure that one of those high-ranking fed boys is the shot caller and Cujo is just his mouthpiece, nah mean?" speculated CJ as they continued to cruise the city.

"Where they get all the yayo from? You know?"

"Dig. Say they knocked a nigga with a lot of them joints or even somebody with a boat full. The shit remains on lock as evidence until after the trial then the feds are supposed to destroy it, but guess what?"

"They don't. They put that shit back out on the street through you and whoever else they're fuckin' with like that."

"Yep. And they jack niggaz for their shit and turn it over to me, no arrest or nothing. Nigga just got his whole trap took."

"Dayum! The muhfuckin' feds is the real cartel," said Rah. "Cujo told you this shit?"

"Yeah, after the two dudes that sntached me up left, Cujo drove me back home in a limo tinted SUV so that niggaz couldn't see inside. He broke it all down to me so that I would feel confident that shit is gravy. Of course, he didn't give me any names and his is the only face I saw," explained CJ.

"So what you gon' do? You gon' fuck with 'em?"

"I already did, otherwise I probably wouldn't be here, nah mean? I got thirty of them joints at a stash spot now. I'm just lining up clientele before I move 'em. I told you all this for two reasons, fam. Number one, you can stop fuckin' with the hustle in ATL and concentrate on school. I'm straight now so I got you. Number two, if Cujo cross me, I want you to promise me that you'll ride for your boy. Don't let that cracker do a nigga dirty and live to laugh about it," said CJ.

Even though he'd be vowing to murk a cop, Rah didn't even have to think about it.

"Word, on all that I love—if something suspicious happens to you, Cujo gon' get it," promised Rah as they touched fists. "On that other thing son, you know a real nigga ain't gon' let his man take care of him like that. I know it's all love, but a man has to get his own, ya feel me?" Rah tried to explain.

"Nah. I can't feel you, but I know that we're both cut from the same cloth and when we feel a certain way about something can't nobody change our mind so I'ma let you have that. At least let me help you get another whip though," offered CJ.

"Fam, I'm good. The insurance company has a check waiting on me. I'll get it as soon as I get back to ATL. Plus, I got about twenty stacks on stash."

"A'ight. When you leaving?"

"In two days, I'ma fly back. But yo, if shit gets ugly up here, I'm just a phone call away," said Rah.

"What's understood don't have to be said, yo."

Kayundra and Rah were chilling at a motel.

"You should get serious about your music, you have a gift that can take you far away from here," Rah said.

"I wouldn't want it to take me far away from you though," she replied honestly.

"Ma, our friendship knows no limitations. I'll never forget how you've been by my side through all of this and I'll always return the love."

"Raheem, I was by your side because deep down I never stopped loving you. Tell me something, do you think that we can possibly be more than friends again one day?" Kayundra asked, sitting across from him on the bed.

Rah thought before he spoke, choosing his words carefully. He didn't want to smash her hope nor did he want to mislead her which is why he had been hesitant to get a room with her when Kayundra suggested that they do so. She wanted them to spend some time alone before she went into rehab and he returned to school.

"Let's just take one day at a time and not make each other any promises. Right now, I just wanna see you remain on your square shorty, for yaself," said Rah.

"Okay. I'm good with that. But if I can't ever have you again I won't have anything to live for."

Rah took Kayundra's hands into his and looked her in the eyes. He saw in her eyes that her words were not idle talk and that bothered him. He kissed her hands and spoke gently.

"Don't say things like that baby girl, or you'll start to believe them. No matter what ever happens, the only reason you ever need to live is for yourself. That alone is reason enough because at the end of the day no one else should be in control of your happiness."

"I know but I want us to be in love again so bad. Like when we were in seventh grade and I gave you my virginity," Kayundra reminisced.

"I gave you mine too," Rah laughed at the shared memory. Kayundra took a deep breath to calm her nerves then she slowly let it out. "Raheem, could we do it all over again? I mean tonight, will you make love to me?"

He told her that he didn't think that was the best thing for her. "You don't need all those emotions messing with your head right now. Just get well ma. What's meant to be will be." His words brought tears from her eyes.

"You see me as a crack ho, don't you?"

"Of course not. I see you as the beautiful girl that I know you to be. But you have to see yourself that way," Rah spoke with wisdom beyond his years.

"I'm trying to. But your love means so much to me. That night after I approached you and realized who you were, seeing the way you looked at me—disgusted by how bad I had let myself fall, I ran straight to the crack house up the street. But I didn't ask anyone there for a hit. I asked them for a mirror. The dude who runs the house thought that I wanted a mirror to snort coke off of. But I wanted to see what you saw. When I looked in the mirror, I saw that I truly had become a crack *monster*. I smashed the mirror against the wall and ran out of there crying. I knew that I had to leave that shit alone. I looked like something out of *Tales from the Crypt*. So Raheem, I know what you saw that night and you probably can't get that vision out of your mind," she sobbed.

Rah took her into his arms and rocked her; kissed her tears away and told her that she was wrong. The vision he had of her in his mind was of her on stage singing a top R&B hit song of hers. It was a prophecy that would come true down the road. But it would come at a price to both of them.

The next day Rah and Kayundra's mother drove her to Trenton where a new drug rehab in-house facility had recently opened its doors. The program in which Kayundra was entering was voluntary and the facility didn't have barred windows or locked fences around the perimeter like a prison.

Kayundra said a tearful goodbye to her mother and Rah before walking into the facility, but her tears were of hope not pain.

The following day Rah's plane departed for ATL, he was returning to school; once again leaving The Bricks. A visit home had almost cost him his life, reminding him how blessed he was to have the opportunity to get out of the hood. However, everyone that he loved still remained in The Bricks, so his heart was still there. And that hood mentality still existed inside of him, in spite of his academic intelligence. That much was obvious even to Rah himself because calling his connect and getting hit off with some pounds of weed and some E was one of the first things he planned to do when he touched down in ATL.

"Is everything okay?" asked the airline attendant perfunctorily.

"Yeah, I'm fine," replied Rah as he pulled out the stationary that he had brought along, then let down the tray flap in the back of the seat in front of him to use as a desk.

Dear Sparkle,

Ca$h

As I write this letter, I'm on a flight back to ATL. I'm looking forward to returning to school, though many of the students will have gone home for the summer. I'm still in the air and already I miss you. I guess you spoiled me with your daily presence while I recovered. I can't thank you enough ma, for the love you showed me. Truly, you epitomize compassion. I want to reiterate that our friendship means a lot to me. Like you said your Mom Dukes told you, don't put too much into titles, it is what's in our hearts that matter more. I hope that by the time this letter reaches you, you will be adjusting well to the program and all that it entails. Remember why you went into the program, for yourself. Not for me or anyone else. You're doing it for YOU! Every night when I look up at the sky and see the "sparkle" of the stars, I will know that it is you winking at me, sending me the message that you're doing just fine. Stay strong.

Love, Raheem.

EIGHT

CJ pulled up on the block in the midnight blue Expedition. The big chrome rims were sparkling almost as bright as the jewels CJ was rocking when he hopped down out of his brand new whip. The forty-two inch platinum chain hung down to just above his waist, the icy Jesus piece that was the size of a tea cup saucer swung from the end of it. Dime-sized diamond earrings adorned both ears and a Cartier with ice told him that it was two o'clock in the afternoon.

"Sup, fam?" he said to each member of his squad, dapping them one by one, beginning with his lil' brother, Eric, who had pleaded his way on the team. Next CJ dapped Kareem and Snoop, the two dudes who had hustled from his spot when he was in jail charged with the four bodies.

"What it do, my dude?" replied Kareem.

"I'm good. Sup, Snoop?" said CJ.

"Getting stacks."

"That's what's up. How you living, Premo?" CJ asked the kid who lived on the top floor of his old building. He had put Premo on the team a week ago because he knew he was ambitious.

"I'm lovely, Black," replied Premo.

Lastly, CJ dapped Guru, a dude who'd been hustling the block for years but couldn't seem to elevate his hustle. Guru was thirty-five and was still slanging rocks until CJ made him crew chief of his squad.

"Sup, Unc?" CJ asked Guru.

"Everything is quiet. You know the haters can't stand to see us with the entire block on lock but after that shit last week, they know to fall back."

"They better know," replied CJ with cockiness, recalling the incident that Guru was referring to.

Those kids that pump outta that spot, two buildings down catching beef with us 'cause their money is starting to come in slow. We got size and prices they can't match yo," Guru *reported to CJ.*

"It's serious like that?" asked CJ

"Yeah, I heard that they're plotting."

"Word? A'ight, they plottin' their own demise!"

Before CJ sent the squad at the kids, he conferred with Cujo who said, "Handle your business, I'll clean it up."

Eric, Kareem, and Premo caught the two kids who had been talking that rah rah shit and left them with their dicks in the dirt a day later. That next day the whole squad was back out on the block pumpin' as if they didn't have a worry in the world.

Although the whole projects knew who had bodied the kids, CJ knew that they were immune from arrest. When niggaz saw that CJ's squad had bodied the kids in broad daylight and weren't in jail behind it, they had no choice but to fall back. Because a squad with immunity to murder is not to be fucked with.

"They know we ain't playin'," said Guru who wondered himself how CJ had gained so much power all of a sudden. But he knew better than to ask.

"Yo, I'ma hit you with ten birds in a minute. I need you to meet Rob Nice at the joint on Central Ave. where we hit him up last time. He gone have a hundred and fifty stacks for you, tell him to have my other fifty in two days. Take Greg, Eric, and Snoop with you," CJ instructed Guru.

"A'ight."

CJ's cell chirped.

"Hey, ma, sup?"

"I found a condo way out in West Orange, you want to come look at it?" asked Tamika who was crib hunting so that they could move out the hood.

"Nah, if it's what you like I'ma be good with it."

"Okay, it's twenty-five a month. Is that too much?"

"Nah, money ain't a thang. I told you, ma, anything you want. And I'ma let you lace that bitch, a'ight?"

"I can't wait! Ooh, I am so excited. I love you CJ," said Tamika.

"Love you too, shorty."

CJ ended the call and addressed his squad for a minute before bouncing.

Later he dropped the ten birds to Guru. Guru and 'em handled the business with Rob Nice with no problem. Now CJ had the one hundred-fifty stacks spread out all over Tamika's bed, and Tamika was butt naked lying on top of the guap. CJ stood in his boxers watching her masturbate as Lyfe Jennings played in the background.

Tamika stroked her pussy nice and slow, locking eyes with her man as she did so. "Umm! You like to watch me play in my pussy? Ooh, I'm getting so wet for you baby," she moaned, sliding two fingers inside of her honey walls.

CJ dropped his boxers and stroked his dick.

"Yeah, daddy, get that dick rock hard for your boo. Yes, daddy, yes, stroke that long, thick muthafucka. I'm rubbing my clit for you boo, thinking about sucking your dick and drinking your cum. You know I love to drink your cream, daddy." Tamika moaned as she rubbed her clit. She was driving CJ crazy, his dick was so hard it felt like a pistol.

"CJ, I'm about to cum. Ooh—oh—oooh—oh—ooh wee—ohhh!" she cried out as she made her pussy melt. Then she stuck her fingers into her mouth and tasted her sweet nectar.

CJ wanted a taste, too. He crawled between her thighs, head first and licked up the honey that now ran down them. He licked his way up to her pussy, softly sucking on the lips as he spread them wide open.

"Oh, yes, baby," moaned Tamika.

CJ continued to alternate from one side to the other as Tamika gripped his head and gently began to grind. He pushed his tongue deep inside of her and Tamika's back arched in a C. When she felt his lips wrap around her swollen clit she screamed out his name.

CJ took her where she wanted to go. It felt so damn good but she wanted the dick and she wanted it now. "I want you to fuck me, daddy. I need to feel your dick inside me right now, don't play," she warned, digging her nails into his back just hard enough to let him know not to fuckin' tease her.

CJ was a fiend for the pussy so he didn't tease. He plunged in deep, started stroking slow then increased his rhythm. Tamika was giving it back just as hard as she was receiving it. "Fuck this pussy! Beat it up! Fuck it, daddy! Fuck it hard!" she cried.

CJ banged in and out of the pussy until she cried out, "I'm cuming, cum with me, baby!" They both exploded and called out each other's name. Cum and body sweat was all over the guap spread out on the bed. Bills were stuck to Tamika's back and ass like pasties.

They laid naked side by side and smoked a blunt as Tamika described the condo to him. "Mama said she's going to help me pick out the furniture," she said. "I am so excited. I can't wait to cook for you and wake up next to you every morning. CJ, you better not get me way out there and be creepin' back down here giving my dick away. Trust, I'ma have my people watching that ass."

"Shorty, hush. You ain't got no peoples," laughed CJ.

"You're my peoples."

"Yeah, ma, I'm ya peeps."

"And him," she said, grabbing his dick.

"Ma, you're crazy," CJ chucked.

Tamika slid down and took him into her mouth. Within a minute CJ's dick went from a boy to a man. Tamika slurped the lollipop until she was rewarded with its cream.

"Dayum Mika, what you tryna do? Drain a nigga?"

"You ain't know? Making sure you don't have nothing left for no other bitch," she admitted.

Tamika knew that CJ had bubbled and he had done it seemingly overnight. Two months ago, he was getting one or two birds at a time. Now he was getting so many it almost made her eyes pop out of her head. Last month, she saw him come up in her crib with thirty-five birds. *Thirty-five!*

"Wow! CJ, where did you get all of that dope?" she had asked him wide-eyed.

"That ain't shit. Stay down with me and you'll see me with five times that many."

"CJ, I'm scared. Did you jack somebody?"

"Shorty, you know I don't roll like that. A nigga just connected now. Relax, you fuckin' with a made man," he told her and the proof was in the pudding.

Tamika saw that with her own hazel brown eyes. CJ had gave her the Q45 and copped himself an Expedition. Now when he sent her to tear the mall up, it was with eight stacks instead of three or four. His ice had been upgraded, they were moving out of the hood, and CJ said that his Mom Dukes was next. Then maybe even Tamika's.

She planned to hold on to CJ like the Jaws of Life.

Tamika had stopped playing with Malcolm and didn't have any holla for any other nigga that tried to get at her.

"CJ, promise me you won't let the money change you," she said, laying her head on his chest.

"Ma, I would never switch up on you, it's you and me for life," he promised.

Meanwhile, way down in Philly, CJ's cohorts were executing a large drug bust.

Stan White had been getting money in South Philly since the late eighties when crack was king. He was one of the very few money-getters left around from that era. All the rest were either dead or in prison, or had been taken down by the same drug that had once gotten them rich.

Stan had escaped those downfalls because he didn't use drugs at all nor did he hit the clubs or flash his worth plus he didn't do dirty business. Now he just wanted to make this one last big move and he was getting out of the game.

But Stan was less than a half hour away from falling victim to the game he was planning to get out of. Jay, his longtime and most trusted lieutenant had gotten knocked with three keys of heroin last month, unbeknownst to Stan. Jay had just come home two years ago from a ten year bid. At forty-three years old Jay didn't think that he would live out the long bid that would come with a conviction for trafficking three kilos of pure heroin, so he offered to give Stan up.

"We want to bust him while a big deal is going down, that way we get him and the supplier. Otherwise, you're going down," the DEA agent had demanded thus Jay tap danced to the cracker's music.

Stan and Jay waited patiently at Stan's grocery store in South Philly for the connect to arrive with ten kilos of heroin and one hundred keys of coke. It would be delivered by someone driving a produce truck just like the one that delivered groceries to the store every few days. Stan already had the money stacked in boxes to pay for the shipment. Jay was trying to figure out a way to end up with one of those boxes after the shit went down.

The shit he had tossed onto Stan to save his own rat ass.

They unlocked the door when the truck pulled up and the driver hopped out. Then out of nowhere, unmarked cars and men with DEA across their chests swarmed in on them ready to blast anyone that moved.

"DEA! Don't move!"

"Get down on the ground! Now!"

Stan's reign was over that quick. The agents cuffed him, the delivery man, and Jay.

Stan didn't realize that there was some shit in the game until the three of them were marched into an abandoned warehouse and forced to lay down on the floor.

"What's going on?" he protested.

"Ole Jay here sold you out. Just thought you'd like to know before you go," one of the agents said.

"Go where?" he asked.

Pow! Pow!

Two to the back of the head was his answer.

"You're next, bro," a second agent said to the driver of the truck.

"Fuck you!" spat the driver.

"Fuck you back," he replied after splattering the man's head.

"Well, Jay, guess who's next," mocked a third agent.

"C'mon, man, please. I gave you these guys like you asked," cried Jay.

"And look how I thank you, right? Some people just ain't appreciative." *Pow! Pow! Pow!* "Rat bastard!"

Back at the grocery store the others were driving off with the whole truck and the boxes of money that they had found inside Stan White's Grocery.

Up in Newark, New Jersey, Cujo received the call from his brother-in-law, celebrated federal Agent Michael Solaski that he'd been waiting for.

"Mike, how did it go?" asked Cujo.

"Like stealing from the blind."

"That easy?" Cujo laughed.

"Yep, they didn't even put up a fight."

"Did y'all get everything that you were expecting?" asked Cujo excitedly.

"Yep, can your boy move all the stuff?"

"We're about to see," he replied.

Ca$h

NINE

Rah was back in ATL, back in school and still maintaining a 4.0 GPA. Academics had always come very easy to him. However, he did study and take his classes seriously in order to keep up a perfect grade point average. Everyone at school was glad to see him back and doing well, they had heard about his near tragedy.

Stephanie, the snow bunny who lived next door to him, was morbidly fascinated when Rah recounted the brawl in the club and being shot afterwards. She wanted to know how it had felt to get shot but Rah couldn't articulate the feeling.

"So, is your homeboy CJ going to go after the guys who shot you?" she asked naively.

"Nah, I told him to let it go." Rah lied.

"He doesn't sound like he would do that," said Stephanie, not knowing how true her words were. "Anyway. I'd like to meet CJ. He sounds so exciting in that bad boy way, if you know what I mean."

"Yeah, I know what you mean—shorty want a thug. A *black* one at that," Rah teased.

"I do not," giggled Stephanie.

"Whateva, ma," Rah laughed. He could see through her denial.

"No. Seriously, I'd just like to meet CJ not date him. I'd also like to meet Kayundra. I'm pulling for her, you guy's story could turn out so beautiful if she overcomes her addiction."

"Maybe so," acknowledged Rah.

"Now Tamika, I am so *not* wanting to meet. I think she and I would have beef," Stephanie said, adopting the black vernacular.

When Rah wasn't in class, studying, or chopping it up with Stephanie, he was back on his grind. The Tahoe had been replaced with an Infiniti SUV, which he was driving now on his way to drop some work to DaQuan.

"What it do, shawdy?" asked DaQuan, sliding into the SUV as soon as Rah pulled up.

"I'm good fam. Grab that foot locker bag out the back, that's you right there. Three pounds of purp' and two hundred pills."

"A'ight. Look, shawdy, I'm a coupla stacks short 'cause I been taking losses like a muhfucka since you been gone. But—"

"No explanation needed, yo. I fucks wit' ya. Get ya weight back up nigga, and pay me what you're short on the re-up," said Rah. DaQuan was good people; Rah wasn't sweating two stacks.

DaQuan handed him a shoe box full of money, grabbed the bag of work off the backseat, and gave Rah some dap.

"I'ma fuck with you later," he said.

"One," replied Rah.

Later that night, Rah was at the strip club, Strokers, getting his mack on with Cream, a stripper with an ass that should've been illegal. Cream was tryna charge Rah a stack to go to the motel with him and spend the night.

"Ma, how many times I gotta tell you I don't do no tricking?" Rah checked her.

"You know what they say lil' daddy, it ain't trickin' if you got it," Cream sang.

"You know who say that shit, don't you? Trick ass niggaz. I ain't gon' charge you for the dick and I'm not paying for the pussy. I dig that you're about ya paper ma but I'm about mine too."

"So why are you even up in here?" she asked.

"I'm just politicking."

"And sweating pussy for free?"

"Nah, I'm just chillin', yo."

Cream peeped that Rah wasn't a trick so she pushed on.

"What's good whoady?" said N.O., a hustla from New Orleans, whom Rah had bumped into a few times around the city. New Orleans niggaz was deep up in ATL ever since Hurricane Katrina tore up their spot.

"I'm good. Sup?" replied Rah.

N.O. slid into the booth Rah occupied. He was a tall skinny nigga; red, with freckles and green eyes. Rah didn't know N.O.'s hustle but he knew that dude was in the life, N.O.'s swag told him that.

"I'm not tryna get in your business dawg, but I be seeing you around, and it looks like you're doing some things. They call you Rah, don't they?"

"They might."

"I feel you. Anyway, I got that work, and I'm always looking for solid niggaz to do business with. Ask around about me and get back at me. I be at this spot a lot, my girl Satin dances here," said N.O.

"Oh, Satin your girl?"

"Yeah, one of 'em."

"Shorty fly," commended Rah.

Him and N.O. chopped it up for a while then Rah left the club and went to holla at one of the many young chicks who was on his jock. All of that pussy up in the strip club had his joint on swole and he needed to get straight.

There was no strings attached between Rah and the jump off that he ran up in. Rah always kept it one *hunnid* with the chicks he kicked it with, letting them know that he was too young to be tryna wife any of them. If a chick started to catch feelings, he stopped seeing her.

Returning home from the jump off's house the next morning, Rah stopped to check his P.O. Box. Back inside his whip, he tore open the envelope and began reading the letter he received from Kayundra.

My Dearest Raheem,

I am doing very well in my recovery. The one aspect that is pure hell is that I do not get to see you or even talk to you on the phone. I think about you so often and miss you so much, I wonder how I managed to live without you in my life over the past four years. I had to be high, right? LOL.

I am writing a song about my feelings for you and how my refound love gives me new hope. Otherwise, I've just been attending meetings here and doing a lot of self-examination. I talk to the other women in the program to try to understand how each of our stories led to addiction. There's this one girl named Porcelin who I talk to a lot. Baby, she is wild! The other day...

Rah continued to read Kayundra's letter detailing some of the things that her friend Porcelin said or done. When he concluded the letter he found himself worried that Kayundra's emerging friendship with the girl might lead to them both relapsing.

Rah didn't want to harbor doubts about Kayundra's commitment to overcoming her addiction so he quickly pushed the negative thoughts out of his mind. As he started up the SUV and drove the mile from the post office to his apartment, he wodered what the future held for him and Kayundra.

His cell phone chirped as he parked in front of his building, interrupting his thoughts.

"Sup, fam?"

"What's good, baby boy?" said CJ.

"Same ol'," responded Rah.

"Go to Western Union. I just sent you eight stacks yo."

Rah started to protest but he knew that CJ wasn't tryna hear it. The love between them was deep like that; if Rah had CJ's hand, he would do the same type of shit for his man.

"It's all love, dawg," said Rah.

"I'm coming down your way soon."

"That's what's up."

"A'ight, son. One."

TEN

CJ was pumpin' crazy work. Cujo had hit him off with one hundred blocks of coke and ten kilos of heroin that his corrupt cohorts had garnered from the drug heist down in Philly. Now CJ's name was ringing all over Newark as "that nigga" cats was tryna see to cop weight from or to get put on.

CJ planned to sell two-thirds of the yayo in weight at eighteen a block, a three stack profit after he paid Cujo fifteen a piece. So CJ stood to clock almost two hundred gees profit off of sixty-six blocks of coke. The other thirty-four he would whip into about fifty blocks of crack—he had a sick whip game—chop 'em up and put stupid sized rocks stones on the block. Off of this work he would profit even more. Of course, some of those profits would be used to pay his squad but he would still be sitting lovely, and the gravy from the ten kilos of heroin would be mad crazy.

"We just need a spot to pump the heroin from. Someplace where it's already jumpin'," he told Guru.

"Kendall and 'em got a bubbling spot over on Avon Ave. We could go over there and put that joint under new management yo," suggested Guru, who was feeling himself because he knew that he was on a squad of head bangers.

"That ain't Bloods' territory, is it?" asked CJ, aware that Bloods were starting to claim many areas in The Bricks. He didn't fear the notorious gang but he respected the fact that they had numbers.

"Nah, not the spot Kendall has, and yo, that piece is a million dollar joint. You know dude, he got that black Escalade with the Batman doors."

"Yeah, I know who you're talking about. Let me check out his spot to see how it's pumpin'. If it's worth the drama, we'll get at him, if not, we'll just pump the shit outta our own joints, nah mean?"

After just three days of watching the traffic at Kendall's spots on Avon Avenue, CJ knew that the location was a gold mine. He had to have that spot as his own so he sent Guru to holla at Kendall.

Guru and Kendall went back to when the Prince Street Projects was the shit in Newark. Back then they both worked for a nigga named Hump. After Hump caught mad fed time, Kendall and Guru parted ways. Kendall had bubbled while Guru never could seem to reach Willie status. Still Kendall respected Guru so he was open to listening when Guru put word out that he needed to holla.

Kendall came through Little Bricks and scooped Guru up.

"Long time, Duke. How you be?" Kendall greeted Guru as Guru slid into the passenger seat of his Escalade.

"Been maintaining, yo. How you?"

"Tryna stay a step ahead of the haters, nah mean?" replied Kendall, who at forty acted like he was twenty-five. He was rockin' a Yankee fitted, Eviso jeans, and Timbs.

"I feel you, baby. Anyway, shit ain't like it was when we was on Prince Street doing our thing. Those were the days yo," Guru reminisced.

"Word. I hate that they blew those projects up. A nigga was eating real lovely off that joint," said Kendall, reflecting back.

"You eating well *now*."

"Oh, I ain't complaining, shit is sweet. I hear you doing a'ight yaself, done clicked with some young wolves," Kendall said as he fired up an Optimo, hit it strong then passed it to Guru.

They were just chillin' in the Escalade, parked outside of Guru's crib in the projects in Little Bricks.

Guru took a pull on the Optimo filled with goodness. "This that shit yo. Anyway, what I wanted to holla at you about is this, my people wanna buy you out."

"Say what?"

"Your spots on Avon Ave, my people wanna buy you out," repeated Guru.

"Or what?" asked Kendall who was a vet and understood how the game went.

"Nah, son, it ain't even like that. My people sent me to holla in peace."

"Yo, this *me* you're talking to. I been doing this shit since the eighties," said Kendall as he put the whip in drive and pulled off, turning on his headlights because it was dark out. "I know how the game goes, I turn down your man's offer then it's on some gunplay shit, 'cause he wants my spots bad enough to take it there."

"Man, you overreacting yo," Guru said.

"Nah, I'm just peepin' game. I guess you with that youngun CJ whose name is ringing all over The Bricks huh?" asked Kendall as they left Little Bricks.

"Yeah, them's my people."

"Dayum Guru, we go way back. You know how I get down. I'm surprised you choosin' sides against me to clique up with a young nigga who thinks he can strong arm the game."

"Fam, I'm tryna tell you I'm not coming to you on no rah rah shit," Guru stated again, although he knew that if Kendall flat out refused CJ's offer, gunplay was definitely the next option.

Kendall didn't utter another word until they reached Avon Avenue. He drove past his spots pointing and talking. "You see all that traffic, the fiends lovin' my shit. I'm clockin' crazy cake. Now why would I wanna give all of this up?"

"I feel you," said Guru.

"No, you don't. But you will," replied Kendall, parking in front of one of his dope houses. He pulled a banger from his waist and put it to Guru's temple. "Call ya peoples and tell him I wanna holla at him. And if you pull out anything but a cell phone I'ma splatter ya head up on the windshield."

"Yo, dawg, you buggin'."

Guru unclipped his cell from his waist and called CJ.

"Sup, Unc?" CJ answered.

"Fam, I'm with those people you asked me to holla at and dude ain't feelin' your offer. Madda fact, it got him heated. Nigga got a strap to my head right now, talking crazy," explained Guru. Sweat poured down his face.

Kendall snatched the phone from him but kept the Nine pressed against Guru's head.

"Youngun, I'm hearin' ya name in the streets but apparently you haven't heard mine. You wanna buy me out huh? Well, here's your answer listen real close." *Boom! Boom!*

The sudden gunshots echoed like a cannon inside the SUV. Guru's head was splattered all over the window and the seat. The gory sight didn't even cause Kendall to blink in regret at what he had done. "Buy a casket for ya man, its game over for him. Let that be your warning to fall back young'un. I'm not the one to press. Ask around," he said as calm as can be.

Two days later Guru's body was found inside the trunk of a burned automobile on Avon Avenue. Kendall had sent the message that he was not to be fucked with. If he thought that the gruesomeness he showed in bodying and burning up Guru, a nigga he'd once hustled with would put fear into CJ's heart, he should've thought again. CJ was a beast because he feared nothing and no one. Plus he had muthafuckaz on his squad who could deliver Kendall to him on a silver platter without there being an all-out street war.

"Let's just bury Unc, then I'ma get at the nigga who murked him," CJ told his crew who were all chomping at their bits to let the streets know that when you fucked with that Little Bricks' squad, mothers had better be ready to mourn their sons.

***

"Daddy, this is my girl, Tamika, that I've been telling you about. Tamika, this is my man Diamond Rick," said Star, making the introduction in the living room of Diamond Rick's crib. Star had moved in with him a month ago, but this was Tamika's first time meeting him. Diamond Rick was definitely eye candy, though he was way too pretty for Tamika's taste. *His ass probably stays in the mirror more than Star does.* She thought as she eyed him up and down.

"How you doing beautiful?" asked Diamond Rick, taking her hand and kissing it.

"I'm fine and you?" she replied.

"Life is wonderful," he said.

I bet it is, nigga. You done added my girl to your stable, got her working the pole in a strip club to keep your pretty ass living like a boss playa. I ain't hatin' on you though. If it wasn't you macking Star, it would be some other nigga.

Tamika wanted to say what she was thinking so bad it hurt her jaws to hold it in.

"Daddy, Tamika wants me to go furniture shopping with her. Is it okay with you?" asked Star in such a docile tone that made Tamika want to throw up.

"Yeah, it's all good, just be back in time for work tonight. It's Saturday and the club is gonna be jumpin'."

"I will, daddy. I'm featuring tonight, right?"

"Yeah, and I know you gonna do your thing."

"I sho' am. I'm going to make you so much money we'll have to haul it out in a dump truck," said Star, pecking lips with Diamond Rick before following Tamika out of the house.

Tamika was so hot she thought her hair might catch on fire.

"I'm gonna make you so much money, Daddy. Eww!" she said mockingly as they drove off.

"Don't be a hater," laughed Star, looking in the mirror on the sun visor.

"Bitch, puhleeze! If you wanna pop your pussy for a living, I'm not knocking ya hustle but you have to be one dumb ho to shake your ass and give the money to a nigga. Shit, the muhfucka owns the club, why does he need your little bit of paper?"

"How about getting you some business and staying out of mine?" Star replied.

93

"You're so caught up in that nigga, you're not even raising those Bay Bay kids of yours. Got your mama raising 'em like she the one fucked and had 'em. That nigga must be mind-fucking you," Tamika went on chastising her girl who wasn't tryna hear it.

"You ain't know?" said Star, sucking her teeth.

"If you like it, I love it," Tamika sighed in exasperation.

They shopped for furniture for the den of the condo out in West Orange where CJ and Tamika had moved. The rest of the condo had already been furnished and decorated by Tamika and her Mom Dukes and the crib was laced. The den was to be CJ's sanctuary so Tamika chose masculine furniture and artwork for that room. She spent almost twenty-five stacks on the Italian leather sofa and recliner, smoke glass coffee and end tables, entertainment center, and plasma TV, all which would be delivered the next day.

After dropping Star back off at Diamond Rick's house, Tamika stopped at a Chinese restaurant to order take-out. Leaving out of the restaurant her eyes locked on a familiar face and his eyes locked with hers. It was the nigga that had grabbed her ass at the club that night, the one CJ had knocked out as he was being put into the paddy wagon.

"Sup, ma?" he spoke as Tamika passed by him and two dudes that were with him. They had just gotten out of a Jeep.

Tamika ignored him.

"Bitch, tell your nigga his day is comin'. Yours too skank!"

"Yo, Darius," said one of the dudes to him, whispering something in his ear.

Tamika's legs trembled as she hurried to her car. Once inside the Q45 she drove off, checking her rearview and saw that the Jeep was three cars behind her. She made a quick left turn to see if the Jeep would follow her. Her heart pounded when she checked her rearview and saw that it had. She quickly speed dialed CJ.

"Sup, baby girl?"

"CJ, that nigga from the club is following me!" Tamika cried frightenly.

"What nigga?"

After Tamika explained the situation to him, CJ told her to hop back on the main street and head to Little Bricks. He continued talking to her as he and Eric, who was rolling with him, headed toward Tamika.

"You strapped?" he asked his baby gangsta, lil' bruh.

"24/7."

"I don't see them behind me anymore," interjected Tamika with relief. Just a second ago she had been so afraid she had almost peed on herself.

"Just keep coming to me ma. We ain't gon' sleep on them niggaz. I shoulda dealt with dude long ago."

When Tamika spotted CJ's Expedition, she finally relaxed. CJ was her protector. She feared nothing when he was around. She pulled into a gas station and CJ pulled up next to her. He hopped down out of the truck, which was sitting on twenty-sixes, and looked around for the Jeep that Tamika had described. CJ's and Eric's hands were at their waists, ready to pop shit off at the first sign of drama. Darius and his mans had fell back, he had only been taunting Tamika, still foolishly thinking shit was a game despite the murders of his homies.

"I'ma get that bitch niggaz ass," promised CJ, later that night, holding Tamika in his arms. "Nigga had my boo shook, he gotta pay fa dat."

Tamika snuggled closer to him, pressing her naked body against his. They were laying in the California king-sized bed in their master bedroom. The satin sheets felt so good against her skin.

"I want you to get him, baby," said Tamika.

"Shorty, your wish is my command."

"Is it?"

"No doubt."

"Well, I wish you would lick the kitty cat for mama tonight."

"Boo, you ain't said nothin' but a word," proclaimed CJ, laying her on her back and stepping to his business.

ELEVEN

"Gurrlll, I had that glass dick in my mouth taking a big blast, one nigga was licking my titties, and another one with some Morris Chestnut lips was eating my pussy, all at the same time. I nutted so hard I saw Heaven's doors." Porcelin romanticized her first time smoking crack.

"Will you please hush, I'm trying to write my boo boo," said Kayundra, becoming irritated with her roomie. "I don't want to hear no crack escapades. There's nothing romantic about being a crackhead."

"It takes one to know one," chided Porcelin.

"Don't I know it," responded Kayundra from the small desk in the room where she sat with pen and pretty blue stationary in front of her.

"Yes you do or you wouldn't be here so don't get all new on me. Anyway, what would you like to talk about? Let me guess—um—Raheem. I'm telling you, you're setting yourself up for heartbreak then you'll run right back to the pipe."

"Porcelin, I am so not listening to you. Why are you always so cynical?"

"Do you really want me to answer that?"

"No. On second thought I don't. All I want is peace and quiet so that I can write my snuggles." Porcelin rolled her eyes and left out of the room. At thirty-two years old, and having gone through mad drama with dudes, Porcelin no longer believed in the fairy tale love that Kayundra spoke of when she talked about Raheem.

Kayundra cleared her mind of Porcelin's cynicism and began a long letter to Raheem.

Dear Raheem,

I hope that I am not overwhelming you with the volume of letters that I write to you. It's just that I think about you all of the time and I can't help but to put my feelings in a song or a letter. When I write to you it doesn't feel like you're so far away.

I miss you more than I ever missed anyone or anything in this world. I know I say that in every letter but it's so true. If I stopped breathing this very minute, at least I will have known what it's like to really love a man. It's strange that you seem so much wiser and focused than me, yet we are the same age. You have a certain sense of calm and purpose that makes it seem that you are prepared for anything that life throws your way. And your gentleness is incomparable. If I had only one day to live, I'd choose to spend those entire 24 hours with you.

Why am I speaking of dying when I've only just begun to LIVE! Baby it feels wonderful NOT to be high. I love the feeling of sobriety! When I think of how foul I was living. I just lay on my bed and cry in shame. It's like I don't even know that person I had become. That shit had me so down and low, I would steal from my own mama. Anything that could be sold or traded for a rock, including my body, was fair game. My dignity too.

Now that I'm no longer living like that, I feel so much better about myself and my future. I thank you for giving me the motivation to change. When you got shot it made me realize that if tragedy could come your way then it could easily come to mine, especially with the foul way I was living. I sat at your bedside and watched in amazement as you fought for your life. That made me realize how precious life is. I feel so blessed to have a second chance and to have a friend like you who loves me for who I am and for what's in my heart.

Raheem, I wouldn't be truthful if I tried to deny wanting much more than a friendship with you. However, regardless to what you say, I know that in order for that to happen I must prove to you that I am stronger than my addiction. Porcelin says that you will never be able to respect and love me completely because you know of my past. She thinks that I'm better off with someone who knows nothing about my recent past. I keep telling her that there is no one else for me but you. No one, not ever. She is constantly reminding me that you are not my man. But I know that you will be. God brought us back together for a reason and I trust in His judgement.

Love, Kayundra –Your Sparkle.

P.S. I have to go to a group meeting. I will write you again soon.

Rah was touched by Kayundra's letter though he was not sure that his sense of purpose measured up to how she envisioned it. True, he was gifted academically and planned to become a journalist but how purposeful was he when he was still hustling and banging niggaz if they violated?

He would ask himself this question in a moment of self-reflection, not only by Kayundra's letter but by a recent conversation with Big Ma as well.

Rah had sent Big Ma twenty-five hundred dollars; she had called to tell him that she was returning the money.

"Why?" he asked.

"Because it's the devil's money Raheem. I know that you didn't earn it honestly. If I accept it from you, I am condoning whatever sin you committed to get that money."

"Big Ma, everyone sins. All my life you've been telling me not to do wrong, that your God will provide a way. I don't see your God providing nothin' for nobody in the hood but hard times."

"Boy, don't you blasphemy His name," Big Ma scolded.

"I'm sorry," Rah apologized.

Big Ma was a Christian and though Rah praised Allah when he was on his Deen, he respected his grandmother's faith.

"Drugs led to your mother's murder and was your father's downfall long before he did what sent him to prison. If you're selling drugs that would really disappoint me," said Big Ma.

"I'm not selling crack," Rah offered in lame defense.

"Drugs is drugs. It don't matter which type."

Rah knew that Big Ma spoke the gospel but the fast money had him hooked. He tried to justify his greed by not slanging crack, the drug that had turned both of his parents into fiends. His mother, Connie, thirst for crack had enticed her to steal two hundred dollars' worth of rocks from a corner hustla. The petty dope boy retaliated by shooting Connie dead in front of Rah and LaKeesha and dozens of other witnesses.

Devin, their pops, was a fiend but he was still a dangerous nigga. He hustled up enough money to buy a strap off the streets then he hunted Connie's killer down and shot the nigga dead just like he'd done her. When the dead boy's uncle let it be known that he was looking to avenge his nephew's murder, Devin murked him next.

For both murders Devin caught life up in Rahway.

Rah respected the way his pops rode on the crab ass nigga who killed his moms; that was street justice with no cut. Though time had disintegrated his relationship with his pops and left them both nothing but faded memories of one another, Rah had love for his old dude. Crack may have broken Devin down but when the worst of the worst happened, he had shown that he would go all out for the one he loved.

"I understand what you're saying, Big Ma," Rah conceded as he let out a sigh after reflecting back on his parents' demise.

He didn't make any promises though because deep down he knew that he wasn't ready to give up hustlin'. Big Ma heard the conflict in his voice so she hadn't pressed him; she knew that all she could do was trust in The Lord. She had done her bone-weary best to instill righteousness in Rah and LaKeesha. It had been a constant battle trying to keep them from being tainted by their environment and now she wondered if she had lost the battle.

Big Ma's words and worry drove Rah to the mosque on the West End. He had not been to a mosque in several years, but today Rah felt the need to kneel amongst Muslims and pray to Allah for strength and guidance.

He did so with genuine humbleness.

However, Rah was not truly ready to submit to Allah's will. The Most High can only guide those who are truly accepting of His guidance. Rah was still straddling the fence even as he walked out of the mosque after praying.

Rah had just walked into his apartment, kicked off his Force One's and was chillin' when his cell phone rang. Not recognizing the number that showed on his caller ID, he answered with a dispassionate, "Yeah?"

"Hi, baby," she chirped, putting an instant smile on his face.

"Sup, ma? It's good to hear your voice. You sound all good and shit," Rah complimented.

"Thank you. It's so good to hear your voice too. My heart is beating so fast," said Kayundra, so excited to be talking to him.

"Yo, where are you calling me from?"

"I'm still at the center. One of the ladies smuggled a cell phone in, she's letting me use it."

"That's what's up."

"I miss you."

"I miss you too, shorty. What you been up to?"

"Getting myself together so that I can sparkle for you. I went to a meeting earlier. It was mostly repetitive of many of the other meetings we've had. This program is Christian-based and it has helped me to face my demons. But no program works, they tell us, unless we make it work for ourselves. Baby, guess what?" she asked changing subject and sounding enthusiastic. "In five days I'll be allowed a visit. My mother will come and she's bringing some home-cooked food. You know I'ma really get my grub on!"

"You gon' eat a little for me?"

"Mmmhmm."

"Tell your Mom Dukes I said hello when she visits you. I talked to her a coupla weeks ago, she's really proud of what you're doing."

"I know, she's my best friend. Besides you, she's the only one who still believes in me."

"You believe in yourself, don't you?" asked Rah remindfully.

"I do," said Kayundra. "Oh, I wrote a song titled "You're like a Dream". Of course it was inspired by you. I'll sing it for you the next time I see you. I wish that could be on my visitation day, but I understand that you can't come. Well, you could come, but I know you don't want to boggle my emotions while I'm going through this program. Anyway, my time is running out and I'll have to give the girl her phone back. Before we say goodbye, I want to read to you a poem I wrote for you. It's just a little somethin' somethin'."

"Blow me away," he said.

"Okay, you ready?"

"I'm ready."

Kayundra took a deep breath to calm her nerves then recited:

"I remember baby, that it was you who told me that love,
does not have to hurt.
That tears on my pillow wasn't the way that
True love works.
That a healthy love never brings you down,
It lifts you up.
When you were hurt you thought that I was healing you,
But in truth, you were healing me.
You helped me to love myself again, to dream, and to reclaim
My self-dignity.
To strive to be the queen that God created me to be.
No matter what life holds for us, baby,
Whether we are destined to be friends or more,
Like woman and man,
If you ever need unconditional support,
Just reach out your hand.
You'll feel me reaching out to you.

Thugs Cry

"Damn, boo, you tryna make a nigga cry?" asked Rah touched by the poem.

"You need to stop! You know you not finna cry," she giggled.

"Your time is up, Kayundra. You're not the only one who has a man to call," Rah heard a woman say playfully in the background.

"Besides, we want you to put on a concert for us," added another voice, which belonged to Porcelin.

"You hear them, baby?" Kayundra said into the phone.

"Yeah. You doing concerts all up in there? You tell them I said they need to be paying you," Rah kidded with her.

Kayundra delivered his message.

"Pay you no damn mind," said Porcelin and Rah heard a room full of laughter on the other end of the line. He could tell that Kayundra was well liked by the other women in the program.

"Let me go, baby, before I have to go postal on this chick about her dang cell phone," said Kayundra.

"Raheem, your girl just frontin', I'll whup her young ass," shouted the lady who the cell belonged to. Her tone made it obvious that her and Kayundra were just kidding back and forth.

"Sing pretty for 'em, boo," Rah encouraged.

"I will. Love you!"

"Love you too, ma."

With Raheem's sweet goodbye still ringing in her ears and fluttering her heart, Kayundra sang her ass off for the women that night. She closed her eyes and thought of how much she loved and needed Rah and tears ran down her face as her self-written lyrics of love, hope, and redemption flowed from deep down in her soul in a melodic beauty that earned her a standing ovation from the fifteen recovering addicts present.

Most of the fifteen women were crying themselves, over-whelmed by Kayundra's emotions and angelic voice.

Ca$h

TWELVE

Kayundra had less than three weeks left before she would complete the ninety-day program. Last week she and the other women enjoyed visits from their families and loved ones. Tomorrow they were all being granted twelve hour passes away from the recovery center; it was one of the final steps in the program to determine if they were ready to return to their homes and be able to live drug free without having to be watched over.

Kayundra was excited about the pass; she was writing Raheem to share her excitement with him. Porcelin was looking over Kayundra's shoulder, all up in her business.

"Girl, all you do is write that nigga. I don't know why you're so sprung on him, I don't see shit he's doing for you," she tried to pour salt.

"Oh trust, he's already done a lot," said Kayundra.

"What has he done for you?" asked Porcelin in a cynical tone.

"He's motivated me to do for myself."

"Tssk! That ain't shit. You can't spend motivation or buy a damn thing with it."

"Material things don't matter much to me."

"Boo, you got a lot to learn and you sho can't learn it from a baby boy."

"Go away, Porcelin. Can't you see I'm trying to write a letter?"

"Okay, I won't talk about your little boyfriend," said Porcelin as she stood in the mirror on the wall in their room, finger combing her shoulder length feathered hair.

"Yes you will. You'll only hush for a minute then you'll start up again, like you always do," Kayundra pulled her card.

Because she had been there and done that, Porcelin thought that she knew everything. She didn't consider herself a crack addict. "I can take it or leave it," she always said at the meetings. She was the type of smoker that was never straight strung out on crack, but neither was she ever quite drug free. She'd been smoking crack for almost ten years. God had blessed her with a bangin' body and a cute face that had thus far withstood her years of addiction.

Porcelin's game hadn't been turning tricks for rocks. She got high and fucked pro athletes and big money dope boys. Still, she was a fiend, though a burner to the head couldn't get her to admit it.

"Ask ya man if he's heard from his boy CJ, that's the nigga I wanna meet, judging from what you say about him. You know me. I love them dope niggaz, young, old, skinny, fat, as long as they got cake and product, I'm tryna see 'em. In a pinch, a nigga with nothing but product will do."

Porcelin saw that Kayundra was ignoring her so she kicked carpet.

The next day Porcelin was filled with exuberance of freedom when she was granted the twelve hour pass. She and Kayundra caught the train to Newark Penn Station then caught the bus to Little Bricks.

"Kayundra, would you and Porcelin like something to eat?" asked Kayundra's Mom Dukes after greeting them with a warm hug.

"We sure would," answered Porcelin, never shy.

Kayundra's Mom Dukes fixed a late breakfast of turkey sausage, egg omelets, grits, and toast. After breakfast the three of them talked for an hour, then Kayundra said, "I'll be right back. I'm going down to say hello to Big Ma."

Kayundra left Porcelin talking to her Mom Dukes while she took the stairs three flights down to Rah's grandmother's apartment.

"Hey, baby, come and give me a hug," smiled Big Ma letting Kayundra in. She was crazy about Kayundra despite her problems because she knew that Kayundra's heart was platinum.

"Chile, you're looking so good!" exclaimed Big Ma.

"Thank you."

"No, baby, praise God. He is so wonderful."

"Yes, He is," agreed Kayundra.

"Just keep faith in the Lord and He'll keep on blessing you. Ain't you a sight for sore eyes!"

Kayundra was blushing all over.

"Where's LaKeesha and the baby?" she asked.

"They just left a while ago. Gone somewhere with her new boyfriend."

"New boyfriend? What happened to the baby's daddy?" Kayundra inquired, being nosey.

"He went to trial and got convicted of murder, that's what happened. Now he's gone to prison and you know she is too hot in the behind to wait on him to come home.

If Raheem were to go to prison, I'd wait on him for eternity, Kayundra thought.

"Anyway, are you out of the program now?" asked Big Ma.

"No, I'm on pass. I have three weeks left in the program."

"That's good. I'm proud of you, and I know God has good things planned for you," said Big Ma, sitting down on the couch and patting a spot next to her. "Chile, you might as well sit down, you ain't gonna grow taller standing up," she joked.

Kayundra sat down next to Big Ma, not minding the smell of Ben Gay that emaciated from her.

"Now you listen to me real good honey. I know you love my Raheem. And I know he loves you, too. Y'all can just save all that friend's nonsense y'all be tryna sell. I may be old but I still know love when I see it."

"I know you do Big Ma," Kayundra happily agreed.

"Raheem is a good person with a good head on his shoulders but he doesn't trust his intelligence. If you're gonna be his woman, you'll have to be strong to make sure he stays on the right path."

"But how do I do that, Big Ma? I'm not very strong at all," Kayundra admitted.

"You'll have to find a way. Otherwise you'll bring each other down," Big Ma said, speaking with the wisdom of her seventy-one years of age. "Just pray," she added, seeing a lack of confidence but a whole lot of love in Kayundra's eyes.

As Kayundra climbed the stairs back up to her Mom Dukes' apartment, she passed by several fiends buying crack from dealers on the stairs. She noted the sunken in faces and lifeless eyes of the crackheads and shivered at the reality that just months ago she was one of them too.

After she collected Porcelin, they walked toward the bus stop.

"Girl, why we gotta catch the bus over to my peoples spot? We both fine enough to charm one of these niggaz out on the block to give us a ride to Springfield Avenue. What's the point in having booty if we don't use it to our advantage?" asked Porcelin.

"No, let's just stick to the plan, the bus will be along shortly," Kayundra objected.

"Watch this," said Porcelin, undeterred. She twisted her butt as she walked right up to a dude named Rakim who was posted between two buildings. He grilled her even though she was looking kinda good, like a smoker does when she's been clean for a few months.

Porcelin was fittin' the hell out of a pair of Seven jeans, thighs thick, booty swole.

"Boo, I know you're on your grind but my mother is real sick and I need a ride to her house so that I can take her some medication," gamed Porcelin, pushing her titties out.

"Fuck I look like? A taxi?" Rakim spazzed. "Yo Kayundra, she with you?"

"Let's go, Porcelin," urged Kayundra, who was back on the sidewalk, not bothering to answer Rakim.

He walked over to where Kayundra stood and looked her up and down. "Damn, yo, where you been? You done got thick as hell shorty." Then he checked out Porcelin, "Ma, that ass got a nigga thinkin'."

"Oh, it's like that?" Porcelin jiggled her butt like a stripper.

Rakim pulled out a few stones. "I got what y'all want, y'all got what I want. Let's make it happen."

"I'm out," said Kayundra. She did not wait for Porcelin to respond; she turned and walked up the street.

If this bitch is behind me, cool. If not, I'm leaving her ass. I'm not letting her get me caught up in anything.

"Aw ho, don't be tryna act grand 'cause yo crack smoking ass done gained a few pounds. Just last month you was suckin' dick for kibbles and bits," hollered Rakim.

To Kayundra it sounded like the whole block was laughing, though in actuality there was only a few niggaz amused by Rakim's put down of her. She wanted to turn around and correct him, it had been five months since she had sucked dick for a rock, not one. Instead of responding to the jeer, Kayundra stiffened her back, held her head up high and pushed on.

Porcelin caught up to her as she passed by one of CJ's spots.

"Basehead Kayundra, does ya friend suck and fuck for a rock like you do?" someone called out.

Porcelin whirled around and faced the nigga that had hurled the insult.

"Yeah boo, I fuck for rocks. The kind you get at Tiffany's— something your broke ass can't afford."

"Ugly ass bitch, ya rotten pussy ain't worth a nic', let alone no damn *Tiffany's*," another block hustla butted in.

"Kayundra, I know you not tryna front. I done ran up in you for some crack residue!" a third nigga interjected, causing mad laughter from his mans.

"Look what you got started!" Kayundra gritted at Porcelin.

"Fuck them mark ass lames. They ain't nothin' but some young tricks. If there was no crack, all of them nigga'z dicks would be brand new, still in the wrapper 'cause they sho ain't got no mack game." Despite her anxiety, Kayundra had to laugh at that.

"Kayundra!"

She turned toward the familiar voice. CJ was getting out of his Expedition, rockin' his chain, a white T-shirt, RocaWear jeans and Timbs. A New Jersey Nets fitted was pulled down low over his brows.

"I see you're back on the block, cluckin'. I told Rah you was gonna fall weak."

"You're wrong, CJ. I'm still in rehab. I'm just home on a pass; I'm not doing anything but on my way to the bus stop."

"That's CJ?" whispered Porcelin. "Damn, that young nigga is fine! Introduce me bitch."

"CJ, this is my friend, Porcelin. Porcelin, that's CJ, Raheem's best friend. And that's Kareem who just walked up."

"Sup," Kareem nodded.

CJ didn't bother speaking to Porcelin.

"If you're with Kayundra, I know you a clucker too," CJ accused.

"Na, ma, say it ain't so. You too damn fine to fuck wit' da pipe," intoned Kareem who then started tryna put his mack down.

Porcelin was only half-listening because who she really wanted to holla at was the Big Dog, CJ.

CJ paid her about the same attention that he would pay to a Jehovah Witness so Porcelin accepted the consolation.

"Give me your number, boo. I'ma give you a call," she told Kareem.

"What, you gon' program it into ya cell phone?"

"Um, I lost my cell baby boy. We gon' have to do this old school, write it down on a piece of paper."

"You got a pen?"

"Nope. Sorry."

"Yo, I got fiddy dollars for a pen," Kareem yelled out, stuntin' hard.

A fiend ran up with an eye liner in hand.

"That'll work yo. But I'm not given yo ass but forty, you been owing me ten for the longest," Kareem said to the baremouthed woman who was only thirty-two but looked sixty.

"That's cool. Can you pay me with rocks?"

"Yeah. Yo, fam, give this bitch two twenty cent joints," he called out to a nigga on the squad. Kareem wrote his cell number on a fifty dollar bill and gave it to Porcelin.

"Get at me, ma."

"I will," she promised.

"If you don't, it's your loss. I can blow my nose on fiddy dollar bills and run out of snot way before I run out of guap, nah mean?"

Kayundra had never been so happy to get onto the bus in her life. After all the jeers, the indifferent expressions on the faces of the other passengers on the bus seemed like welcoming smiles.

Porcelin wasn't tripping. Little Bricks wasn't her hood, so the insults hadn't been as personal to her as they'd been to Kayundra.

The anecdote for them taunting will be redemption. Only God can judge me, Kayundra reminded herself. Time will prove them wrong about me.

"Them nickel and dime niggaz think they are all that just because they're street pharmacist. But I gotta admit, even at my age, I still love the fuck out of a hustla'z swag," said Porcelin, seated next to Kayundra on the bus. "I like that damn CJ. Is his young ass always so damn mean?"

"Towards me, he is," said Kayundra with regret. She badly wanted Rah's best friend to like her.

"I bet I can soften his ass up."

"I bet you can."

"What's wrong with you? I know you didn't let those niggaz upset you? They just frontin' 'cause their mans were around. Get them alone and they'll give up their re-up for some of what we got."

"Porcelin, aren't you tired of all the bullshit? I mean, don't you want to be respected?"

"No. I just wanna be high and get paid."

When they reached Porcelin's cousin's house on Springfield Avenue, Kayundra realized that it was a crack house as soon as they walked in the door. Baseheads were sitting on the floor of the furniture-less, bare-floor living room, getting blasted.

"Girl, I'm outta here!" Kayundra grilled Porcelin and hissed.

111

"Don't bug out, I just want to spend a few minutes with my cuz then we can bounce.

Porcelin's cousin, Camilla, had visited her at the rehab house so Kayundra had already met her. She smiled at Porcelin as she came from out of a back room of the raggedy house, pulling up her Capri pants with a fat greasy man behind her. The man ogled Kayundra and said "I wish I could get this dick hard again, you look like a good piece of ass."

Kayundra just ignored him.

"Leave her alone, Tiny. She's tryna stay clean," said Camilla.

"Not trying, I *am* staying clean," corrected Kayundra.

She arrived back at the rehab house with three hours to spare before curfew at eight. She had walked out and left Porcelin at the crack house. The house matron asked why she had returned so soon. "And where is Porcelin? I thought that you two were together?"

"I wasn't feeling well so I came on back. I left Porcelin at the mall, she's cool." Kayundra lied, tryna cover for her friend.

"She'll get herself in trouble," said the house matron. "Here, I need you to pee in this for me." She shoved a cup in Kayundra's face.

When Kayundra submitted the urine sample, the matron asked, "Is everything okay?"

"Are you asking if I've used drugs while out on pass?"

"No. Had you relapsed I don't believe that you would have returned from pass so early. But I am suspicious of your story, and I suspect that your early return has something to do with Porcelin," said the matron, who had a very keen sense for detecting game. Dealing with addicts for more than ten years had her on point.

Still, Kayundra stuck to her story.

"If Porcelin has violated her treatment, you aren't helping her by covering for her. Remember, we talked extensively about *enablers*."

"No, she was fine when I left her," said Kayundra. The house was quiet because no one else had returned from pass yet. She went to shower after being told her urine sample was clean of drugs. After showering and putting on pajamas and a tee, Kayundra began writing a letter to Raheem. An hour later, other women began returning from pass one by one.

"So, how was your day?" inquired one of the women, speaking to Kayundra.

"Uneventful," she said, not wanting to recap her day. Also, she was worried about Porcelin.

"Did you get some dick?" asked another.

"No, I did not. The only person I'd get with like that is way down in Atlanta, Georgia."

"Yeah, we know. Raheem, right?"

Thirty minutes before curfew, ten women had returned, leaving five still out. The ten women started placing bets on which of the five would not return at all. Kayundra refused to place a bet, she was hoping that everyone would return although the situation she'd last seen Porcelin in was as dangerous as dangling from the roof of a high-rise by a piece of thread.

Two more women returned five minutes before curfew, leaving three unaccounted for, Porcelin amongst the absent. A chorus of applause erupted when Porcelin came bouncing into the day room where all the women had gathered, beating curfew by only thirty seconds.

"How many of you *dope heads* counted me out?" she half-joked.

Relieved laughter answered her, but the joy subsided quickly as they realized that two women had not and probably would not return.

A while later, Porclein was seated at the foot of Kayundra's bed. Kayundra was in bed with her back against the headboard, about to read *Thugs and the Women Who Love Them* by Wahida Clark.

"Girl, why did you leave me?" Porcelin whispered.

"You know dang well why I left Porcelin. I don't appreciate you taking me to a crack house! You may think that shit is cute, but hello, we're supposed to stay away from those places!"

In typical Porcelin fashion, she dismissed Kayundra's feelings. "Stop overreacting. If being in a crack house makes you wanna get high, that ass wanted to do it all along."

"No, that's contrary to what the counselors have been telling us about addictive behavior and things that can trigger a relapse," argued Kayundra.

"What the fuck do they know?" shot back Porcelin, sucking her teeth.

Kayundra just shook her head.

"Well, did you get high?" she could not resist asking.

"Nope. You think I'm a fiend? I told y'all bitches, I only get high when I *want* to. I got me some young dick and some money though."

"From who?" asked Kayundra, laughing.

"Kareem," answered Porcelin, pulling out a small roll of bills and waving them in Kayundra's face. "And I got me some rocks." She flashed eight rocks in individual small baggies.

"Have you peed in the cup?"

"Not yet. I figured that tree monkey would test us when we returned so we'll smoke this after I go give her a little pee," Porcelin said, smiling deviously.

The smile hadn't had time to leave her face when the matron came to get her to pee in the cup. Porcelin smoothly slid the crack up under the blanket folded at the foot of Kayundra's bed. When the matron turned her back, Porcelin tossed a straight shooter to Kayundra then followed the matron out of the room.

Kayundra made sure that the coast was clear, then she peaked up under the blanket. The rocks stared up at her like the whites of death's eyes. The longer she stared at the crack, the larger the rocks appeared to be, until their presence became the size of boulders; large enough to crush all the months of drug-free living Kayundra had built up.

Her eyes were locked on the eight rocks; her hands involuntarily caressed the glass straight shooter, the type that her lips were so familiar with. It was like a battle of wills between her conscious thoughts and her subconscious desires.

It's the best high on earth but what about all the shameful shit it made me do? Be like Porcelin only get high when you want to. Control the drug, don't let it control you. But I can't control it, that's how I ended up here! Raheem would be so disappointed in me. But he's not even my man. How will he know if I just get high this once?

Kayundra made sure that no one was coming into the room before reaching under the blanket and cuffing the rocks, all eight of them. With crack and paraphernalia in hand, she tip-toed to the bathroom down the hall.

Ca$h

THIRTEEN

CJ was hotter than a steam iron. They had buried Guru two weeks ago and he wanted to avenge the grizzly death of his comrade. Kendall had bodied Guru, threatened CJ, and was riding around Newark like that ass was bullet proof.

"I'm sending the goons at his people tonight! We hittin' three of his spots simultaneously, wettin' everything breathing," he said to Kareem, though Cujo had warned him not to turn the streets red with blood.

"That will bring heat," the detective had explained.

"Yeah? Well guess what? It's yo job to cool shit off. Ain't that what you told me? I make a mess, you'll clean it up. Those were *your* words so get ready to do a lot of cleaning up," snapped CJ.

Now CJ was ignoring Cujo's calls.

"Fam, you're the boss and I'ma ride if you say ride, but we don't have a beef with that nigga'z whole squad. If you wanna control those spots, we're gonna need those niggaz to pump work for us. Let's just chop off the head and replace it with yours, nah mean?" suggested Kareem. "My dude Flip is down with that squad and son ain't too happy with his position; he feels like he has put in a lot of work for Kendall and deserves to be his top lieutenant. But Kendall played him, gave the position to a kid named Bo, 'cause Bo fucks with Kendall's niece, a shorty from Bergen Street."

CJ read the play correctly.

"So, you saying we can step to your dude Flip and get him to set Kendall up for us to bang him?" CJ asked.

"Yep and we gotta bang Bo too."

"Is Flip official?"

"Yo, how official can a nigga be if he sets up his people?" asked Kareem.

"That's what I mean. So let's play it like this: holla at the nigga and we'll get him to bang Bo himself, then deliver Kendall to us. I want that ass personally. What your dude want for doing this? Let me guess, he wanna be HNIC of Avon Ave."

Kareem smiled. "That's the golden nugget."

"A'ight, but you know I'ma bang his ass eventually. Can't trust a nigga like that," said CJ.

"I ain't got no problem with it. My loyalty is to you my nigga," vowed Kareem.

Two nights later, Bo stepped out of his shorty's house on Bergen Street and caught a chest full of lead.

Kendall made immediate plans to get back at CJ who he believed had bodied his lieutenant. In the meantime, he had no choice but to elevate another one of his people to street lieutenant, the position that Bo had held down. He chose Flip; Kendall's choice was like he had just signed his own death certificate. Kendall only had one week to live but of course he had no way of knowing that.

While he waited for Flip to deliver on his end, CJ was dropping work all over Newark. Little Bricks was pumpin' like the projects on Prince Street used to pump back in the day before they were demolished. CJ was also looking for that nigga Darius, Tamika's antagonizer.

Tonight though, CJ was taking a break from the drama. The only thing pressing him was that Tamika was blowing up his phone, leaving crazy voicemails and texts. He turned the cell off and refocused his attention on Tricia, who was sprawled out naked across the bed.

"I don't know why I'm still fuckin' with yo ass after you made me play myself, just so you wouldn't lose that bitch," she pouted, mad at herself because she could not leave CJ alone. She was hooked on his swag as well as his dick game.

"You fucks wit' me 'cause I'm a boss nigga and because you my bitch," he said arrogantly, nibbling on her neck and finger fucking her pussy.

"Eat me out, CJ," she moaned but he ignored her.

"You did it once before, back when we first used to mess around."

"Shorty, that was then, this is now. I be hearing shit about you fuckin' with other niggaz. I'm not eatin' behind the next niggaz dick yo."

"Man, I'm not fuckin' nobody but you," Tricia swore, which was the truth but CJ wasn't buying it.

"Whateva. I'm not licking the kitty cat, sorry, ma."

"Get up then, 'cause if I'm not good enough for you to eat, I'm not good enough for you to fuck. I bet you be eating that bitch you got at home."

"Don't worry about her, just play your position."

"And what is that?" she asked in a half moan, because CJ was now rubbing her clit.

"My freak bitch. Now open your legs wider and tell me you want me to fuck you."

"Okay. I want you to fuck me CJ."

"And what else?"

"Treat me like your ho."

CJ was ready to run up in Tricia when something told him to turn his cell back on. He followed his instincts and did so. Five minutes later the cell rang, interrupting him in mid-stroke.

"Don't answer it. Please," begged Tricia. She was just about to have an orgasm.

"Got to, shorty," he said, looking at the screen and seeing that it was Eric calling. "Yo, wassup?"

"That nigga, Darius, who was following Tamika in that Jeep she describe," Eric began. "Yo, me and Premo just snatched that bitch nigga up."

"From where?"

"Bumped into him on Grafton, coming out of that record joint owned by those Jamaican niggaz. One of the homies that was at the club the night that shit popped off pointed the pussy out to us yo."

"Where the nigga at now?"

"In the trunk of Premo's car."

"Is his eyes shut?"

"Not yet."

"Handle y'all business and don't be joyriding around with the body. One," instructed CJ.

"One."

When CJ finished boning Tricia, he took a quick shower and headed home. On the way out to West Orange, he called Eric to make sure that him and Premo were okay.

"Yeah, we handled it," said Eric.

"A'ight, where you at?"

"Chillin' at the crib with a shorty."

"Where mama and Brianna?"

"Man, you know where Mom Dukes at and Bri next door, spending the night with her lil' friend."

"A'ight, lil' bruh, I'ma fuck witchu later. You make sure you strap up 'fore you run up in shorty, fuck around and one of these lil' hot ass hos give you that grown man," warned CJ, speaking of AIDS.

When CJ walked into his crib, he found that Tamika was not there. *It's damn near midnight, where the fuck can she be?* he wondered, dialing her cell phone.

"Hello?"

"Where the fuck you at?" he snapped, though he was the one who had been out creepin'.

"I'm at the club where Star works," she said over the music.

"Fuck you doing there?"

"Having some drinks. Fuck you doing over at that bitch Tricia's house?"

"Ain't nobody been over Tricia's house." CJ lied.

"Well, why was your car parked in front of her building?"

"'Cause I parked it there. I was riding with Eric, since you spying on a nigga, you oughta know."

"Nigga, you are such a liar!" She dial toned his ass. She didn't know for sure that he was lying, but she didn't trust his ass. Her Mom Dukes had told her about CJ's whip being parked outside of Tricia's building.

CJ called her right back.

"What CJ?"

"Bitch, you must got another mouth stashed somewhere, 'cause you gon' make me bust the one you talkin' so mufuckin' slick out of!"

"I'm not your bitch! Ya bitch is the bald-headed ho whose house you been over to!" Tamika screamed into the phone as hot tears ran down her face. She could not believe that CJ would disrespect her like that, calling her a bitch.

"Yo, I'm sorry, ma. You know a nigga don't mean that shit," he checked himself. "Fa real Mika, you know you're wrong for being in a strip club. How did you get there anyway?"

"I caught a cab."

"I oughta make yo ass walk home," he threatened.

"Hmmpf! You'll grow old waiting."

"What?"

"Nothing. Come pick me up."

CJ fell up in the strip club ready to blast on the first nigga or dyke bitch that he saw in his girl's grill.

Tamika was chilling alone at the bar, having shooed niggaz off, when CJ found her. Star walked up at the same time as CJ, all she had on was a G-string, a lace bra, and stilettos.

CJ grilled her like it was *her* fault that he had to come collect wifey from a strip club.

When they got home, CJ didn't say a word, he went into the kitchen with some blocks and started whipping them up in the microwave.

Tamika came up behind him and wrapped her arms around his waist. "Baby, I'm sorry," she cried. "I get lonely out here by myself and when you won't answer your phone it drives me crazy."

"What, you don't trust a nigga? I'm out hustlin' for us. I'ma cop you another whip. I just didn't want you pushin' the Infiniti anymore 'cause that nigga know it. That's why I sold it. But you ain't gotta worry 'bout that bitch nigga no more; we got at that ass tonight," said CJ.

Tamika knew what he meant.

121

"CJ, please don't let the money change you," she said, crying.

"Neva dat, baby girl." He promised something that he was not equipped to stop from happening. "I'ma always love you; you can trust in that." At least that part would prove to be true.

"Sup, fam?"

"I'm good," replied Premo, touching fists with Flip.

"This my peoples CJ."

"What's good? The whole city on your jock yo," Flip told CJ, who just nodded. Fuck the dick riding; CJ wanted to know what the business was. "So, how's it going down Black? You done rocked the nigga to sleep for us?" he questioned

Flip, staring at him with a piercing glare.

"Yeah, he's meeting me at this building he's leasing on Evergreen Place in East Orange. He's supposed to be turning it into a music studio but ain't shit in there yet. I'm supposed to hit him with some guap and pick up some work from him."

"How much work?" asked CJ, still staring at Flip, who looked like Flava Flav.

"A bird of heroin and two bricks of coke."

"How much guap you suppose to have for him?"

"Just seventy-five stacks, money from the last two nights. Shit been slow."

"Aight, when this go down, you get to keep the cake, and I'ma give you a third of the work but you can't pump it from our spots once I take over, understood?" instructed CJ.

"Yep," agreed Flip.

The sun had just retreated when Kendall pulled into the lot in front of the building where he was meeting Flip. He didn't see Flip's car in the lot which was empty so he parked and walked toward the building. A figure stepped out of the shadows.

"This is for Guru, nigga!"

Kendall's hand went to his waist after hearing the threat, but his draw wasn't fast enough. He was up against three shooters, two of which had just appeared.

CJ, Premo, and Flip let loose.

Boc! Boc! Boc! Boc! Boc! Boc!

Kendall's body jerked before he hit the ground, twisted and bloody. CJ walked up and stood over him.

"It's ova ol' school!"

Boc! Boc!

Two to the hat rack.

Ca$h

FOURTEEN

"So, you flushed the rocks down the toilet?" asked Rah. He was talking on the cell phone to Kayundra. She was using the phone that the woman at the rehab house had smuggled in. Kayundra had just told Rah everything that had happened when she went out on pass.

"Yep, and I smashed that damn straight shooter into a million little pieces. Porcelin is still mad at me."

"I'm proud of you, baby girl. That Porcelin chick sounds like a hot mess."

"Oh, she's definitely that," said Kayundra.

"Well, in two more weeks you'll be done with the program. I know you're looking forward to that. You got any plans?"

"I'm going to get a job and I'm going to continue to write songs. Maybe I'll try to get into the music industry but not right away. I don't think I'm ready for that, it's too much pressure. What I would really like to do is come visit you in ATL," Kayundra held her breath as she nervously awaited Rah's response.

She screamed with joy when she heard him say, "I can make that happen. Just tell me when you wanna come, how long you plan to stay, and I'll get you some plane tickets. I'll send you some money to go shopping for new clothes to bring with you too, 'cause I know that butt done got swole up."

"Yes, it has," she laughed. "I'm looking real fine baby, and my skin is so clear. But you don't have to send me money for new clothes. My mother promised to handle that."

"I got you anyway, shorty," he said.

"Can you afford all of that?"

"Ma, I might be a college dude but I still know how to get mines," Rah reminded her.

When Kayundra hung up from talking to Rah, she felt like she was floating on a cloud. Two weeks could not pass fast enough.

As for Rah, he was anxious to see Kayundra, too.

In the meantime, though, he still had to stay on point with his classes and continue to make it do what it do in the streets. His man Don and 'em had caught heat behind a shootout with some niggaz on the Westside and had to bounce back to New York for a minute. So now Rah was fuckin' with N.O. Shit was still sweet.

Rah went and scooped up DaQuan to go to the strip club. They hit The Blue Flame this night.

Inside, they ran into a thirsty nigga named Paco, who was from Zone Three like DaQuan. Paco was a short shabby dude who was too slick for his own good. He pushed up on Rah and DaQuan.

"What it do, shawdy?" he smiled a mouth full of platinm at DaQuan.

"You know me, keepin' it pimpin'," DaQuan replied, dapping him.

"I hear ya, shawdy, I see you rollin' wit' rich folks. What's da business Rah? Fuck wit' me, I'm leaking."

"Paco, why would I fuck with you? When you done shitted on every nigga that has tried to give you a helping hand. C'mon dawg. I keep up with the streets," said Rah, not mincing his words.

"Ahh man, it ain't even like dat playa. I ain't never shitted on a real nigga. Those dudes you referring to tried to pimp a nigga. You feel me?"

"Every one of 'em huh?"

"Shawdy, tell him how these niggaz be tryna handle a muhfucka." He tried to enlist DaQuan's help.

"You talking to him; tell him yaself," said DaQuan.

Paco's reply got twisted in his lying tongue and never came out. Finally he said, "Rah, just front me a halfa brick at a fair price and I got you."

"I don't fuck with coke, yo."

"Oh, well, you got some purp or some cush?"

"I got both but I'm not tryna fuck witchu, son."

"Why not? Damn, you scared to give a nigga a play?"

126

"Nah, I'm scared of what I'll do to you if you play with my guap. That's real talk."

"I'm not gonna play with ya guap shawdy. Fa real, fuck wit' me one time."

Rah wasn't tryna hear it. A big booty stripper was on stage making her ass clap and Paco was all up in his ear fuckin' up his groove.

"A'ight, yo, I'ma fuck witchu. Gimma ya number and I'll get at you tomorrow," said Rah agitated.

He programmed the pesty nigga'z number into his cell phone then he returned his attention to the bodacious chocolate honey on stage with the stupid booty. Paco went off to agitate someone else.

"Rah, I know you not gon' fuck wit' that nigga, shawdy don't pay," DaQuan stated what Rah already knew. But Rah was on some other shit.

"Yeah, I know. But I'ma fuck with him anyway. Niggaz like Paco think shit is sweet. Niggaz like me were put here to show 'em that this ain't no fuckin game," he said.

Two weeks later, Rah was looking for Paco, strapped with two burners. Paco only owed Rah five stacks but it was the principle that had Rah heated.

Nigga 'bout to find out how Newark niggaz get down. These niggaz in ATL might spare his ass, but I'ma heat up his muhfuckin' forehead.

But Paco could not be found.

Kayundra came through the arrival gate at the airport carrying a brown leather overnight bag that matched well with the brown velour sweat suit she was wearing and the brown suede Baby Phat sneakers. Her hair was cut and styled into feathers. Her dark chocolate skin tone had returned to its richness. Even her teeth, which smoking crack had discolored, were regaining their natural whiteness; Rah noted when she smiled at him just before dropping her bag and running into his arms.

"It's so good to see you," she cried tears of joy.

"Same here, ma. Damn, you lookin' good."

"You think so?" Kayundra blushed, enjoying the feel of his arms around her.

"No doubt," he kissed her softly on the lips and Kayundra's heart fluttered.

They held hands as they walked to baggage claim to retrieve the suitcase that Kayundra had brought along. When they reached Raheem's apartment and stepped inside, Kayundra was greeted with shouts of "Welcome to the ATL!" by Stephanie, Hakeem, DaQuan, N.O., and a few classmates of Rah's. Of course, she didn't know any of them; still, she was overwhelmed by the reception.

The get together lasted for a few hours then Rah's friends left them to spend some time alone.

"Thank you for everything," said Kayundra. "This is already the best day of my life."

"It gets better, ma."

They chilled in the Jacuzzi in the den, drinking V-8 Splash while vanilla incense burned and Jaheim played in the background. Kayundra had on a red two-piece bathing suit that showed off the thickness that she had regained.

Rah had on silk boxers. His well-toned chest and defined abs felt so good to Kayundra's touch.

"C'mere, ma," Rah guided her onto his lap so that she was straddling him. "You know I've been dreaming of this for months," he said, unfastening her top.

"Me too," moaned Kayundra as he cupped her mouthful of titties, caressing both dark chocolate nipples with his thumbs.

"Can I taste 'em?" His mouth covered one nipple before she could reply *yes*.

As Rah alternately sucked both of her breasts, he gripped her hips and grinded her on his dick. Kayundra bit down on her lip in passion as her whole body became aflame.

Her mouth found his and their tongues intertwined. The familiarity that they both felt from the years that they were together when they were younger erased any awkwardness that may have existed between them otherwise; yet everything seemed brand new, especially for Kayundra. It was a new beginning with an old love.

Rah eased her bikini bottoms to the side and felt her wetness with his fingers. They were both anxious for each other's body so the foreplay was cut short and they found themselves in the bedroom panting as Rah put on a condom and entered Kayundra.

She had given him her virginity back when they were both thirteen years old. So much had happened since then, but Kayundra didn't want to think about any of that now. She just wanted to enjoy being made love to.

They made passionate love throughout the night; when they awakened in the morning they were tangled like two pretzels.

"I could lay in your arms forever," she told him when he awoke with her head on his chest.

"That would be nice ma, but I wanna show you the city."

"Okay. Last night was so wonderful, I hope we'll have many more nights like that," she said, drawing circles on his chest with her tongue.

Before Rah knew it, she had him inside her mouth, sucking him to another erection. He wasn't complaining; he was feeling the same insatiable passion for Kayundra as she felt for him.

After he released his pleasure into her mouth, Rah laid Kayundra on her back, spread her thighs and reciprocated the ecstasy.

Kayundra spent two weeks in ATL, enjoying every minute of it. Rah took her to Six Flags over Georgia, where they got on all the rides, screaming like kids on the roller coasters, eating cotton candy and having a blast. They also went to White Waters amusement park, visited the Martin Luther King Jr. Center, the Underground, the historic Auburn Avenue and many other tourists spots.

129

When Rah had to go handle business, Stephanie usually kept Kayundra company. Kayundra knew that Rah was still in the streets; he didn't lie to her.

"I just don't want anything to happen to you," she told him as she prepared to catch her flight back home.

"I'm not out there like that," he said.

"Please be careful," she begged of him as they kissed goodbye at the departure gate in the airport.

"I will, baby girl. I'll send for you again soon. A'ight? You my girl now, right?"

"Of course I'm yours, baby," Kayundra replied with sincerity.

"And I'm yours, shorty," pledged Rah.

"All mine and no one elses?" she asked, because the type of love she had for him would not allow her to share.

"You already know how I get down, Sparkle." She loved when he called her that. "I ain't a playa. When I commit; I keep it one hunnid."

Kayundra had no doubt that she could trust in his promise, she knew from the past that he was a man of his word.

"I'm going to miss you so much," she cried.

"Nah, ma, none of that. No more tears," he said as he wiped her tears with his thumbs and kissed her softly.

"Why am I such a crybaby?" she asked, chiding herself.

"It's all good but from now on, only happy tears, okay?"

Kayundra nodded then it was time for her to board the plane. They hugged and she did not want to let go of him, afraid that if she did she might awaken to find out that this was only a dream and that her life was still in shambles.

Finally, though, she had to let Rah go and go board her flight. She did so with her head in the clouds long before the airplane ascended to that altitude.

With his shorty headed back home, it was time for Rah to hit flip mode from gentle lover to head banger.

Thugs Cry

Nigga I warned you not play with my ducats. Now you about to see that shit ain't as sweet as you thought it was, he sneered as he thought about Paco.

Ca$h

FIFTEEN

Now that CJ had bodied Kendall and taken control of his heroin spots up and down Avon Avenue, money was coming in like the dope game was raining it down on him. "Butta Love", the stamp on CJ's packages was what the junkies wanted.

Pumpin' heroin and coke, CJ was getting cake hand over fist. His name was ringing loud all over The Bricks and hos was on his dick like groupies on a rap nigga.

CJ stayed running up in different chicks, enjoying the perks that came with his meteoric rise in status. Niggaz hated but only from a distance, 'cause him and his squad were beasts. They didn't hesitate to put a toe tag on a fool.

Tamika was finding out that a lot of other things came along with her man becoming the made-man she had always wanted him to become and she was salty about a lot of it. Especially that he would leave the house early in the day and stay gone until the wee hours in the morning. She didn't give a fuck what CJ said; business didn't take all day and night to fuckin' handle.

If CJ isn't home by ten, I'm going to my cousin's party by myself. I just reminded him last night that Danyelle's little birthday get together was tonight, Tamika fumed to herself as she tried to decide what to wear.

"Fam, I heard you had basehead Kayundra down in ATL with you for two weeks," CJ said, talking to Rah on his cell phone as he headed home. "Don't try to lie yo; LaKeesha already told me," he chuckled.

"What I'ma lie for, nigga? Like you my bitch or something?" Rah joked.

"'Cause you don't want me to know that you sprung on a crackhead."

"Son, don't call her that shit. Shorty don't get high no more. Anyway, yeah me and baby girl kickin' it strong. You hatin'?"

"Neva dat, yo. Do you, playboy. It's one love no matter. Fuck all that though; how you livin'? You need me to send you a grip?"

"Nah, I'm good. What's good with you?" inquired Rah.

"Got shit on smash," said CJ. "I'ma come fuck witchu soon."

"That's what's up."

"I'ma gut that snow bunny you been telling me about. 'Cause if that ho got an ass like Ice T's bitch I gotta have it. Oh, remember that lil' bitch Tasha Montgomery? She used to wear braces on her grill, thick ass glasses on her face and shit? Yo, I ran into shorty at a spot on Chancellor a coupla months ago. Fam, that bitch is fine as hell now."

"I know; I saw her at the club the night all that shit popped off. I meant to tell you, ma was feelin' ya swag," recalled Rah.

"Yeah, I know. I gutted the bitch, now she won't stop blowing up my phone," revealed CJ.

"I thought she had moved to D.C.?"

"She had but the bitch back in Newark now."

"Yo, she got that wet-wet?" asked Rah.

"It ain't nuthin' special. Want me to put you on her so you can sample the pussy yourself?"

"Nah, I'm good," Rah declined. He told his man that he was going to honor his word to Kayundra.

"You buggin', yo!" CJ laughed.

"Real talk," said Rah.

They hung up just as CJ pulled up to his crib.

Tamika was half-dressed and pouting when CJ walked through the door.

"Did you forget that you're supposed to take me to Danyelle's party tonight?" she asked with attitude.

"Nah, that's why I came home early, it ain't even ten o'clock yet. Why you got the screw face boo?" He walked up behind and wrapped his arms around her.

Tamika said, "Because you're neglecting me."

"The neglect is in the nature of the game, not in my heart. That's why I'm puttin' hustlin' on the shelf tonight so I can spend some quality time with you." CJ nibbled on her ear.

Tamika didn't respond passionately like she usually did when CJ did that so he walked her over to the window where they could see out into the parking lot.

"What's that parked next to my Expedition?" he pointed.

"My whip," answered Tamika. Two weeks ago CJ had copped a BMW 740i for her.

"Is that neglect?" he asked.

"Money and gifts don't buy happiness. I need for you to start spending time with me like you did before all of this."

"What? So, you want me to take your whip back to the dealership and stay at home with you for a few days, huh?" he asked being sarcastic.

"No, I want both—the luxuries and your time," demanded Tamika.

"A'ight, ma, I got you."

They arrived at the party in matching gear, which was being held at Danyelle's house on 13th Avenue. Tamika wore a sheer black Versace dress that was as small as a handkerchief. CJ wore a black Versace two piece suit, a gray silk shirt with open collar, and black Gators. Tamika loved to see him in a suit; she had bought him the one that he was rockin'.

They both were jeweled up like the ghetto supastars that they now were.

Danyelle's sister, Nee Nee, let them in.

"Hey, girl," she greeted Tamika with a false smile and a hug.

"Hey." *Bitch, don't front. You don't like me and the feeling is mutual.*

Nee Nee, who was short, and thick in all the right places stepped back and looked Tamika up and down, nose turned up.

"Girl, you might as well be naked," she hated.

"My man likes it."

"Anyway," Nee Nee rolled her eyes. "What's up CJ? Why you so quiet?"

"I walk light and carry a big stick," CJ quipped.

"I bet you do," smiled Nee Nee, looking at his crotch.

"I bet you'll never know," Tamika checked her.

"Don't bet against me, cuz. You know when the cat's away the mice will play. See you around CJ," replied Nee Nee over her shoulder as she walked away.

Nee Nee's last remark was barely audible over the loud music that was playing. Tamika heard it though and she said, "I'ma kick that bitch ass," ready to run up behind Nee Nee and cold cock her but was restrained by CJ.

"Chill, don't let that shit get you twisted."

"What the fuck did you say that bullshit for? *You carry a big stick!* Were you flirtin' with that bitch?" Tamika asked, turning her anger on him.

"Hell nah. I wouldn't fuck Nee Nee with a dog's dick."

"Just make sure you don't fuck her with *this* dog's dick," said Tamika, jabbing her index finger into his chest.

"Neva ma." He pecked her on the lips. "And I'm not a dog. I'm your nigga."

They made their way from the living room into the kitchen, where someone had told them they could find the birthday girl.

"Hey, Miss Thang. Don't y'all look cute! What's up, CJ?" spoke Danyelle when she saw them enter the kitchen.

"Hey big cuz. Happy b-day," said Tamika with a genuine smile. Danyelle was Tamika's favorite cousin. She was thirty years old, married with four kids and she was built like Sponge Bob which meant she was no threat to Tamika so they got along great. Danyelle got to live out her suppressed fantasies through Tamika's wild stories and Tamika got a voice of reason from Danyelle.

"Sup, Danyelle? Happy Birthday," said CJ.

"Thanks. Tamika must've threatened to put her thighs on lock to get you to come with her," Danyelle teased as she fixed plates of fried chicken and potato salad.

"Hmmpf! That nigga won't let me, he stay wanting to run up in this," Tamika boasted to other bitches in the kitchen, more so than to Danyelle.

"Sounds like another Shawn," said Danyelle, cutting her eyes toward her husband who was at the fridge getting more beer. "That's how we got four kids."

"I heard that," said Shawn.

"I'm not tryna have no babies, don't be jinxing me," said Tamika, and they all laughed.

CJ left Tamika in the kitchen kicking it with Danyelle. He was going back out to the truck to get Danyelle's present, which they had left on the backseat. Nee Nee saw that Tamika wasn't around so she stepped into CJ's path, pressing her body all up against his.

"Can a bitch get some of this?" she touched his crotch.

"We might can do something but you can't be talking all crazy in front of my girl," said CJ, removing her hand.

"Okay, you gon' give me your cell number so I can get at you?" She wanted to fuck CJ bad, just to show Tamika that her shit wasn't all of that.

"I know how to get at you," he said.

"Let me give you my number," she insisted. She called out her digits.

CJ waited until he got outside to his truck before programming Nee Nee's number into his phone. He could've had any bitch at the house party 'cause they all knew of him and his status in the streets. Nee Nee wasn't the baddest chick there by far. Really she couldn't touch Tamika. So why CJ wanted to creep with her, he didn't know.

I guess it's just the dog in me, he conceded.

Ca$h

SIXTEEN

Paco sat inside the holding cell at Delkalb County jail pondering his options which were two. He could either take his medicine like an official nigga would or he could turn bitch and flip on somebody to save his own ass.

He had just got knocked delivering an ounce of hard to a nigga on Flat Shoals Road. It was his third fall; he was on parole so he knew his ass was in a sling. Paco didn't want to snitch out the nigga who he had bought the hard from because the dude was from his hood. He didn't want his homeboys to know that he was a rat.

Ima give 'em Rah. Kill two birds with one stone. Get my ass outta the sling it's in, and get that young Jersey nigga off my back.

Paco feared Rah because he was quiet and laid back, traits of the most vicious killaz. He had been ducking and dodging Rah for more than a month. Now he had the perfect way to get rid of him.

When the narc who arrested Paco had him brought to the interrogation room, the rat bastard was eager to cooperate.

Rah felt the sexual intensity between his man and Stephanie as soon as he introduced them. CJ's thuggish demeanor, handsomeness, swag, and all that she had heard about him had Steph fawning all over him. CJ had never seen a white chick with an ass like hers plus she had blond hair and blue eyes. Features that represented a true blue blood heritage so that turned him on even more than the phat ass. It wasn't that he fiened for a blue-eyed she-devil; rather, when he fucked her, he would be sticking dick to the whole white race.

That was a big fuckin' turn on.

Two nights later, CJ was raw-doggin' the snow bunny at her spot. Steph was sprung. CJ had put the black dick on her like she'd never had it before and he continued dicking her down, night after night, while in ATL for ten days.

Rah took CJ to the strip clubs and other hot spots in the city. He introduced him to N.O. and DaQuan, and the four of them balled out of control. CJ parlayed with a coupla other cats he met through Rah, choppin' it up with them about future business.

When CJ bounced back to New Jersey, he left his number with N.O. He also left twin seeds growing inside of Stephanie, but neither of them knew that then.

Rah's computer beeped and a small red light blinked on and off, letting him know that he had received an e-mail. He typed in his username and password, and his latest email came up on the screen.

Dear Raheem,

I think about u so much. It seems like I'm 13 yrs old n having my 1st crush =). I guess this is the way true luv is, regardless to one's age. I'm so happy to be a part of ur life, n have u a part of mine. The distance is a small price 2 pay 4 true luv. I don't kno if I really deserve u, but I promise never 2 do n-e thing to make u regret being with me. I am enjoying my job at the hospital in the laundry, the women who work with me r a hot mess! I saw my friend Porcelin over here n the pj's last week. The next morning when I walked 2 the bus stop 2 go 2 work, she was still over here, walking up and down the block with no coat on. So you can guess what that means. N-E way, baby, they are having a big talent search at The Apollo in New York in a few weeks. I want to audition but I'm kind of afraid. I'm going 2 do it, though. Wish me luck. Luv u, baby.

Sparkle.

Rah was about to email Kayundra back when his cell phone chirped. He recognized Paco's number and answered with a harshness in his tone.

"Yeah nigga, sup?"

"I'm tryna holla at you Raheem. I got that bread I owe you. Things went crazy for a minute but I got you. And I need to cop again. I got the bread up front this time," said Paco.

"What you tryna get?" asked Rah, slipping in more ways than one. Not only was he talking reckless on the phone, he hadn't noticed that Paco called him by his government, though he usually called him "Rah" or "shawdy." Paco was using Rah's government for the benefit of the narc who was recording the conversation.

Paco had exaggerated Rah's status to the drug agent, who was thirsty to bust the big drug dealer Paco made Rah out to be and perhaps earn himself a promotion.

"I need 'bout five pounds of purp, some X, and a key of coke if you got it," Paco said.

"I told you son, I don't fuck with coke. How much E you need?" asked Rah, talking himself into a drug conspiracy charge.

What saved him from catching a more serious case was his distrust of Paco. Rah really thought the nigga was tryna set him up to get jacked. So when he met up with Paco the next day, at the pre-arranged time and place out in Dekalb County, Rah didn't bring along any work.

Paco paid Rah what he owed him in marked bills. The narc's were filming the meeting from across the street, using a camera with a zoom lens plus Paco was wired. DaQuan, who was rolling with Rah in case some funny shit went down had hopped in the backseat and let Paco sit up front.

"You got the weed and the X pills?" Paco asked Rah, sweating though fall had kicked in and the summer heat had disappeared like nigga'z respect for the code of the streets.

"Nah, I'ma have to holla back at you about that later," said Rah, studying his face and sensing something foul.

"Damn man. I got people depending on me. When you think you'll be straight?"

"I'ma get at you," was all Rah would say no matter how Paco rephrased the question.

"I don't trust that nigga," said DaQuan after Paco had gotten out of the car and they were driving off.

"Me either, that's why I'm not fuckin' with him no more. I wanted to mark his ass—just on the strength."

The narc's didn't pull them over and arrest them because they wanted to bang them with some drugs. "We'll have you try again in a few days," Paco was told.

When he tried to call Rah later that week, Rah's number had been changed.

Rah tried to block out the ominous feeling that he was left with over his dealing with Paco but something just didn't feel right. So he chilled out on hustlin' for the time being, and invited Kayundra down for the weekend.

They were lying in bed, satiated from a long night of good sex when Rah's apartment door was kicked in. He heard the loud crash and recognized it for what it was. However, thinking it was some niggaz pulling a home invasion, Rah jumped up and grabbed his strap off the dresser, ready to go out like a G.

"Police! Freeze!"

"Drop the weapon!"

Rah realized that the crackers were official popo so he complied. As they led him out in cuffs, he mouthed to Kayundra, "I'm sorry. Get in touch with CJ."

Kayundra nodded her understanding as tears poured down her face.

CJ didn't hesitate. He flew down to ATL and gave Stephanie the money to bond Rah out of jail. They had decided it was best, for appearances sake, to have her post Rah's bond.

CJ also gave DaQuan's people money to bond him out. DaQuan had been arrested the same morning that Rah's door was kicked in. CJ and DaQuan wanted to go mark Paco's whole family because they were sure that they wouldn't be able to find his bitch ass, but a cooler head prevailed.

"It's just a conspiracy and gun charge," said Rah, "Ain't no sense in adding murder charges to it, unless we can find Paco. I'm not touching his family. They haven't done me any dirt."

142

They couldn't find Paco. He was hid safer than a nigga'z stash. So CJ went back to New Jersey to handle his growing empire. Kayundra wanted to remain in Atlanta to be by Rah's side while he awaited the outcome of the charged he faced but Rah wouldn't hear of it. He did not want it to interfere with her job or the outpatient program that she was involved in as part of her recovery.

"I'm good baby," Rah reassured her. "Go on back home and I'll see you again soon. I apologize for getting you caught up in my shit. Even though you weren't arrested, I hate that you were here when the shit went down."

"Raheem, I'm down with you through whatever," Kayundra said.

"I know that. So make sure Big Ma doesn't find out about this."

"Baby, my lips are sealed," she promised, making the gesture of zipping them.

As winter kicked in and Kayundra shined at the audition at The Apollo, Rah wondered if he would have to go do a bid. Because he had used a cell phone to conspire to distribute drugs, the feds had decided to pick up his charges. CJ got Cujo to holla at his people on behalf of Rah and a deal was worked out where Rah would serve thirty months in federal prison.

"That's the best we can do for your boy," Cujo related to CJ. "And we can get the kid, DaQuan, sixteen months."

"For what? He ain't do shit," protested CJ, knowing how everything had went down.

"Wrong place, wrong time. Sixteen months, unless he wants to roll the dice, which I advise against."

"I'll relay the message."

DaQuan didn't want to roll the dice and neither did Rah. The bid would not only dash out his journalistic dreams, it would break Big Ma's heart, but Rah had to swallow these bitter pills.

"Let's do this. The sooner I go in, the sooner I touch back down," he advised his attorney, through whom the official plea was offered.

"You want to wait until after the Christmas holidays? It's only a few weeks away," asked the attorney.

"Nah, man, I don't celebrate Christmas," replied Rah.

The toughest thing was when he had to inform Big Ma that he was going away to serve a bid. Rah manned up, though and flew up to New Jersey and delivered the news to her face to face, enduring her tears and disappointment.

The next flood of tears came from Kayundra when it was time to tell her goodbye.

"Stay strong," he urged her.

"I will," she promised as she wept in his arms.

SEVENTEEN

Tamika was in the bedroom watching a Tyler Perry's Madea's Family Reunion on DVD and smoking a blunt. She heard CJ come into the house and go into the kitchen.

She pressed pause on the DVD player and went to see what he was doing; she had cooked dinner and left him a plate in the microwave. When she walked into the kitchen in her Prada pajamas she saw CJ stacking twenty kilos in the cabinet above the sink.

I thought a hustla wasn't supposed to shit where he eats.

Tamika didn't know that CJ was immune from arrest. And a nigga running up in there on a jack move was highly unlikely. Besides, their crib being tucked away in an affluent gated community, the streets knew that CJ wasn't to be fucked with.

After stacking the work that he would drop off to Kareem in two days to sell to a nigga in Irvington, CJ sat down at the kitchen table feeding money into a money counting machine.

"Oh, you don't know how to speak to nobody?" Tamika asked, stepping into CJ's view.

"Hey, boo." He kept his attention on the task, but Tamika was determined to get his undivided.

She sat down on top of the table, dead on top of the pile of money.

"Can't you put business aside long enough to kiss me and ask how my day has been?"

CJ smacked lips with her.

"How was your day Tamika?" he asked so perfunctorily she didn't even respond. She just stood up and glared at him then stormed back to the bedroom and locked the door.

Sleep on the couch, nigga!

Tamika fell asleep hoping CJ would come knocking on the bedroom door, begging her to let him in.

When she woke up, he was already gone. It was Christmas Eve, her birthday.

Tamika's cell phone chirped. The ringtone told her that it was her mother calling.

"Good morning, Mommie."

"Good morning, baby. Happy birthday. Are you coming over to get your present?"

"Maybe later," said Tamika dryly.

"What's wrong?" asked her Mom Dukes.

"CJ. He doesn't love me anymore," she cried. "It's my birthday. I should've woke up to roses and breakfast in bed. Instead, when I woke up he was already gone."

"Maybe he's handling business."

"No, he's not. I locked the bedroom door and made his ass sleep on the couch last night. Mama, he didn't even come to the door and ask me to let him in. And you know that is not CJ. If he doesn't mind sleeping on the couch, that means he has someone else. Before he started making all this money, he would've dropped to his knees begging me to let him in bed. Now, because he has all this stuff and women are falling to his feet, he acts as if he can do without me."

"Show him that he can't. Pack up your clothes and come home and don't go back to him until he gets his shit together," her Mom Dukes advised.

"But what if I leave him and he doesn't want me back?"

"He'll want you back I promise you. And if he doesn't, you were going to lose him anyway."

"I'm scared to do that, Mommie. I don't want some other chick to end up with him," admitted Tamika.

"Chile, you gotta show that man that you won't play second to the streets. If you allow him to take you for granted, you'll be crying a lot more often than just on your birthday."

"You're right, Mommie," acknowledged Tamika, though she was not ready to test CJ. "I'm going to see what today brings before I do anything though."

They talked, woman to woman, for the better part of an hour. After hanging up from her Mom Dukes, Tamika called CJ.

146

"Sup?" Tamika noted that he answered like she was one of his boys and not wifey.

"Nothing. I'm not just calling to see what you're up to. What time did you leave this morning?"

"'Bout six-thirty."

"Why didn't you come to bed last night?"

"You locked me outta the bedroom."

"You should've knocked. Maybe I would've unlocked the door."

CJ didn't respond.

"Do you have anything special planned for today?" Tamika asked, trying to give CJ a hint that it was her birthday.

"Nope. Just the usual, getting this guap. Oh, don't bother what I left in the cabinet."

"Don't worry, CJ, I'm not gonna bother your precious stuff. I wish you wouldn't bring it to the house though," she said.

"I got this, ma."

"Bye CJ. I love you." Her heart ached.

"I'll holla later."

Tears dripped down from Tamika's eyes as she looked at the phone in her hand.

Across town, CJ, Star, Danyelle, and some members of CJ's squad were decorating the club where they were throwing Tamika a surprise birthday party. CJ hadn't told Tamika's Mom Dukes about the surprise party because he felt she would've let it slip out. He had heard the hurt in his girl's voice a minute ago.

She thinks I forgot that today is her birthday. Neva ma. I might creep but you still a nigga'z heart.

He was doing it up big for Tamika's surprise party. Free food and drinks for everyone, all night long. Male strippers for the women, female strippers for the niggaz. RZA and Method Man were going to perform. And CJ had spent twenty stacks on gifts for his boo. He wanted to show her that she was still special to him.

Tamika wasn't feeling special at all, she spent the whole day at home waiting for CJ to call and remember that it was her birthday, a call that did not come.

The sun had gone down and the wintery night's wind whistled outside her windows. She tried to call her Mom Dukes but got no answer. Same thing with Star and Danyelle. It was as if everyone had forgotten about her or were busy doing other things. Malcolm called to wish her a happy birthday and to invite her over but she was not that desperate.

She tried to call CJ but he did not answer his phone.

Nigga probably laid up with Tricia or some other bitch.

At hope's end, Tamika called her hairstylist.

"Joylynn, I need you to do me a favor. CJ won't answer his cell phone when I call. I need you to call him on the three-way and see if he answers, he won't recognize your number."

She gave Joylynn CJ's number and she made the call for her.

CJ answered on the third ring.

"Oops, I have the wrong number," pretended the hairstylist. They could hear loud music in the background. She hung up.

"Thanks, girlfriend," said Tamika, fighting back tears.

"No problem. Trust, I understand. I'm thinking about getting me a dildo and saying to hell with niggaz, they're too much damn heartache."

Tamika faked a laugh.

When she hung up with Joylynn, instead of crying her eyes out, Tamika set out perfumed candles all over the condo and put a bottle of Moet on ice. She put on a sexy Vicky Secrets thong and bra, six inch red stilettos, and a short mink jacket. As soon as CJ stepped through the door she was going to attack him with a sexual flury that would remind him that he had that good-good at home.

The hands on the grandfather clock in the living room read 8:15P.M. Tamika laid across her bed and waited for her man to come home. When a half hour more passed and CJ still hadn't walked through the door, Tamika popped the Moet. Two full glasses later she was mad as hell. And drunk.

148

Okay, nigga, you think I'm a weak bitch that you can just walk all over? I'll teach your ass not to neglect me.

She went to the kitchen and got his twenty kilos of coke out of the cabinet, making several staggered trips to carry them all into the bathroom.

Then she went back to get a butcher knife.

On the way back to the bathroom, Tamika detoured into the den and slashed up the Italian leather sofa. Next, she staggered to the bedroom closet and cut up all of CJ's clothes. She did so with such a fury that she cut her hand and blood got all over her mink jacket. But Tamika was too zoned out to care. Her hair was sweated out and she was breathing hard as she made her way back to the bathroom. Her cell phone rang on the sink counter just as she plopped down on the floor where she had dropped the yayo.

"Hello!" she shouted into the phone.

"Hey, girl. Come to that new club out in Arlington. Your man is here with some red bitch draped all over him," said Star, trying to bait Tamika to her surprise party.

"Fuck that nigga! Whoever she is, she can have him," replied Tamika in tears.

"Come to the club!"

"No! Fuck CJ!"

"Bitch, you sound drunk."

"I am," she cried.

"Hol' up. I'ma come pick you up," said Star, with CJ, Danyelle, and Tamika's Mom Dukes standing next to her. They had let Ms. Jerkins in on the surprise at the last moment.

"No bitch, don't come pick me up. Just tell CJ that I said I'm flushing all of his shit down the toilet; all twenty keys!"

She dial-toned Star and cut open a block. Her cell phone was screaming; she knew that it was her man calling.

Muhfucka, you haven't called me all fuckin' day, too late now!

Tamika broke one of her nails ripping the wrapping off of the block of Peruvian flake as the phone continued to ring. Then it went to voicemail.

By the time she had flushed the whole kilo down the toilet her cell phone was ringing again, persistently.

"What muthafucka!" she answered it.

"Tamika, don't do nothing crazy."

"You hear this nigga?" she dropped half of another block into the toilet and flushed it. The compressed powdery substance dissolved in the toilet water and flushed away. "Say goodbye to your precious drugs!"

"Tamika, stop! Please, baby listen—"

"Nah you listen, black muthafucka!" Flush. "That's two down, eighteen to go!"

"Tamika, nooooooo!"

Flush. "That's for the bitch you're with."

"Star, please talk to her!" CJ pleaded, passing Star his phone.

"Tamika—"

"Stay outta my business bitch!" Tamika screamed at her and hung up the phone.

Tamika cut open another brick and sent it to the sewers of New Jersey. Then vomit rose up in her throat and she threw up all over the commode and the floor. It did not deter her though, she was determined to flush the remaining sixteen bricks.

Her cell phone rang again. This time it was Danyelle.

Tamika answered, "I don't wanna talk!" and hung up.

Seconds later, her Mom Dukes called. Tamika ignored her call and flushed another of CJ's bricks. Then another and another.

It was seventeen down, three to go, when she heard hurried footsteps come running into the bathroom. She vomited again then looked up to see CJ and Star standing in the doorway.

CJ stared with an open mouth at the seventeen empty kilo wrappers.

"Bitch, is you crazy!" he shouted.

Tamika stood up, looking insane as hell in her stilettos, mink jacket, and Vicky Secrets get-up. She had the butcher knife in her hand.

"Fuck with me and you'll find out, cheatin' mutherfucka! And ya mama's a bitch!" she screamed back at him, and crouched down ready to attack.

CJ pulled out his burner.

"I oughtta blow your stupid ass brains out. Put that knife down before I shoot you in the face."

"Go ahead, you don't give a fuck about me anymore no way! C'mon, nigga. I'm not afraid of you! I'ma show you I'm not no weak bitch!"

Star saw that Tamika was out of her mind and did not fear the gun in CJ's hand.

"No, Tamika!" she screamed just as her girl lunged at CJ, knife arcing through the air.

A single shot rang out in the bathroom like a loud clap of thunder. Tamika laid face-down on the floor as CJ looked down at her in regret, blood dripping from a slash across his forearm.

"Oh, my God!" cried Star, falling to her knees and cradling Tamika's limp body in her arms.

Ca$h

EIGHTEEN

CJ had reflexively squeezed the trigger when the knife slashed through the sleeve of his cashmere Coogi sweater that he had on, laying his forearm wide open. The bullet missed Tamika and shattered one of the overhead fluorescent bulbs in the ceiling.

Tamika had lunged for his heart but her foot had slipped in a puddle of vomit, causing her aim to come up short. She banged her head hard on the floor when she fell, knocking herself out cold. Star thought that Tamika had been shot until she cradled her in her arms and saw no blood and realized that Tamika was still breathing.

"I can't believe this shit!" gritted CJ, holding a towel up under his forearm to catch the blood. He looked at the empty kilo wrappers and shook his head in disbelief.

Star wet a face cloth and gently wiped Tamika's forehead until she regained consciousness. Once her head cleared, Tamika wanted some more of CJ's ass but Star restrained her.

"Do you realize how much guap you've fucked up?" sneered CJ. "All because you're so gotdamn jealous. I wasn't out creepin' on your insecure ass. I ignored your calls all day because I was setting up a surprise birthday party for you. Star knew about it all along. I didn't tell ya Mom Dukes until tonight."

Star was nodding her head, cosigning CJ's claims.

"There's a club full of people waiting to surprise you. But fuck it, you done fucked up everything! This too! He pulled out a small velvet jewelry box, opening it to reveal a clear blue diamond set in platinum band. It was an engagement ring.

Tamika wanted to curl up and die when he flushed it down the toilet.

"I ain't marrying yo' crazy ass! And I'm selling the whip I bought you, all of your jewels and the designer shit too."

"I'm sorry CJ. I thought—"

"Nah, you didn't think, you just reacted!" he cut her off then stormed out of the bathroom."

When CJ went to the closet to change shirts and saw that all of his gear had been cut to shreds, he stalked back into the bathroom with a murderous unit on his mug. If Tamika had been any other chick he would've twisted her fuckin' neck.

"It's silly bitches like you that bring a nigga down. Maybe I would be better off with Tricia, someone who knows how to play her position yo. Or maybe I should've chose Star or just let ya psycho ass stayed with Rah," hurled CJ at Tamika.

Then he stormed out of the crib, headed to the hospital to get his forearm stitched up.

Tamika cried on Star's shoulder after CJ left. Finally, Star helped her to her feet and stood her in the glass mirror on the bathroom wall.

"Crazy bitch. I just want you to see how busted you look right now. Ass hanging out, titties too. Vomit and blood all over your mink, and a bump the size of a plum on your big ass forehead."

"And I done flushed a half million dollars' worth of CJ's coke down the toilet and he didn't even kick my ass. I guess he does love me," said Tamika.

She studied herself in the mirror and couldn't help but to laugh at how ridiculous she looked.

"Bitch, you're retarded," laughed Star.

CJ wasn't laughing at all. He had called Nee Nee and told her to meet him at the emergency room. Now they were laid up at the motel; he had just blew her back out and they were sharing a blunt.

"I still can't believe Tamika done that," said Nee Nee, trying to fully capitalize on the situation. "I would never do anything like that. A real bitch knows how to play her position; don't let my cousin bring you down baby. She doesn't know how to rep for a boss nigga like you."

"I'm seeing that now," CJ agreed more out of anger than actuality.

For the next four days he laid up with Nee Nee.

154

Not because he wanted her, it was just his way of getting back at Tamika for what she had done. The seventeen blocks that she'd flushed didn't hurt him, he was sitting pretty. Cujo had just hit him with a hundred and fifteen of them thangs and five of heroin.

Tamika's Mom Dukes had called CJ to plead forgiveness on behalf of Tamika. CJ played hard for a minute but he still loved his girl, and Nee Nee, with her hatin' ass damn sho couldn't replace Tamika. In just four days, CJ was burnt out on Nee Nee's pussy and she had nothing else to offer.

Nee Nee had caught feelings though. So she had the screw face when he told her that their rendevous had reached its end.

"I'm going back to wifey."

"Whateva!" replied Nee Nee, feeling played.

Tamika was at home, missing her man like crazy. She knew that she had fucked up and she wanted to fix things between herself and CJ but she didn't know how.

"He's still heated. Just give him time to cool off," Danyelle had suggested to her a few days ago.

The days seemed too long and the nights were lonely as hell. Finally, after four miserable days and nights, CJ walked through the door. He didn't speak to her but at least he had come back home.

For two days, Tamika walked on egg shells, afraid to say anything but wanting to say so much. At night when they went to bed, CJ slept with his back to her and pushed her hand away when she tried to touch him. All Tamika could do was wait for his anger to subside.

Eventually CJ said, "I oughta make you work two jobs until you pay me back all the money I would've made off the work you flushed."

"Whatever you want me to do baby, just let me make it up to you."

"Don't ask me to buy you shit for *three years*," he said, grabbing a number out of the air.

It wasn't what Tamika wanted to hear him say, she would've preferred to hear him say that he still loved her but at least it was something. His statement told her that he was back to stay.

"CJ, three years is a long time. By then my hair will be so nappy. Can't I at least ask for salon money?" she asked, putting a finger in her mouth and batting her eyes.

CJ smiled. "Girl, bring your crazy ass here," he pulled her onto his lap.

NINETEEN

CJ

For the past three years, my chokehold on Newark has been mad strong and I've spread out to Elizabeth, Jersey City, and even Irvington where I drop weight to some Bloods, they got Irvington on smash.

Still Little Bricks is home base, though I got most of Newark sewed up. Now there's these niggaz who call themselves The Goon Squad, from Hawthorne, who wanna test my team's G. The Goon Squad is under the command of a nigga called U-God, a beast. I give the nigga his props, his squad's murder and hustle games are official. I've been keeping an eye on The Goon Squad the last coupla years, any spot that I didn't have locked they scooped up. Anybody that opposed them got smashed.

As long as The Goon Squad didn't step on my toes, I wasn't sweatin' 'em. But I guess U-God is no longer happy gettin' a small slice of the pie. The other day him and his squad fell up in the after-hours club I have on Springfield Ave.

"Yo, CJ let me holla at you," said U-God.

I lead him to my private office so that we could chop it up alone. But some of my crew was posted just outside the closed door.

I sat behind my mahogany desk. U-God, who is brown-skinned, about five-nine, and medium built, was rockin' a Sean Jean denim hook up and black Timbs. He wore an iced crown medallion on a platinum chain that hung down to his waist. He had the eyes of a killa, much like my own.

Real recognize real so I had always shown U-God the same respect, in passing, that he showed me.

He sat down in the chair across the desk from me.

"What's on your mind?" I asked.

"Yo, I'ma cut to the chase. You been raping shit for the past few years; I salute you on that. Real talk, I admire how you put it down. Niggaz can't fuck witchu so they don't even try. Well

I'm cut from a different cloth, nah mean? I'm sure you know about me, my rep speaks for itself."

"And you said all that to say?" I asked when U-God paused.

"I wanna eat like a king too. In fact, I'm gonna eat like one or die trying. Now, the way I see it in order for me to eat better you gotta eat a little less, which means a war or an understanding. It's your call."

Because I had learned to hear a man out before rejecting him I asked, "What kinda understanding you tryna get with me?"

"We divide Newark 60-40. Right now it's 80-20, your way, and those numbers gotta change. No disrespect intended," said U-God who had come home from a ten year bid down South, five years ago, determined to come up or lay niggaz down.

He had done both.

U-God was pushin' thirty-five years old and probably figured he had no more time to waste or nothing to lose. A bid can make a nigga go all out when he's released.

"What do I get in return for giving up a bigger share of the city?" I posed to him.

"You get to live and ya people do too. If you make me go to war with you anybody connected to you can get it. That's not a threat lil' homie, that's just how I get down."

I smiled. But a smile can mean many things, just as a kiss can mean "the kiss of death". I didn't feel disrespected and I damn sho' didn't feel intimidated. It amused me that U-God had the balls to come up in my spot and kick it like that. I respected both his rep and his ambition but he had me fucked up. I wasn't breaking him off a piece of my empire.

U-God must've saw the answer to his proposal in my eyes. "Youngin', greed befalls a man. Share the plate or get a lot of people marked because you wanna feast alone."

"May the strongest squad prevail," I said, firing up a blunt and kicking my feet up on the desk.

A week passed. I warned the team to stay on point but The Goon squad hasn't come at us yet. My team is more than a hunnid strong while U-God and 'em 'bout twenty deep. So I guess dude is hesitant to pop shit off because I got numbers. Still, I'm not waiting for son to bring the drama to me. I'ma send my killaz at that ass soon.

Meanwhile, these two jack boys named KD and Ghetto, both from Big Bricks, have been snatchin' up niggaz after they cop weight from my people and robbing 'em, causing the streets to whisper that we ain't playing fair.

"Niggaz saying we selling mufuckaz work then have 'em jacked" Eric tells me at a meeting of my top people—Eric, Kareem, Premo, Snoop, and Flip, the cat that we got to cross out Kendall for us. I was gonna body Flip not long after that move, 'cause I figured that if Kendall couldn't trust the nigga, I couldn't either. But Flip proved to be inexpendable with the way he handled my spots on Avon Avenue.

I say to Eric, "We're getting soft. It's been so long since niggaz tested our gangsta, we startin' to relax. The streets sense that, that's why these incidents are starting to happen. Two, three years ago a nigga would rather take some dick up the ass than violate us! Y'all niggaz so busy ballin', stuntin', and fuckin' different shorties, y'all ain't on point anymore. Got all our foot soldiers putting in all the work while y'all muhfuckaz just lay back and get fat off the hog!"

My response was to Eric but the rest of my niggaz know that my venom is directed at them too. Don't nobody say shit 'cause they know not to interrupt me when I'm going the fuck off.

"No more clubbin', stuntin', nuthin! Until I say so. Y'all niggaz understand?"

Five heads nodded.

"I want every one of y'all back out on the block, showing niggaz that shit is still gully."

After the meeting, Kareem pulls me aside.

"Fam, I didn't wanna say nothin' but every one of our customers who got jacked by KD and Ghetto bought their weight from Flip. Five niggaz got jacked, and all five of 'em copped from him. That's too much coincidence yo."

"I noticed that," I acknowledge. *I know this lil' ugly Flava Flav-lookin' nigga ain't stupid enough to violate.*

"You want me to get at him?" asks Kareem.

I give it some thought.

"Not yet, lemme check it out first." I decide, 'cause shit ain't always the way it first appears. Betrayal warrants death which is irreversible so I wanna be sure before I fit Flip for a coffin. Based just on past behavior though, it's not looking good for ol' Flip.

"What about KD and Ghetto?"

"I'ma handle that ASAP."

"You don't have to get ya hands dirty, me and Snoop'll get at them fools," suggests Kareem, anxious to murk something.

"Nah, I'ma put in work myself, remind the team that I still pop these things." I pat the Desert Eagle on my waist.

As I leave the apartment in Little Bricks where the meeting was held, my phone vibrates on my hip.

"Sup?"

It's Flip. I cut the conversation short because I'm not sure how the nigga is gettin' down these days. The last thing I need is an enemy on my team.

Later, I share with Eric what Kareem suspects of Flip.

"Bruh, I don't believe Flip would get down like that. You know Kareem salty with him 'cause Flip bagged a shorty that Kareem had been tryna get at," says Eric.

"What? So you sayin' Kareem would get Flip murked over a bitch? Nah, Kareem ain't shady like that. But Flip—I don't know."

I ponder the situation for a few. *A'ight, I know how to handle this shit. But first I'ma get at KD and his man; make an example outta them niggaz so muhfuckaz will be reminded that I handles mine.*

Me, Premo, and Snoop been casing out these niggaz, KD and Ghetto for the past two days. Tonight we parked a coupla houses down from this gambling joint in East Orange where they're known to hang out. The way KD and Ghetto been lickin' my mans, their grip should be on swole, so even if they're losing their shirts up in the gambling joint this wait could be hours.

With murder on my brain like inoperable cancer, I'm not going anywhere. I'll wait these two niggaz out until nuns start giving muhfuckaz STDs and Fiddy fuck Vivica again.

My wrist piece reads 12:15 A.M., a quarter past midnight.

'Bout 2:50 A.M. Snoop whispers, "There they go," from the backseat of the whip we were rollin' in. Premo behind the wheel. I'm ridin' shotgun, strapped.

"Turn on the headlights and drive normal," I instruct Premo.

He does exactly as I instructed but Snoop's trigger finger is so happy, he lets loose a little too quickly. KD catches a coupla slugs to the shoulder from Snoops fo-five and staggers back. Then my piece barks angry and loud, leaving KD on the pavement leaking vital organs. But that nigga Ghetto done jetted. We bust at that ass in vain. Muhfucka quicker than street justice.

We peel off, me and Snoop both spittin' lead at Ghetto who's dodging and ducking. Nigga dips between two houses and he's ghost.

"Fuck!" cusses Snoop.

"It's all good my dude. We'll get up with that ass sooner or later. Nigga can run but he can't hide, not in Jersey, we own this bitch!" I exclaim.

When I get to the crib, an eight hundred thousand dollar joint in New Haven that I copped last year, Tamika is already sleep. I look down at my ghetto queen and get all nostalgic and shit. Me and shorty been through in the last three years: she done caught me with other bitches, found out about me fucking her cousin Nee Nee, all types of shit, but she still holding a nigga down. And she has learned not to do no stupid shit outta jealousy like she did three years ago when she flushed seventeen bricks of coke of mine.

Remember that shit?

Yo, I can laugh at it now, but back then wasn't a damn thing funny. I told her not to ever do that shit again or I would put my foot up that ass so far, my toes would come outta her mouth.

Baby understands that I need her to show mad trust and loyalty, 'cause the game is hard enough without a nigga having to battle with his girl.

All Tamika has to do is look around at all the splendor that I have her living in and she can see that she a nigga'z heart and soul. Ain't nothing changed since she first became my girl. Fuck the other hos I be cuttin'; where a nigga sticks his dick ain't got nothing to do with his heart. Ma laid up with me in a six bedroom, eight and a half baths joint, got a brand new BM drop, jewels and clothes galore. So she gotta know that I love me some her.

I bend down and kiss Tamika softly on the lips and her eyes flutter like the wings of a butterfly.

"Mmm, what time is it?" she asks.

"Go back to sleep shorty. I'ma take a quick shower then I'm coming to bed. You know I got a flight to catch later today."

I gotta fly down to ATL and fuck with my nigga Rah. Fam has only been outta the joint six months but he's doing good. I be kidding him like, "You a Muslim now—ono more dope game." But that's not really the case.

Yeah, my nigga came home from that bid focused on some legit shit, but he ain't trying to front like he won't get back on his grind. In fact, I hit his dude DaQuan off with some work through Rah, who mostly concentrates on promoting celebrity parties and running the two night clubs I loaned him the guap to open up.

"Nigga, you should open a strip club, them joints hot in ATL, right?" I'd suggested.

"Yeah, they pumping but I'm not into exploiting my sistaz," he'd replied.

"Whateva, fam," I said.

I gotta go down to ATL for another reason too. I'm going to visit my seeds. Yep, a nigga got twins by that snow bunny, Steph.

Fucked *me* up, too!

That's what running up in bitches raw will get a nigga.

Nah fool, Tamika don't know about my seeds. Can't tell her that shit. She find out I got seeds with a white girl—man, I don't even wanna think about how she would react.

I got this, though.

Just roll wit' me.

Ca$h

TWENTY

STEPHANIE

It's already seven A.M. and I'm running behind schedule. I have to finish dressing the twins, Leron and Loran, drop them off at the daycare center out this way, and then fight morning rush hour traffic from Norcross, where I live, into Atlanta where I work as a real estate developer for Worldwide Commercial Architecture.

I've grown to love Atlanta but I can't stand the rush hour traffic. There's absolutely no way that I would live in the inner city, particularly Fulton County, where the crime rate is appalling. I have a nice three bedroom home in a quiet suburban spot north of Atlanta, away from the plethora of danger that lurk in the heart of the city.

Okay, let's rewind this story a bit. The twins are two-years-old. Loran is cute, and very combative like her daddy. She is the typical daddy's girl. So much so, that when CJ comes in town to visit I'm relegated to the status of "nanny," not mother. Leron is the quieter of the twins and not as affected as Loran by CJ's long periods of absence.

I became pregnant with the twins during the first week that CJ and I were together. At the time I was certain that the twins were a double dip of punishment from God for being so stupid and caught up in CJ's magnetism, that I had a full week of unprotected sex with him. Now I see my children as a wonderful blessing. But it was far from a blessing, in my mind, when I first found out that I was pregnant.

CJ was my lover and I was sure that our feelings for each other were more than sexual but I wasn't fooling myself. I knew from Raheem that CJ had a girl back home that he loved, though CJ lied about it. However, I was more concerned that CJ's heart belonged to the streets.

I didn't want him to think that I was trying to trap him. Nor did I want to have a child by a man that wasn't already my husband. I knew that CJ's being black was going to be an issue that would get me disowned by my parents, whose mindsets are still back in the 60's. Also, the last thing I wanted to become was some drug dealer's baby mama. Contrary to what you may have thought, I'm not a candidate for The Jerry Springer Show.

So I was faced with serious choices.

Would becoming a single mother of twins hinder my education and future career? I had to decide what I would do if CJ nutted up, which he did.

"C'mon, shorty, don't even try to play me like that! What? Next you gon' ask for abortion money, right? When I give it to you, you hittin' the mall. That game is played out, yo."

"CJ, I'm not playing a game. Here, look—those are the pregnancy test results from my gynecologist. See, it says right there—positive." I'd shown him the papers and pointed out the results of the test.

"Like yo ass can't get fake results?"

"The results aren't fake! You'll see, when my stomach starts poking out in three or four months."

"Fuck! White hos tryna baby trap a nigga now!"

I stared daggers at him.

"I did not plan to get pregnant! In fact, it was you who did not want to use a condom, CJ," I reminded him.

"Ain't like you was beggin' me to wrap up," he countered as he paced back and forth in my living room.

"Well, what's done is done. I'm telling you because you have the right to know. I was hoping I'd have your support but I see that I misjudged you."

"Yeah, I misjudged you too shorty. How I know I'm the father? Shid, college ain't nothin' but a fuck fest, I know you got other male friends," he accused.

"Of course I have male friends but I don't sleep with them." My words were not only true, they dripped with indignation. Because I had slept with him so quickly, CJ was implying that I am loose, which was not true.

"Yeah—yeah—yeah," he replied sarcastically.

Thugs Cry

"Okay CJ, I see clearly now what you think of me. I won't bother you again, but I want you to be aware that I will be filing for child support. Not to antagonize you, but to do what's best for these babies I'm carrying. Good bye, CJ," I said showing him the door.

I didn't hear from CJ again until I was in my fifth month of pregnancy. Then one day, out of the blue, he showed up at the student center at Georgia Tech looking for me. Needless to say, I did not run into his arms. I still cared for CJ and with his twins growing inside of me, I probably even loved him but our last confrontation had left me hurt, mad, and feeling like CJ thought that I was white trash, unworthy of having his children.

"The streets make him skeptical of everyone, particularly females," Raheem defended CJ when he called from prison and I explained the situation to him.

I wasn't concerned with what CJ thought of other women, he had no right to put me in that category. I was ready to go ballistic on him right there in the student center but his tone had improved.

Eventually, CJ warmed to the idea of fatherhood. No, let me correct myself: he gloated over the fact that I was carrying twins. Like, making two babies at once proved that he was more than the average man. To erase all doubt from CJ's mind whether or not he was the twins' father, I welcomed him taking a paternity test after they were born. The test proved to be a 99.9 percent certainty that he is in fact Loran and Leron's dad.

I give CJ credit for stepping up and providing financially for the twins and even for me while I concentrated on getting my degree. That was the one thing that I asked of him. There was no way that I was going to drop out of college and place myself in the tedious position of being dependent on CJ forever. The fact of the matter was, and still remains, that the twins and myself can never count on CJ being in our lives from one day to the next.

The life he lives is as uncertain as skydiving without a parachute.

After I graduated from college, CJ wanted me to find a job closer to New Jersey and move there so that he would not be so far away from the twins. However, I absolutely refused to subject myself and the children to the collateral dangers that might come with us living in close proximity to their dad. Let's not tip toe around this, CJ is one of the biggest drug dealers on the East Coast. Danger comes with that distinction.

So this is where we stand today: I'm going on with my life and my career, raising the twins in Norcross, Georgia, while CJ still resides in New Jersey and continues to do what he does. I have no intimate knowledge of his drug dealing and that's how I want to keep it.

CJ is still with Tamika and I'm sure that he has an assortment of other women. I'm white, not dumb! Yes, I'm still intimately involved with CJ but I'll go out on an occasional date with other guys. I won't bring other men around my children though, and if I ever become intimate with someone besides CJ, I'll know it's time to move on from CJ completely.

I allow CJ to provide for his children but I do not depend on it. I do not accept large gifts from him or allow him to provide for us in any manner that would allow the government to seize my home, car, or bank assets if CJ ever takes a fall.

Of course, CJ is always welcome to visit.

Now if you know CJ, then you know that I wasn't able to just lay down all of those stipulations without some conflict. Because, above all, CJ has an ego that must be appeased. So I had to get him to understand that the stipulations protected the twins' best interest.

When it comes to my dating other men, CJ has yet to come to terms with that. He looks at it like this: I gave birth to his children, therefore, I belong to him.

"I'm not one of your possessions CJ," I constantly have to remind him. Because if I allow CJ's willpower to overrule my principles he'll control me just as he does nearly everything in his life.

If it wasn't for Raheem's friendship and sage advice, I'd be close to psychotic trying to deal with CJ's domineering personality and explain to Loran and Leron why their daddy doesn't call for visit for months at a time.

Raheem has only been home for eight months, but in that time he and Kayundra have taken to the twins like a blood uncle and aunt. They live out in Powder Springs, Georgia, not far from me.

So that's where things stand.

CJ is supposed to come in town tomorrow; he has some business with Raheem, concerning their nightclubs to handle. Also, I know he's going to try to talk me out of what I told him I was going to do. However, my mind is made up.

I will no longer allow CJ to hide the twins' existence from Tamika.

Ca$h

TWENTY-ONE

TAMIKA

I been putting up with CJ's bullshit for so long. I'm sick and tired of being *sick and tired!* I guess he has forgotten that I'm the same bitch who loved his black ass when he didn't have nothing but hood dreams. I've been trooping for him for four years, through all types of drama. Who held heat, drugs, and secrets of his? Me, that's who.

Who stepped up and took care of Brianna, his younger sister, when their crackhead mama was too strung out to do it? The nigga done gave me headaches, heartache, and herpes; and I've loved his ass through it all. Nigga done creeped with Nee Nee, knowing how much I despise that trick; slung dick all over Newark and I forgave him for it all, but this right here is just too much!

It's been a month ago, to the day, that I was sitting on the back patio of the baby mansion that CJ copped for us last year, when I heard the doorbell chime. I was thinking, okay, this has to be CJ's mother because no one else just pops up at our house uninvited. In fact, only a handful of people know where we rest at.

I get to the front door, not really wanting to be bothered with Miss Wanda because, although she's off the pipe, she still has a foul mouth and can get on my damn nerves.

Anyway, I looked out the peephole and there's this white chick standing on the porch. I opened the door.

"Yes, how may I help you?" I asked, trying to be courteous, thinking: *She must be a neighbor.* I smiled at the little boy and girl with her. *Ain't they so cute? Makes me want to have a baby.*

"Tamika, can we come inside? There's something you should know," said the white chick.

I'm staring at the two light brown toddlers that she had in tow, and I know what the fuck she had to tell me before I invited her in and listened in shock as the words came out of her mouth.

CJ came home to a real fuckin' surprise that day, finding his little secret half breed family sitting in our living room, my face twisted into a scowl.

"Fuck you doing here?" he snarled at Brittany Spears. His jaw was twitchin' like I've seen it do a few times before when he's extremely mad.

"I'm not allowing you to keep us a secret any longer," she'd said.

I was thinking, okay he's about to kick Snow White's ass for bringing this bullshit to where we lay our heads. But nah, the muthafucka folded. Had the aw-fuckin'-dacity to ask *me* to understand. Acted like he was proud of the two rug rats. Like I was supposed to smile at 'em and be friends with their cracker mama. Not hardly! I held my composure in front of the bitch who was sitting in *my* living room on *my* ten-thousand dollar sofa, like I was supposed to pack my shit and move out! So that her and those two ugly crumb snatchers could move in with my man.

I was two seconds off of that ass—trust!

They could have made a family violence video out of the scene at our house after the bitch and those two child support cases left.

"So, that's how you doing it?" I asked CJ. Then wham! I punched him in his lowdown face before he could answer. Tears were pouring down my face as I did my best to kick his ass for old and new.

CJ is not weak so he didn't just wear an ass whuppin' even though he was in the wrong. He popped me upside the head a few times. But I scratched his ass up so bad, nigga looked like a pinstripe suit. Would've shot that ass if I could've got my hands on a gun before he bolted out the house.

"Don't run, muthafucka!" I shouted as I ran to the door with the .380 that CJ had taught me how to handle. Lucky his ass was gone.

A week later, CJ came back home, flowers in hand, begging me to forgive him. Had the nerve to ask me to have his child. I wanted to spit in his fuckin' face!

"Nigga, I wouldn't have a baby by you if it would cure world hunger and AIDS," I said, tossing the flowers back to him and putting my hands on my hips. "If I wasn't the first to do it, best believe I'm not going to be second or third. I don't try to be like other bitches, they try to be *me*. If a cracker done it, it can't be all that special."

"Oh, so that's how you feel?" asked CJ, looking hurt.

"That's *exactly*, how I feel! Furthermore, you made those kids in the street, so that's where you go to visit them. They are not welcome in this house."

"Mika, don't make me choose between you and my seeds," he'd threatened, like I was some punk bitch who'd be afraid to lose him.

"You're right, CJ. You don't have to choose, I'll choose for you. Obviously you expect your illegitimate children to be welcome in the house where I lay my head. Well, this is one time that you have seriously got me twisted! This yo' shit, and it's too big for me anyway. So hook me up with my own place like you promised to do if we ever broke up and I'll be just a memory," I said then went and packed my things.

Now I'm living in a fly three bedroom house not far away from CJ. The Victorian style crib cost a little over three hundred thousand. It doesn't have the opulence of the baby mansion but it's laced.

I talked Mama into moving in with me so CJ doesn't try to regulate. And you know that the deed is in my name. I have my BMW, crazy clothes, jewels, $250,000.00 in cash, and ten kilos of cocaine stashed away.

What?

Did you think I kept watch over so much of CJ's money and drugs all time time without squirreling something away for myself in case the nigga got brand new on me? I thought I told you once before that my mama didn't raise no fool.

CJ is still my man, though we have separate addresses now. He still takes care of me—I'm not about to work—because he owes me that for all the shit I've held him down through. I guess I still love him, in spite of everything. But I can't forgive him for what he did. A white bitch?

That shit hurts!

I have never given any other nigga the pussy since becoming CJ's woman. Maybe that needs to change? I mean, I'm not going to suddenly become some nigga'z jump off, but if the mood hits me I'ma get mine. I'll just do it twice as slick as CJ tries to be.

One thing the past four years have taught me is that when a nigga gets caked, he expects everybody to bow down at his feet. I respect what my man has accomplished in the streets but I'm not that bitch to kiss his feet.

"CJ needs to be reminded that other major niggaz check for you," Mama schools me.

"You're right, Mommie. Now that CJ's dirt has come to light I'ma see what some of these other niggaz are talking about," I say.

A short while later, mama's new boyfriend comes by to take her out.

"Don't give up the booty too quick," I whisper in her ear and we both laugh.

My girl, Star, calls from L.A. to invite me to an award show where she is being honored for being the new hot thing in the adult entertainment industry. Oh wait! Y'all didn't know? Yep, girlfriend turned being a slut into a career. Two years ago Diamond Rick had Star and his other girls make an amateur girl-girl porn video, and he sold copies of it underground. The DVD became so hot, a company out in Los Angeles purchased the rights to distribute it. Diamond Rick ended up with most of the

174

money from the distribution deal, but Star and one other girl signed contracts with the largest adult video company in the industry.

Now that Star has fame and a little money, and all types of men on her bra strap, you know you can't tell that bitch that her shit ain't the best thing since blueberry pie. When she comes back East to feature at one of the upscale strip clubs, they be advertising it all over the radio. And the hooker travels with a full time body guard.

I'm happy for my girl, though. The ho always has loved to fuck. Might as well get paid. I'm just glad that she kicked that fake pimp to the curb.

"Do you think you'll be able to fly out here for the show?" she asks.

"I'll try, but you know how CJ is," I say, not needing to explain.

My other line rings.

"That's him now. I'll call you back."

"Okay. Muah!"

I click over.

"Hello."

"Sup, ma? You wanna go to the club with us tonight?" asks CJ.

"Us meaning?"

"The clique. With all the shit that's been going on in the streets, I want niggaz to see that my team is still as strong as ever."

"Okay, come by and pick me up," I say.

It's the beginning of summer so we're all rockin' lightweight summer gear. I'm wearing a D&G white mini skirt with a red and white spaghetti strap halter that shows off my diamond belly ring; red and white Guiseppe stilettos and matching clutch purse. My hair and nails banging; baby diamond chandeliers hanging from my ears.

CJ and his crew are thugged out in street gear, but all of them are iced like igloos. We roll up to the club in The Bricks in a convoy of fly whips. I'm with my man of course in his brand new Maybach.

When we step in the club all eyes are on us. The DJ jumps right on our dicks (of course I don't have one of those but you get my point).

"Ladies and gentlemen, hustlaz and hos, playaz and fly chicks, the young don has just fell up in this muhfucka!"

The spotlight finds CJ, me on his arm. *Bitches better know.* CJ's whole team, over a hundred niggaz, roll up behind us.

"Y'all clear out VIP and make room for The Bricks most official team yo! Show respect for the realest," screams the DJ into the mic.

We invade VIP like we own the whole club.

Soon, the bubbly is flowing, weed smoke is in the air, and CJ is sporting me like old times.

"These hos can't compare to you ma," CJ whispers in my ear. We're hugged up in a booth.

"Well, you need to start treating me like you realize it," I tell him, putting my tongue in his ear.

CJ turns his head so that he can suck my tongue.

"Mmm," I moan.

"I know I fucked up big but I love you more than anything in my life Mika. More than the guap, the whips, and the street fame. More than anything you can name," he says, nibbling on my bottom lip.

If CJ's words were food, they could be candied yams, that's how sweet he whispers them into my mouth. I want to gobble them up and ask for seconds. But y'all know I have to speak my peace.

I pull my mouth away from his and asks, brows arched but knitted, "If you have that much love for me nigga, why didn't you kick *Brittany Spears* ass for coming to our house and putting you on blast, breaking up our happy home? Better yet, why you creep in the first place?"

CJ tries to kiss me again. I lock tongues with him for a half a minute, "Answer my question nigga."

He sighs, "What can I say ma? Man, I just slipped. Stephanie gettin' pregnant was an accident and—"

"An accident? What? Was you walking down the street not looking where you were going tripped over something and fell between her legs?" I asks sarcastically. "That's an accident! If you ran up in her willingly with no condom on, those kids ain't no accident."

"I was drunk yo."

The nigga lies like I'm Suzy Fu Fu.

I jump all in his shit. The pain of his betrayal comes out in a torrent of tears and accusations. "I never would've thought that you were on some jungle fever shit," I conclude.

"Girl, you know it ain't like that. But dig, I didn't bring you out tonight to argue about that shit. I wanted you to roll with us to show muhfuckaz that we still holding each other down. Bitches been all in my grill lately, talkin' 'bout they heard you had bounced. So I know mad niggaz been tryna get at you."

I fix my mouth to deny it but CJ cuts me off.

"It don't matter man. I know you ain't gon' play yaself. Can't no other nigga compare to this," he boasts, tapping his chest with a fist. "Our thing is platinum baby. Whose name tatted on your breast, ass, and neck?"

"Yours," I reply. *Daymum, I love this nigga.*

"I can't have these knuckleheads thinking I can't hold on to wifey, 'cause then they'll start thinkin' that a nigga can't hold his crown. Nah mean? Come back home, shorty," pleads CJ, looking into my hazel browns.

"Oh, that's the only reason why you want me to move back in with you? To prove something to niggaz?"

"Hell nah! Shit just ain't the same without coming home to you. I bought that big ass joint for you ma. It ain't a home without you in it."

CJ looks so sad that he has me feeling guilty. I feel myself about to cry. I have forgiven CJ for too much shit already. I still love the ground that he walks on but if I continue letting him get away with creepin', one of these days I'ma lose him for real. Because when a nigga starts taking his girl for granted her position is in serious jeopardy.

Alicia Keys *Why Do I Feel So Sad* plays in the background as if the DJ is locked into my emotions. I wanna move back in with CJ, but I have to hold my ground. At least until he realizes that he has to clean up his act or risk losing what he claims to love above all else.

I turn my head so that CJ can't see the tear cascading down my face.

I see Kareem with some first-night-pussy on his lap. Kareem likes his women real easy, like Rah's sister, LaKeesha, who he has a daughter by. Then again, the whole hood is gonna have a baby by her at the rate she's going. She already has two babies by two different niggaz, now she's pregnant with the third, by your guess is as good as mine.

Not my problem, though. I don't fuck with Miss Hot Ass. Don't really got much to say to Rah either, now that he's home. See, I blame him for hooking my man up with that white bitch.

CJ's crew is wildin' in the club, spraying bubbly on hos, making it rain, the whole nine. I watch bitches watching me, wishing that they could switch places with me, not knowing that its hell being CJ's wifey.

CJ comes back to my place with me after we all leave the club. He used every persuasion in the mack encyclopedia to get me to go back to the baby mansion with him, but ever since his white bitch set foot inside those doors, the place was no longer home to me.

Mama is asleep when we get back to my house. CJ picks me up in his arms at the door, carries me to my bedroom, and proves that the sexual chemistry between us is as hot as ever. He caresses me with his tongue until I cuss God for creating a muthafucka who can make me feel so damn good. When he enters me. I cry out his name.

TWENTY-TWO

RAHEEM

I'm at the crib. A simple two bedroom joint that me and Kayundra copped out in Powder Springs when I came home from the Feds last year. Shorty is getting ready to hit the studio and do a piece with Scare Me, a new rapper who fucks with Young Jeezy.

While my boo is at the studio, I'ma swing by the nightclubs that I own. One, the Starnight, is an upscale joint in Buckhead that caters to the professional crowd. The other, Club Sparkle, is on Flat Shoals Road in Decatur; it's not as upscale as the Starnight but it's a magnet for ballers and the array of chicks they attract.

Since I'm not on paper, there is no PO to tell me that I can't do this or that, or associate with felons. Still I'm striving to get to the guap without having to slang. Straight up, that lil' bid gave a nigga time to think, reflect, and weigh my options. Journalism is out but I'm still determined to be a success.

Big Ma is disappointed that I have given up my scholastic dreams. But I told her like this, "Big Ma, I know that life hasn't been easy for you lady. You lost your only child to drugs and violence then you had to raise two knuckleheads in an environment that undermined everything that you tried to instill in us. But you did the best you could," I'd said, placing her gentle hands in mine.

"You gave us mad love and guidance. Me and LaKeesha just wanted to do what we wanted to do. The world can't blame you." I wiped a tear that trickled down her sweet face then continued, "I know I've disappointed you so far but at the end of the day, your teachings will shine through. Just keep me in your prayers beautiful woman. I love you," I'd concluded, hugging her.

Big Ma just wants the best for me and LaKeesha.

I drop a jewel on CJ from time to time because I wanna see my nigga walk away from the game not get carried away because of it. I don't beat his ears up with advice though; 'cause if push came to shove I'd get back on the grind myself. So fuck being a hypocrite. No matter what, that's my nigga 'til the end. Fam held me down the whole time I was on lock, like the solid nigga he's always been.

He moved Kayundra to Jessup, Georgia, where I was serving my bid, so that she could visit me every week. Even after she found a job CJ continued to make sure that she wasn't without. Kept my commissary laced too.

Real niggaz do real things.

When I touched down, he asked, "What all you need, fam? I already got you one of them Chrysler 300 joints on deck. That bitch got a chameleon paint job so it flips colors and looks like you pushin' a different whip every time you bend a corner."

Then he hit me with twenty stacks saying, "Go cop a wardrobe, fam. You done got mad diesel!"

Now that's mad love, yo.

I'd bumped into N.O. soon after opening the Starnight. He was still ballin', but since I wasn't trying to fuck with no work we really didn't have nothing else to chop it up about.

"Be easy, whoadie," he'd said.

"You too." I'd dapped him.

As he was about to walk away, he turned and asked, "Did you hear what happened to Don and 'em?"

"Yeah," I'd replied.

A few months before I was released I had read in the *Atlanta Journal/Constitution* that Don and his crew had caught crazy fed time for mad bodies, drug trafficking, possession of illegal weapons, and whatever else those dirty ass feds could pile on.

Just keepin' it gangsta, I was more than a bit concerned that I might get tied in with the clique. But they all bit the bullet and took their medicine like men which is an anomaly, 'cause these days niggaz will implicate their own mamas in some shit to walk.

"Baby, I'm about to go to the studio," says Kayundra as she comes into the den where I'm at the computer working on a manuscript. She bends down and places a cherry red kiss on my cheek.

Shorty the truth, yo.

She trooped for me every step of the way, my entire bid. Put her singing dream on hold until I touched down. Not once did she backslide on drugs, miss a visit, or wrap her legs around another nigga. That's the type of loyalty and dedication that is to be treasured.

"Okay, I'll see you later tonight," I say, still typing. "Come by the club when you're done at the studio."

"Which one?" asked Kayundra, putting her hand up under my wife beater and rubbing my chest.

"The one that's named after you."

LaKeesha calls a minute or two after Kayundra leaves for the studio.

"What's good?" I ask.

"Nothin'. I need a loan," she replies, cutting straight to the chase.

"How much?"

"Five hundred."

"A'ight, I got you. I'ma send it through Money Gram. How's my nephew and niece doing?"

"They're good. You and Kayundra want them to come stay with y'all for a while? I swear, I need a break before this other baby comes."

No, you need to stop having all these babies and do something with your life.

I don't verbalize my thoughts because I've been on LaKeesha's case real hard since coming home. Lately, I've decided to switch up, maybe positive words will encourage her to get her shit together.

"Let me holla at Kayundra about that," I say in regards to us keeping my nephew and niece for a while.

Damn, I can't think of anything positive to tell her. So I ask her for Kareem's cell phone number.

"What do you wanna call him about?"

"Sis, will you please just give me his number?"

"Rah, what's good?" Kareem greets me after I identify myself. But I'm not about to act all buddy buddy with him, not the way he's dragging my peeps.

"Son, you gettin' crazy guap, right?" I set him up.

"Fa sho," he responds.

"Fuck my sister gotta call down here asking me for money then?"

"Yo, Rah, whatchu speakin' on?"

"Nigga, you doing my peeps dirty and that shit don't sit right wit' me."

"Hol' up nigga!" he snaps back. "Me and La ain't like that no more. She's carrying the next nigga'z seed; if she need some money, that's on *him*."

"When was the last time you hit her up with some money for your daughter?" All I hear is silence. "Yeah, that's what I thought. Nigga, be a man about the shit and take care of yours, then my sister wouldn't be struggling."

Kareem begins to retor, something breezy probably, but must've thought better of it. I know that he doesn't fear me, he's a killa. So it's respect that makes him say, "I feel you Rah. I'ma call La and work something out with her. Word."

"A'ight, son. One."

Respect given, respect shown.

When CJ comes in town the next day, I have to get in my nigga'z ear about the same shit. He's mad at Steph for blowing up his spot so he isn't going to visit his children.

"Yo, fam. I'm not tryna hear no lecture," he jokes as he fires up a blunt and sits at my computer and begins reading the urban street lit novel that I'm working on.

"Oh, you gon' be an author now?" he quips.

"Yeah, Insha Allah. You know I've always been nice wit' the pen. Now that I'm a convicted felon a journalism career ain't really a viable option anymore. At least not if I try to go the traditional route so I'ma try my hand at writing street novels, them joints is hot."

"Yo, it's a chick got a publishing company in East Orange that fuck with them type of books. I be seeing advertisements about her company all around Newark. I think shorty did a bid in the Feds, something like ten joints. Kept it gangsta too."

"Yep. You talking 'bout Wahida Clark. I wrote her when I was on lock, she seems like good people. I sent her the first five chapters of my joint a few months ago and she hit me back saying that her and her editors is feeling it, and for me to send the rest."

"Word? So when yo shit comin' out?" CJ jumps the gun, picking up several books published by Wahida Clark Publishing that I have sitting on the desk.

"Shid. I can't even find the time to finish writing it, and you asking when it's coming out." I chuckle.

CJ fires up a blunt and flips through the pages of *Trust No Man* by Cash, nodding his head.

"I'ma have to read this joint yo," he says, setting the novel down and grabbing the sequel, *Trust No Man 2: Disloyalty Is Unforgivable.*

"That shit is butta, fam, I'm tellin' you. Dude put it down." I say, though tryna get CJ to read a book is gonna be like tryna get all the brothaz and sistahz on lock freed.

"This shit sound like that fire," he says, reading the blurb on the back cover from Kwame Teague, the author of those *Dutch* joints, who's from the Bricks. "Don't they got these joints on audio?" asks CJ, now sweatin' *Thirsty* by Mike Sanders.

"I think so."

I switch the subject back to Steph and the twins.

"You still on that yo?" CJ replies. "Fuck being an author, yo ass need to be an Imam, 'cause you always got advice for a nigga." Clowning.

"Like steel sharpens steel, men sharpen men," I jewel him.

"I feel you, yo."

Ca$h

He still doesn't go visit Steph and the twins.

TWENTY-THREE

CJ

Winter comes in with a bang. Snow covers the streets of Newark like piles of cocaine, and the wind and cold dares a muhfucka to come outside. I'm up to the challenge though as I hop outta my whip, hoodie pulled tight, head ducked like a fullback running up the middle of the goal line.

"Close that damn door!" Mama yelled as Eric lets me in. My lil' bruh don't live with our Mom Dukes, he has his own spot. Mama called us over to talk to us.

I copped Mom Dukes this joint on Munn Avenue just outside the hood a coupla years ago. Offered to move her to the 'burbs but she wouldn't hear of it. She's been on and off the pipe for the past few years, but I think she's back fuckin' around now because she's been seen in the projects a lot lately, and I know what that's about.

I close the door and touch fists with Eric, go hug Mom Dukes, who's sitting on the sofa smoking a Newport, looking vexed.

"It didn't take y'all but three days to come by and see what it is I wanted," mama says sarcastically. "I bet if Tamika calls you, you would fly over there to see what she wants."

"All you do is fuss," I say and pull her ponytail.

She smacked my hand.

"You ain't no better, Eric," she directed her aim at him. Like me, Eric ignoreed her.

"Ma, you need to clean up around here. Fa real, it don't make no sense, yo."

"Hire me a maid!"

"I'm just sayin'."

"You ain't sayin' shit! Start cleaning up if you got a problem with the way it look in here," she checks Eric, cigarette smoke coming out of her mouth in little clouds that break up and disappear.

"Brianna!" I call out and my lil' sister who's now fourteen with the body of an eighteen-year-old. She comes downstairs with her cell phone glued to her ear.

"That's all she do, talk on the phone all day," says mama. Bri rolls her eyes.

Mama peeps it. "You and Eric spoil Miss Thang too fuckin' much, that's why she think she's grown."

"I do not," disputes Bri.

Mama right about one thing, me and Eric do spoil Bri. But she deserves it because she's an A student and she minds mama most of the time. I don't try to shelter Bri, I give it to her gully, lettin' her know how lil' niggaz gon' try to come at her to hit it. And Eric got lil' dudes scared to even speak to Bri.

"Bri, clean up the house yo," I tell her.

"Okay." She gets right to it.

"So, ma, what you need to talk to us about?" asks Eric, plopping down on the sofa next to her. I sit in the armchair adjacent to them.

Mama mashes out her cigarette.

"I need an increase in my allowance," she says, sounding like a teenager.

Me and Eric look at one another and silently communicate that it ain't going down. We both pay all of mama's bills and are blessing her lovely enough already.

Mama fuckin' wit that crack again. That's why she's asking for more guap, I think.

When we refuse to increase what we give her each month, our Mom Dukes goes off into left field ranting about Eric following in my criminal footsteps.

"Y'all asses gonna end up dead or under the got damn jail! I'm not lettin' y'all corrupt my baby. Brianna! Don't let me catch yo ass acceptin' anything else from either one of yo drug dealin' brothers! You hear me, got dammit?" Mama screams over the noise of the vacuum cleaner which Bri is running across the carpet.

"Umm-hmm," says Bri as if to say, *how many times have I heard this before?*
We just let our Mom Dukes scream and cuss; we all know how she do. She be talkin' shit but in her own way she's proud of us. Done heard her tell a bitch, "I ain't got no boys, I raised two *men*. Both of 'em know how to get what they want, and it don't matter if I smoke crack or not, let a bitch violate and see don't CJ and Eric make the muthafuckin' coroner file a report. And my baby Brianna, their pride and joy, smartest girl in her whole school. Gonna be like Condoleezza Rice."

The love in our fam ain't text book but it's the love that we know and understand; it's gully, nothin' fake about it. Sociologist might call it dysfunctional, but "dis" functioning good as a muhfucka.

Since we're not paying mama's tirade no attention she puts me and Eric out.

Eric goes to check on my spots in Little Bricks. I go fuck with Cujo, he has some work for me. Cujo's cohorts knocked off a big shipment of coke down in VA last week so I'm about to get broke off. Plus Cujo has twenty-five keys of heroin for me.

I go handle business then begin dispersing the work to my most trusted people who in turn are responsible for getting it to the street team that pump it. Everything is gravy until one of my spots on Springfield Avenue gets robbed and all three of the lil' niggaz that were pumpin' from the house are found bodied in the basement. Two days later, another one of my spots gets hit and I lose another lil' nigga.

Word on the street is that U-God is coming for my crown.

A'ight, nigga, you think you're built for this? Yo' team ain't strong enough to fuck wit' mine! I'ma show you why they call me The Young Don.

I get my team together and tell 'em, "We gunnin' fo' them niggaz wherever we see 'em, wherever they rest at. I want U-God and all them bitch niggaz that call themselves The Goon Squad. We killin' mamas, girlfriends, babies, dogs and cats, anybody and anything connected to their squad is fair game!"

We are in the main room of my after hours' joint which I've closed down for business with all this shit going on. My top niggaz and a coupla dozen of our most tenured street soldiers are present. I let Kareem finish giving my directions to the team while I pull Flip to the side.

"Let's take a walk yo. I need to holla at you," I say to him, zipping up my black leather Rocawear bomber coat as I lead him outside. "Let's sit in your whip," I suggest.

Inside Flip's money green Escalade with the peanut butter leather interior, I look out the rolled up the passenger window to make sure our enemies ain't on the creep. In the driver's seat Flip does the same then starts the engine and turns the heater on full blast. Ironically, Biggie's joint "Warning" is bumpin' from the system.

I turn the music off and speak to Flip in a tone that's like a banger pressed against his temple.

"Flip, I'm suspicious of you yo, shit 'bout to get crucial and I can't afford to have a nigga up under me that can't be trusted."

"Fuck you talking about, fam?" he asks, genuinely looking like he has no clue.

"Nah, son, you don't get to ask any questions." My hand comes out of my coat pocket grippin' a tool, and it's not the kind that you make repairs with. "I'ma talk, you gon' listen until I tell you to speak, nah mean?" I grit with the fo-five ready to do what it do.

I assume Flip is strapped too, but his ass bet' not reach or I'ma seal his fate.

"I'm listening, yo," he says.

I look him in the eye.

"Those kids KD and Ghetto jacked five muhfuckaz that shopped with you. They didn't fuck with nobody else's people on our team but yours. So, I been wondering, how them thirsty niggaz get all in yo mix like that? Convince me that you wasn't down with the licks or I'ma rewrite that ass with KD!"

Flip looks me back in the eye.

"Fam, why would I make a dope fiend move like that? You got a nigga eatin' hella good. What them niggaz lick for, two or three joints each time? Like twelve altogether? All coke?" I don't answer, I just let him go on. "Man, that's trick-off guap compared to all the heroin I'm touching through you. If I was gonna stick you I'd stick you when you hit me with ten or fifteen of these joints, but that ain't how I'm gettin' down."

I'm not convinced. I click-clack one into the chamber.

Flip sighs and adds, "CJ, you lookin' at me sideways because of that shit with Kendall way back. But yo, nigga was handling me like a peon! Wouldn't give me what I had earned then got real breezy when I complained about it. Nigga didn't have no love or respect for me so I didn't have no loyalty to him. With you it's different, you give a nigga whatever he earns. I done put in mad work for the team yo. Ain't never violated, not one time and that's on my dead Mom Dukes. The snake ain't me my nigga. Be careful of the dog that brought you the bone."

I'm looking in Flip's eyes, weighing his words, reading his body language, using my street-honed ability to see into the hearts of men. If what I'm reading is true, that can only mean one thing because I don't believe in coincidences.

I ponder that for a sec' then extend my fist.

Flip puts his to mine.

I'm a street warfare strategist so when I strike at U-God and 'em I hit hard, merciless and in three different spots at once.

I send a ten-man crew, headed by Snoop, to smash U-God's stash spot on Hawthorne Avenue. They do a kick-door, bodying four niggaz and a bitch, and coming back with eight keys of coke, a whole block of heroin, and seventy-three stacks in cash.

Hit dat ass in the pocket!

While that was going down, Eric and Flip snatched up U-God's baby's mama coming out of a hair salon on Park Avenue. Left the bitch face down with red streaks in her new hairdo that her stylist didn't put there.

"Shorty stiff in the snow," Eric quipped.

Hit that ass in the heart.

*You feel me now, U-God? Not yet? Okay, now I'm 'bout to
fuck with ya head.*

Like I said, I'm a street warfare strategist so I've done my
homework.

Me and Kareem park at the curb in front of the old woman's
house in Elizabeth on a quiet side street. We get out of the
nondescript Chevy truck carrying shovels and a snow blower.
We go to the side door and ring the doorbell.

"Coming," says a voice that sounds elderly.

Granny comes to the door and asks, "Who is it?" her voice is
polite.

"Mrs. Lowdell, we're here from A Helping Hand, an agency
that assists senior citizens."

"A what?"

"A Helping Hand," I repeat, speaking louder in case she's
hard of hearing. "We're volunteers who assist elderly people
like yourself with chores that you may not be able to do
anymore."

"Oh, isn't that nice," she declares and opens the door,
greeting us with a grandmotherly smile, reminding me of Rah's
Big Ma with her short wide frame and salt and pepper hair
wrapped in a bun.

"Yes ma'am. We're going to plow your driveway and walk
for you today. Can I please come inside and call the agency to let
them know where we are?"

"Sure."

Me and Kareem step inside and close the door behind us.
Gospel music is playing throughout the downstairs.

Minutes later, I'm smoking a vanilla Black-n-Mild, leaned
against the mantelpiece in the old woman's living room.
Kareem is seated on the plastic-covered sofa next to Granny,
burner in hand.

Although I did my homework and knew that Mrs. Lowdell, a
widow, lived alone, I still checked the house to make sure that no
one was in any of the other rooms or the basement. When I

returned back to the living room, I had a smirk on my face as I thumped ashes from the "Black" into my gloved hand.

Kareem shut off the gospel music so I didn't have to speak over that annoying shit.

"Well, well, well! Guess what I found down in the basement, Mrs. Lowdell?" Her eyes got big as eggs.

"That's not mine," she quickly declared.

"Yeah, I know that. But you know what's in it," I say, in reference to the safe that I found.

"I don't! I asked my grandson not to put it down there. If that's what you came for please take it and leave."

"Uh, I'ma do that but first you're gonna call your grandson and tell him that someone wants to talk to him."

"Look here, young man! You can't come in my house and order me around," she protests.

"Oh nah?" I walk over and slap a proverb outta her mouth.

"The Lord is my shepherd…"

"Shut da fuck up! Call your grandson or the Lord gon' be more than your shepherd, he gon' be ya Landlord!"

Granny makes the call from her cordless.

"Somebody here wants to speak to you," I hear her say into the phone before passing it to me.

"What it do baby boy?" I say like me and him cool.

"Who dis?" asks U-God.

"N.W.A."

"Who!?"

"*Nigga Wit' an Attitude* aka the Young Don. You think this shit is a game, homie? I take it personal." I hang up the phone and leave the bitch nigga stressing over whether or not I'ma body his grandma.

Fuckin' wit' his mind!

We don't do Granny but we snatch up the safe, leaving U-God another three hundred stacks lighter in the grip.

A war is costly nigga.

Two days later, U-God retaliates. The Goon Squad bodies two of my lil' niggaz that pumped from my spots on Berger Street and Elizabeth Avenue.

The next day, I'm knocked to my knees; Brianna gets shot down in broad daylight while visiting a friend in the projects where we used to live. Murdered like she was a street thug, not a fourteen-year old innocent child.

At her funeral a week later, I cry like a baby as I look down in the coffin at my precious little sister. Tamika does too. Rah walks up and puts a hand on my shoulder.

"I'm here for you, fam, just give me the game plan," he whispers.

"Nah, go on back to the 'A' after the funeral. I got this." I give him a gangsta hug, appreciating that he was down to ride even though he's sworn off the streets.

Halfway through the funeral service mama faints and has to be rushed to the hospital. Eric sheds a few silent tears but he hasn't said a single word since the day Brianna got killed. I know that revenge is on his mind.

"Stay outta the streets, it's about to get real ugly," I warn Tamika a few days later.

Bodies drop on both sides but we're gunnin' them niggaz down three to one, and since The Goon Squad was only twenty-something strong in numbers to start with, before long there's only U-God and three others left standing and I haven't lost any of my top niggaz.

But the streets are an inferno! Jake all over the place; niggaz gettin' sntached up and questioned like it's the 60's.

"This ain't fuckin' Columbia! You can't do all of this killing. I told you that once before," Cujo snaps at me.

We're inside the vacant warehouse where we often meet.

"White nigga, don't tell me what da fuck I can't do! I handle the streets, you handle your ilk. Nigga killed my sister; the blood ain't gon' stop flowing 'til I wipe out every last one of those bitches!" I spazz on him.

192

"You're killing innocent people! Aunts, cousins, neighbors, people that don't have anything to do with this!" Cujo barked back.

"My sister didn't have nothing to do with it either!" I remind him. *Yeah, what about dat? That's why I bodied anything close to them niggaz. Would've banged the nigga'z grandmom, too, but the bitch was ghost when we went back to do her.*

"I'm sorry about your sister but all of these unnecessary murders won't bring her back."

"I'm not tryna hear that shit!" I spit and turn around and walk out of the warehouse.

"You're becoming uncontrollable!" Cujo yells at my back.

"Suck my dick!"

One of U-God's mans has a sister who is a school teacher at Shabazz High. Me and Eric leave the bitch nodded inside her Honda Civic in the school's parking lot.

Now U-God's man's mama has to bury a daughter just like my Mom Dukes had to do.

"I see you're gonna do shit your way!" Cujo snarls as he cuffs me and shoves me into the backseat of a police cruiser being driven by a jake in uniforn. The jake has to be down with Cujo because Cujo ain't watching his mouth. "Lock his ass up and make sure that he don't get a bond! Charge him with assault on a police, attempted murder, and attempted escape, anything that will keep him in jail while we settle our problem. Otherwise, he's going to fuck up a good thing!"

I'm taken to jail where I remain for twenty days on those bogus charges. It's only after U-God's and the remaining three Goon Squad nigga'z bodies are found inside a vacant warehouse that I'm released.

I know that Cujo and 'em dealt with them niggaz because their bodies were found inside the same warehouse where I've often met Cujo.

The victory seems bittersweet because I didn't get to smash U-God myself. But the next squad will think hard and long before coming for my crown.

Ca$h

TWENTY-FOUR

TAMIKA

Things had gotten so crazy after Brianna got killed I was afraid to venture out of the house. CJ, Eric and 'em was turning all of Newark into one big cemetery, and Miss Wanda lost what little piece of mind that she had before tragedy claimed her daughter. While all of this was going on, Nee Nee called me to say, "Cuz, I know we've had our run-ins but we're still family."

"And?" I'd interrupted the bitch.

"I think you need to leave CJ's ass alone before he gets you killed."

"Really?" I'd laughed. "Why? So you can try to fuck him again? Bitch, puhleeze!"

"No, for real. I don't wanna end up having to come to your funeral."

"Ha! Trust, you won't be coming to my funeral because there's no way that your cum guzzling ass will outlive me." I'd laughed at her again.

"See, that's why I don't fuck with you. Bitch, you ain't all of that!" Nee Nee said like the hater that she is.

"Maybe I'm not but I'm more than you. I would rather die by my man's side than turn my back on him. Jump offs like you can't relate to that," I said and hung up on her ass.

But I admit to being afraid that loving CJ was going to end up costing a bitch her life.

Then CJ got locked up and held without bail for two or three weeks. I was really shook with my man not being out here to protect me. Still, I went down to the jail to visit him every visitation day. That's how I ran into one of his other bitches!

Oh, so he's pulling this shit again? I'd said to myself, but I didn't even confront him this time.

Two can play that game.

While visiting CJ at the jail I met this chick named Lemora who was also visiting her man. Lemora and I became friends fast, but I didn't tell her *who* my man was, not then. Her and I went out partying in New York and guess what?

I got me some dick!

It was good, too. My "revenge fuck", I call it.

Now that CJ is out of jail and whatever beef that he had in the streets seems to be settled. I'ma see how he acts. I've been hollerin' at this young nigga named Nard on the low. He's a cutie with potential. I'm headed to meet his young ass at the movie theater now.

As I back out of my driveway, I turn on the radio and they're playing the hottest single in the land by this new rapper out of ATL named Scare Me.

You won't believe who is on the song with him!

TWENTY-FIVE

RAHEEM

Allah is truly the Most Beneficent, I think as I look in the mirror one last time before peeking over at Kayundra who is in the doorway of our bathroom, all ready to go. I'm wearing a black and charcoal gray pinstripe Armani tux, black gator square-toe shoes. Kayundra looks beautiful in a long silk Prada dress. Her hair is pinned up, allowing the tear drop diamond earrings that she's wearing to flaunt their magnificence. A limo awaits outside to take us to "Sparkle's" album release party.

Yep, you heard me! Kayundra is in the game!

Ever since her record with Scare Me topped the charts four months ago and critics acclaimed the collab an instant classic the likes of that joint Mary J and Method Man hooked up on back in the day, the music world has been anticipating Sparkle's solo project. One mag predicted she'll have the year's hottest R&B album. Her lable mate, Scare Me, already has the rap game on smash with his triple-platinum selling debut CD, fueled by the single *Through Whateva* on which Sparkle first appeared.

Through Whateva has been nominated for a Grammy in the rap category and numerous BET music awards. That alone has Sparkle's name bubblin' and her own CD hasn't even hit the stores yet.

Preston Myers, the CEO of Platinum Entertainment, the record label to which my girl is signed, is a young brother who seems to have the astuteness of Diddy or a Damon Dash. Before Kayundra signed with Platinum Entertainment she had been close to signing with Universal, but she backed out of the deal when the A&R at Universal wanted to "create" a different background in regards to Kayundra's past, than what is true. He also wanted her to sing pop instead of R&B.

Preston promised us that if Kayundra aka Sparkle signed with Platinum, the label would not try to hide her past or change her style. So far, Preston has been true to his word and he's going all out for Kayundra with her debut CD. Preston hired a team of superstar producers to work on Sparkle's joint, including Pharell Williams. Scare Me appears on one song and T.I. appears on another.

The stretch limo glides toward the upscale ballroom on Peachtree where Sparkle's album release party is being held. Inside the chauffeured vehicle me and baby girl are joined by her Mom Dukes who flew in from New Jersey for the occasion. We collected her from the Peachtree Plaza Hotel where she has a suite for the weekend.

When we reach the ballroom and step out in the warm spring night air, the paparazzi spots Sparkle, whose face has become well known from the video for the hit song she did with Scare Me and flash bulbs blinds us.

Sparkle, who's that fine chocolate brotha escorting you on his arm?

What happened to Scare Me? I thought you two were dating?

What do you think about people comparing you to Mary?

Smile for the camera.

How does it feel, girl?

The hordes of paparazzi and radio and video show personalities rain questions and requests at Kayundra.

I'll tell you how it feels as soon as I wake up. Right now I'm trapped in a wonderful dream!" she replies and flashes her beautiful smile, which makes her sparkle, as we are escorted through the horde and a throng of fans by ballroom security.

We're seated inside the ballroom's auditorium at a VIP table with Preston, Scare Me, his man Young Jeezy, and several suits from Platinum Entertainment. Sparkle is seated between Preston and Scare Me. Myself and Sparkle's Mom Dukes, who is Sparkle's manager, are seated at the end of the table. We don't trip, this is Sparkle's night.

The entertainment begins with other Platinum artists performing. An hour and a half later the ballroom grows quiet with anticipation of Sparkle taking the stage to perform the single that will be the first release from her CD entitled *A Long Journey.*

Sparkle comes on stage to a deafening roar of applause, whistles, hoots, and shouts. She smiles and raises her hand for silence. The crowd quiets down.

"Before I perform for y'all," she says into the mic, "I want to thank God first; He knows my journey and he brought me through. I also have to acknowledge my mother, thank you so much Mom.

"To my soulmate—baby you know who you are and how very much you mean to me. No matter how far I go in the music world, I owe it all to you because you believed in me when I had stopped believing in myself. I love you baby.

"Last but certainly not least, thank you Preston, and all the dope producers that worked their magic on my CD. Scare Me, keep scarin' 'em off the mic."

Soft melodic music begins to play and I see Kayundra transform into Sparkle, belting out song after heartfelt song, captivating the audience. I smile with pride as I recognize joints from when Kayundra first began writing songs, right after going to rehab. Other songs, she has sang to me at home. Now on stage, those same songs come from a depth inside of her that entrance me.

Scare Me joins Sparkle on stage for the final song, the hip hop meets R&B joint, "By Your Side." The single might be on Sparkle's CD but Scare Me murdaz it! The audience goes crazy after he spits his first verse:

You know how a nigga was livin' when we first hooked up, boo/ in these streets doin' what a nigga gotta do/ so don't ask me now to give it up/ just hold me down, we gon' live it up/ And nah, I don't need you to show ya ass like Trina/I need a quiet shorty on my side like Nina/calm and steady and seldom seen/yet lethal when she step on the scene, nah mean/I be lovin' you 'cause you not petty, always beggin' for baguettes/Dolce and Gabbana and other designer shit/Lil Kim wanna be bitches, like poison, make a nigga so sick/them and their gold digging clique/that's why niggaz don't wife them hos/be like my man Kimbo slice them hos/get high, cut and dice them hos/neva see our peeps throwin' rice on them hos/Mom Duke sharing advice with them hos/my mans thankin' Christ fa them hos/so don't change ma, you gon' Sparkle in the end/you ain't gotta pull up, get out, tits out/to chase his benjamins/you ain't gotta fuck fast, lose class, tat his name across ya ass/to be dude's girlfriend/when he bounces for another chick, what happens to the tats then?/are you just a rat then?/I'ma leave you wit' some wiz/let dude handle his biz/If he a real nigga he know what real is/and when it's time to ride, you not a bitch, you a bride/ya name might not be Nina but you'll be by his side.

"Scare Me's gritty rhymes accentuated Sparkle's soulful voice to form a melodic street ballad that is sure to be as hot as their first collab' earlier this year on Scare Me's triple platinum CD *I Came To Take The Throne,* reports *The Source* a few days after the record release party.

"Sparkle's first CD is soulful and deep—deep—deep! She sings about her battle with drug addiction, self-hate, and self-doubt before finding love and inner peace. Her lyrics make it clear that she's been through hell, but now it's her time to Sparkle!" reports BET's Roxy.

On Atlanta's 107.3 the host says to her listeners, "There's a buzz going around that rapper, Scare Me and Platinum Entertainment label mate, Sparkle are doing more in the studio than making hits. But I don't know unless my eyes deceived me, I coulda swore I saw a fine brotha sportin' Sparkle on his arm last week at her album release party and it wasn't Scare Me. Take my word for it y'all."

I'm in my whip, on my way to a meeting with a client who balls for the Atlanta Hawks, when I hear that on the radio. A few minutes later, my phone chirps. I put my Bluetooth in and answer.

"What's good?"

Thugs Cry

"Baby, are you listening to 107.3?" Kayundra asks with detectable anger in her voice.

"Yeah, I'm listening. And I heard that."

"I'm about to call my publicist and have her to call the radio station and demand an apology! I want a quick end to that false rumor about me and Scare; it's disrespectful to you."

"Ma, I'm not stressin' over that shit. I know what the deal is yo. That's the nature of the beast, that's the entertainment industry. Yo listen! That's yo joint they're playing." I say, smiling as Sparkle's single "A Long Journey" plays on the radio. Just hearing that joint has a nigga teary-eyed because I know what type of journey it's been for shorty. To fans, it's a song. To myself, it's a chronicle. I'm so proud of my girl I wanna roll down the car window and yell, "That's my baby's joint they're bumpin' on the radio!" but my swag is too humble to get down like that.

While the song fills up my whip I say over the volume, "Shorty, you can't go calling every radio station and magazine that reports rumors about you. You're in the limelight now ma; remember what Preston said, 'a lot of what's printed and reported about entertainers is exaggerated or straight up false but it helps their popularity.'"

"Still, it's disrespectful to *our* relationship."

"As long as you and I know the truth I'm not trippin' yo." I assure her 'cause I'm not an insecure dude."

"Okay, sweetheart. I love you."

"Love you back. I'ma call you as soon as I get done meeting with Josh Smith. I'm gonna do a party for him."

"Alright, baby. Don't be sweatin' none of the Hawks' cheerleaders. Let me find out," Kayundra teases.

"Nah, baby, neva dat."

When I get home, Kayundra and I talk while grubbing on the JR Crickett's hot wings that I brought home for dinner. I describe to her the lavish party that I'm planning for my man Josh Smith's birthday and show her the invite list; all of ATL's big name athletes and entertainers are being invited.

"You are too! Josh specifically told me to make sure that you had an invite," I tell her.

"He did not!" she playfully punches me in the arm. "He doesn't even know who I am."

"Nah, fa real ma, he told me he loves your CD," I say honestly and Kayundra blushes.

With her first single blazing the charts, the label as well as Freeda, Kayundra's mother/manager, have lined up dates for Kayundra to appear live on various video shows such as 106 & Park, syndicated radio shows, and even Oprah who is interested in the story of Sparkle, overcoming her brief but serious addiction to crack and how that battle influences her music.

What's apparent to both myself and Kayundra is that her life is about to become a whirlwind of appearances, travel, and performances, and she hasn't even scheduled a concert tour yet.

I'm happy for my girl but she's concerned that all of the travel will tear down our relationship.

"Few relationships withstand the superstardom, rumors, and the temptations that come with the life," is the consensus of our friends.

"Do you call her Sparkle now?" asked CJ the other day when he was in town. I suspected that my nigga was being sarcastic.

Still, I'd replied straight up, "Sometimes because that was my pet name for her before all of this."

CJ nodded his understanding then surprised me by saying, "I gotta give her props, she can sing her ass off."

"Yeah, she do the damn thing."

CJ shook his head as if in disbelief.

"She deserves her shine dawg," I'd said, to which he'd responded.

"I guess so. I just hope she don't forget that her ass wouldn't be shining if it wasn't for you."

"That's not true, fam, but let's not go there. I appreciate the love nigga; it's been there since we were snot-noses. I just wish you wouldn't be so hard on my girl. She's good peeps; the fame won't change what's in her heart for me."

202

"I feel you," said CJ. "I just wanna see you get ya just rewards for all that you did for the girl. Remember, I saw her when the only *sparkle* she had came when she put the flame to a rock."

"Son, Allah blesses those who deserve blessings. Real talk though, my reward is seeing shorty drug-free and living her dream."

"That's what's up then," he conceded.

"Anyway, what's up with you? Shit done simmered down?" I inquired.

"I'm the last nigga standing, yo," he boasted.

"Be safe, bruh."

"I'ma do that always," he'd promised before saying he'd hit me up later.

The house phone rings while me and Kayundra are talking.

I wipe my hands on a hand towel and answer the cordless. "What it do?"

"Is that how you answer your phone, my brotha?" A hint of playfulness is in the caller's voice.

"Oh, what's good, Wahida?"

"As sailum alaikum."

"Wa alaikum as sailum."

"I'm waiting on those other chapters," says Wahida Clark, The Queen of Thug Love Fiction and my prospective publisher.

"Yo, I can't lie. I haven't been writing," I admit.

"I know how it is, get at me, though. And give my congrats to Sparkle."

"Will do."

"A'ight. Peace out."

I hang up and say to Kayundra, "Wahida Clark said to give you her congrats. Maybe we can get her to write you into her next novel."

"Nope. Too much drama be going on in her books, but I love 'em," replies Kayundra who is a big Wahida fan.

Ca$h

TWENTY-SIX

SPARKLE

Wow! Sometimes it all feels like a dream!

That can't be my song on the radio and atop the R&B chart. Is that really me in that video on BET? My face on the cover of Essence and Don Diva? Am I Sparkle for real?

Wow! Every time I pinch myself I realize that this is really happening to me. Three or four years ago, who would've believed that I could accomplish all of this? The first two singles from my CD both reached the top of the charts, now the third single, "By Your Side", my collab with Scare Me is number three on the R&B chart and number two on the rap chart.

I've appeared on so many radio and television programs in the past six months I've lost count. Some days I love it; other days I just want to go back to being unknown. I love performing; it's all the other stuff that wears on a sistah. I know, I should be happy, right? But I am not and I know why.

Wait, let me back up a bit.

My music career may seem to you an overnight success story; that's hardly the case. Even while Raheem was incarcerated I had begun trying to break into the music industry by sending copies of my demo to various industry heads. What I quickly found out was that there are a lot of horny bastards in the industry and they aren't all male. Niggaz and chicks wanted to sample my "goodies" in exchange for listening to my demo. I wanted to get into the industry but I refused to lay on my back to do so. I had stooped that low for crack, I wasn't about to go out bad again.

I never told Raheem about the indecent proposals I'd gotten from those who I'd approached with my demo because I was afraid that if I ever got my big break he might wonder if I had given in to one of those unscrupulous industry heads.

When Raheem came home from prison and I recommitted myself to getting a record deal, I was fortunate to know someone

Ca$h

who passed my demo on to Scare Me, who was about to drop his
debut CD. Scare liked my voice and asked me to do a collab with
him. And as they say in this industry—"the rest is history, baby."

Now here I am with a double platinum CD that has produced
three hit singles; I've just begun a thirty-two city concert tour
with Scare Me, Young Jeezy, Keisha Cole and a couple of lesser
known artists; the five concerts we've done so far have all been
sellouts, and the reviews are insane!

So why am I alone in my hotel suite in Chicago crying my
eyes out? Because—

I am pregnant!

*Preston and Mama drive me to the abortion clinic after
finally convincing me that having an abortion is the best thing to
do under the circumstances. They both argued, "You have to
think about your career."*

*"Other recording artists have had babies—Lauryn Hill,
Erykah Badu, my homegirl Faith," I rattle off a few names.*

"And their careers plummeted afterwards," says Preston.

"Un-huh," Mama cosigns.

*"I can't kill this baby, Raheem would never forgive me," I
say.*

"He doesn't have to know."

*"Mommie! How can you stand there and suggest that I
deceive the man I love?"*

"Mmmpf! You gotta do what you gotta do."

*Maybe Mama and Preston are right, but I keep hearing
Lauryn Hill's voice singing, "Now the joy in my world is in
Zionnn..." Her song reverberates in my mind like it's chanted by
my subconscious.*

Lauryn gave birth to Zion; are you going to kill your child?

*Now I'm stretched out on the examination table, legs spread
wide in stirrups. The pain is almost unbearable.*

"Push! Push! I see the head!" says the doctor.

I scream and push harder.

206

A moment later, I hear a tiny voice wail. The beautiful sound of my baby.

"It's a boy," exclaims my doctor wiping him off, wrapping him in a warm blanket then handing my son to me.

I hold him in the crook of my arm, crying tears of joy. "Ooh, you look just like your daddy. You precious boy," I coo.

Suddenly the doctor yanks my beautiful baby out of my arms and shoots him in the head with a gun almost as big as the baby!

"You wanted an abortion, right? Well, that's your abortion bitch!" the doctor snarl, then tosses my dead baby in the trash can.

I scream and scream and kick until...

"Wake up! Kayundra, honey, wake up!"

I open my eyes and see mama sitting on the edge of the bed in my suite. The bed sheets are wrapped around me like a satin straight jacket.

"Honey, what were you dreaming about?" asks mama, wiping away my tears then untangling me from the bed sheets.

"I don't know, mama." I lie.

"I'm calling Preston and I'm telling him that you need a break. And I say that as your Mom, not your manager."

"I'm okay."

"No, you're not. You need rest; I'm calling Raheem," says mama, pulling out her cell.

"Really mama, I'm okay. I just had a bad dream."

I cover her cell with my hand, preventing her from calling my man, who I know will demand that I shut it down.

Two weeks later the tour is in Charlotte, North Carolina, when I pass out on stage in the middle of my performance. I wake up in the emergency room to find doctors fussing over me.

R&B SONGSTRESS FAINTS DURING CONCERT. HER BOO TO THE RESCUE! Reads the headlines in the entertainment section of the local paper the next day.

Below the headline is a picture of Scare Me lifting me from the stage floor into his arms. I don't have to read the accompanying story to know its contents. I worry that the photo and story will be picked up by national newspapers and magazines and will embarrass Raheem, who is flying into Charlotte today. Mama called him this morning and told him what happened.

My record label issues a press release explaining the episode as "extreme exhaustion." I'll miss the next four concert dates then rejoin the tour in VA.

Immediately, rumors pop up that I'm back on drugs. To dispel the rumor, following the advice of Preston, I give an on-air interview from my hospital bed so that my fans can see that I'm not inside some crack house getting beamed up.

"I'm fine everybody. Just exhausted. I love you guys!" I cheese for the TV cameras and wave to my fans out there.

The nasty rumors quickly fade and I'm set to rejoin the tour. Only the doctor who examined me in the emergency room and Quida, one of my backup singers who I've befriended, know that what really caused me to faint on stage was my having an abortion the day of the incident. Having loss a lot of blood during the procedure, it was foolish of me to try to go on with the show. Doctors can't divulge a patient's medical information to the public and Quida won't tell it, we're tight as thieves. So my secret is safe.

I do feel guilty; maybe that's why I've begun to do a little light drinking. Only champagne, and I've taken a few tokes on joints. Not too often though because when I smoke weed it makes me feel worse about what I did than I felt before I smoked the shit.

Maybe I need to attend an aftercare meeting? Could I be on the verge of backsliding?

If I were to attend a meeting while on tour and word leaks out, the rumors will start up again. I need Raheem on tour with me. He was only able to stay with me three days when he flew into Charlotte after I had passed out on stage then he had to return to Atlanta to run the clubs and do another party for some celebrity. The success of the party he did for Josh Smith has others calling him to hook them up. I'm happy that things are going well for Raheem but I still wish that he was here with me. Absolutely no one can comfort me the way he can.

Adding to the stress that I'm already under, Preston is pressing me and Scare Me to play up the rumor that we are a couple.

"It'll boost interest in the label," he predicts.

"I feel you on dat," Scare Me agrees with him.

"The label is already bubblin'! Our concerts are sellouts and our faces are everywhere. I'm not playing my man like that," I vehemently protest.

"Sparkle, fans wanna see a star with another star, not with an average Joe. No disrespect to Rah," responds Preston, only concerned with the label, obviously.

So I go off!

"Dude, it *is* disrespectful to my man! I'll give up this shit, walk away from it all, before I give up my man. Before I prostitute myself for your damn label! Raheem was there when none of the fame existed for me; when the only people who was a fan of mine was crack dealers! Raheem gave me the name 'Sparkle'—gave me my sparkle back. So you can take this career that I now have and flush it down the damn toilet for all I care. I'm not Scare Me's woman, I belong to one man only— Raheem!" I stand up from the table at the steakhouse, where the three of us are having dinner and stormed out.

"Take me to the hotel!" I snap at the limo driver.

Alone, again, in my hotel room, a thousand miles away from my boo boo—and mama is back in Jersey—the urge comes over me to do something that I have not done in over four years.

Ca$h

TWENTY-SEVEN

TAMIKA

Dayyum! I thought that I had seen it all when my girl Star parlayed being a ghetto ho into becoming a star in the porn industry. Uh, excuse me. Let me correct myself, *adult film industry*, as Star likes to refer to it. But porn by any other name is still porn, right?

I thought so.

As I was saying, I thought that I had seen it all. Now Basehead Kayundra is an R&B star. Lord what is this world coming to? And the bitch got the nerve to call herself *Sparkle!*

First, a jump off dyke sucks dick and fucks her way to fame, now a fiend is on the cover of *The Source*? I could see if that fiend was Whitney but Kayundra! Just a few years ago she was selling pussy for crack fumes, now she's all on BET in magazines with a nigga so thugged out and fine if he was to hold her hand and walk down the street, you'd swear he was walking his dog.

The rap nigga Scare Me, who is rumored to be fuckin' Kayundra (I'm not calling her no damn Sparkle!), is all of dat. Like LL, Pac, and Tyrese rolled into one. I guess if the rumors are true, Kayundra has kicked Rah to the curb now that she's a big star.

I'll keep it real, the dope fiend bitch can sing and her CD is butta. Now people in the hood are acting like they're a star just because someone from Little Bricks has made it. All I can say—and this ain't hatin, it's the truth—is that Kayundra 'bout to have enough money to smoke crack until her heart burst.

"Don't be so cynical," Danyelle admonishes me. Me and big cuz are on the phone talking about Kayundra.

"I'm not. I'm just calling a spade a spade and a crackhead bitch a crackhead bitch," I say.

Danyelle can't help but to laugh.

"I predict that within two years the bitch will be back in the projects on crack again, sucking dick for a rock."

"Girl, you're crazy! I'ma talk to you later." Danyelle laughs. "Bye."

Speaking of rocks, the other day CJ bought me a diamond so clear I could see through it. And it's the size of a grape. I still refuse to move back in with him though. Why should I? He's still married to the streets and all that comes with it, including other bitches. So I'm doing me. I've accepted that I can't stop his ass from creeping no matter how much good coochie and slow neck I give him; no matter how hard I ride for his ass. Bottom line, he's a ho.

A bitch ain't just sitting around twiddling her thumbs while CJ runs up in different bitches. I got myself a young sweet dick nigga on the side.

Yep it's Nard, the one I was hollerin' at. His eighteen-year-old dick can stay up long and strong, but hard dick and bubble gum ain't never been enough for a bad bitch like myself, even if it's just side-dick. Nard has a little something going on over on Dayton, where he's from. Nothing major but he's on the come up. I hit him off with a couple of kilos that I stole from CJ to help him bubble.

I'm the flyest bitch his young ass has ever gotten some holla from. My hood diva style, the fly whip I push, and the sexy clothes I wear had him sprung from the jump. Like every nigga in Newark, Nard has heard of CJ. In fact, he worships him without even realizing it. Once he found out that I'm CJ's wifey, he wanted some of this hood celebrity pussy so bad he would've shot Obama had I told him to.

A thorough bitch like myself has too much game to give up the punani easily to a baby face nigga whose pockets are lightweight. I knew that he was dying to run up in *this* then run and brag to his friends, "I fucked that nigga CJ's broad yo!"

I wasn't about to clown CJ or myself like that. Besides, I had to train Nard from the start or he would be impossible to train later.

212

"If I said that I am a boss bitch, would you disagree with that?" I posed the question to Nard one day we were kicking it on the phone.

"Nah, shorty, you as boss as they come," he'd quickly agreed.

I dial toned his ass.

When he called back. I said, "Listen up, boo, call me back when you learn that my name is not 'shorty'." Another dial tone.

I was going to instill in Nard so much respect for me that he'd damn near be calling me "ma'am" by the time I let him hit this. I ignored his calls for a week before deciding to end his suffering. I made him apologize but I didn't chump him. I'm molding a man not a mouse. I'm going to turn him into a boss hustla and the average ho's dream while keeping him looking up to *this* bitch. Much like it used to be with CJ before money, power, and all the other shit changed him.

Don't get it twisted, I know I'm still CJ's wifey and it's not like he's dragging a bitch. Trust, he keeps me designer down to the thong. But I'm not CJ's *everything* anymore, like when he used to stand outside slangin' rocks in below zero weather tryna come up; knocking on my door so that he could step inside and warm up. Then it was back on the grind, getting it up so that he could keep me happy.

Back then, if CJ wasn't on the grind, he was chillin' with me. I was second to nothing.

I'm training Nard to see a bitch in that regard. I had him on probation for three months; even set certain standards Nard had to hustle up to before I could take him seriously.

"Any nigga in his right mind would want to fuck me. Most wanna claim and possess me, buy me things and show me off. Few deserve to do either and only one has earned the right to do them all," I told him.

"I guess you talkin' 'bout CJ. Yo, I get tired of hearing about that nigga!"

"I give CJ props Nard, because he has *earned* that. Only a trifling ho fails to acknowledge what's real. Imagine how you would feel if you did all the things for a chick that CJ has done for me and the bitch acted like what you did for her wasn't nothing," I explained in order to repair the damage done to a man's pride when you throw another nigga up in his face; a superior nigga at that.

"I feel you," Nard humbled down.

"If you're the nigga that I believe you are, one day I'll speak your name with that same respect. And the streets will too. Just remember, behind every major nigga there's a woman. She may play the background or just stay at home and make sure that everything is butta when her man comes out of the streets and needs the comfort of her touch to relieve the stress that the game puts on him, but she's necessary to his success.

"The streets don't know it but without me CJ wouldn't be running things; he'd be in prison, waiting for me to send him commissary money," I explained.

Me and Nard were chillin' at his brother Man Dog's crib in East Orange that day. Man Dog, who is five years older than Nard had started kicking it with my girl Lemora; the two of them were in the bedroom making the bed creak. I wasn't giving Nard the pussy; I was giving him something more valuable: I was giving him game.

"Why you even hollerin' at me? I can't give you shit compared to what CJ gives you," Nard replied, sounding discouraged.

"That's where you're wrong baby," I said, kissing him softly. "You can give me *devotion* which CJ does not."

And that wasn't game.

First, I had to help Nard grow his bank up because a devoted nigga with small stacks can't please a bitch. Nard eyes did a double-take when I hit him with two whole kilos the next day.

'Handle yo business baby. Just don't shit on a bitch."

It took Nard about a week to flip the kilos. Once he was ready to re-up, I hit him with another two. After that, I encouraged him to find a connect, which he did.

So now I'm going to give Nard a little reward.

I pick Nard up from Man Dog's place and we get a room at a hotel way out in South Orange.

At the hotel, Nard is anxious to get what I've been denying him for the past three months.

"Slow down, baby," I say as he tears out of his clothes.

I take in his physique as I slowly peel off my tight Capri pants.

Packing about eight inches—that'll work, six pack, nice chest. Okay, we can do this.

When I'm naked, I turn around to place my clothes on the dresser and to give Nard a shot of this phat ass. I make it wiggle for him.

"You like that?" Talking over my shoulder.

"Mmmhmm," he replied, walking up behind me and rubbing my booty.

I reach back and stroke his dick.

"Wrap up, baby, I'm ready for some of this," I coo.

I allow Nard to fuck me hurriedly. I understand that I'm the bitch of his dreams so he's excited. I knock his young ass out cold with a bomb shot of this good pussy of mine. Then I wake him up with a lot of spit on his dick. I spend the next two hours teaching him how to please me.

"Every woman is different. What turns on one chick might turn off the next so you have to learn to listen to my body talk; it'll let you know what it likes," I tell him as I wrap my thighs around his head.

Nard isn't CJ but naked with my eyes closed, I hardly know the difference by the time I finish teaching him how to take me there.

Lemora and Man Dog aren't kicking it anymore which is cool because I have begun to see envy in the bitch. Bottom line, she resented the fact that I had schooled Nard so well that Man Dog now works for him. Lemora can't stand seeing me with the money-nigga, while she gets the lieutenant. She now knows that CJ is my man and she's envious of that too. I should've known that I can't become cool with a bitch; they are just too damn petty and envious.

I pull up over Lemora's crib, going to pick up the five hundred dollars that I loaned the bitch two weeks ago.

"Whud up, girl?" Lemora greets me, letting me into her apartment.

"Nothin', just came to pick that up."

She grabs my hand and admires my new rock.

"Nard?" she asks.

"Of course not! His money isn't grown enough to be able to afford this. CJ bought me this," I say.

"You must lick that nigga'z ass to get him to cop you jewels like that," Lemora cracks.

"Nah bitch, I do what those that don't know can't tell you and those of us who do know won't tell you." I shut her down.

The envy in her eyes is as thick as bifocals.

"Anyway, let me get that so I can bounce."

"Oh, I don't have it all," the bitch claims.

I let out an exasperated sigh. "How much you got?"

"Seventy-five."

"Seventy-five! Bitch I know you're kidding."

"Nope, that's all I got," she says hands on hips.

I'm tempted to slap the ho silly but instead I just say, "Lemora, you're a jealous-hearted bitch! By right, I should be all up in your shit about my money but five-hundred is not even worth breaking my nails over. So keep that shit and try to buy some game with it, 'cause you'll never bag a money-gettin' nigga until you learn not to hate on the next bitch!"

I leave the bitch standing there with her hands on her hips, wishing that she was me.

TWENTY-EIGHT

STEPHANIE

Things have reached the point to where CJ is going to have to decide if he wants to be a part of Loran and Leron's lives or not. I will not continue to beg him to come visit his children nor will I continue to allow him to pop in and out of our lives at his convenience.

It's been almost a year since I went to New Jersey with the twins in tow and confronted CJ's woman with the evidence that CJ had fathered my children. I had found out where CJ lived by going through his wallet. Maybe I was wrong for that, but I was tired of CJ hiding us from Tamika as if our existence meant less to him than his relationship with her did. Which I see is true because since the incident CJ has only visited the twins once.

I'll call Raheem up. Maybe he can talk to his boy.

I get right into the gist of my problem as soon as Raheem answers his cell.

"Raheem, I hate to bother you with my problems but this situation with CJ is really sad. I can't get him to call or visit the twins with any consistency and it's having an adverse effect on Loran and Leron."

"Steph, I don't know what to tell you. I've talked to CJ over and over again about that but I can't make a man do what he doesn't wanna do. I was hoping that he was just mad at you and that he would visit the children more often once his anger dissolved. But—I guess that's not the case."

"I'm going to demand that CJ set up a visitation schedule where he'll visit the twins every other weekend and call to speak with them at least twice a week. If he does not agree to that, I'm not going to allow him to see them at all," I say as my emotions get the best of me and I begin crying. "How can CJ just act as if the twins don't exist? What type of man does that?" I sniffle.

"I don't know what to say Steph," Raheem replies and I find myself getting upset with *him*. Of course I have no reason at all to be upset with Raheem; he has always given me a shoulder to cry on, and he is a wonderful "uncle" to my babies.

"You don't have to say anything Raheem," I say. "Just listening to my problems is enough. I'm sorry, how is Kayundra doing? I don't get to see her much now that she's a big star."

"She's good. Still on tour."

"I'm so happy for you guys. Well, I'm going to call CJ and see if we can come to some type of agreement concerning his visiting the twins."

"A'ight. Steph, don't make it seem like a confrontation or CJ will call your bluff," Raheem advises me, but I am so done with catering to Mr. CJ's ego.

"I won't be *bluffing*," I say with conviction.

"Good luck."

It is time for CJ to realize that being a parent is an everyday responsibility. The little bit of love that he shows for our children, sporadically, never fills them up, it only teases them. Just when the twins were getting accustomed to their daddy visiting and calling, he just stopped. I try to fill the void but Loran and Leron aren't always appeased.

"Mommie, I want my daddy!" cried Loran yesterday.

"Where's daddy?" Leron chimed in.

How can any parent claim to love their children and not even pick up the phone and check on them for months?

What really melts my butter is when CJ, after months of neglecting the twins, pops up out of the blue with a carload of clothes and toys for them, like he's fucking Santa Claus.

My children don't need Santa Claus in their lives, they need a father all year around.

I have given up trying to encourage CJ to get out of the streets before it's too late. Something that, yes, I've tried to do in the past. CJ thinks that he's invincible. I hate to say it because he's the father of my children, but CJ's demise is imminent and I predict that when it happens it's not going to be pretty. CJ believes that he can outrun fate; that he does not have to reap what he has sown.

218

I beg to differ.

I love CJ *and* I hate him. I love him for what he could be and I hate him for what he is. Not the "drug dealer" part of him; I knew what he did for a living from the start so I can't put him down for it now. It's his arrogance and his lack of devotion to our children that I despise.

I guess in the back of my mind I believed that I could get CJ to love me and the children; a challenge that I have obviously lost. CJ does not love us, he never has. Who and what he loves is manifested in where he spends his time, the streets and his street woman, Tamika, is what and who he loves. Every time the children cry for their daddy and I call or text him and get no answer, I hate CJ more and more.

This time when I call he answers his phone.

"Sup?"

What's up? After ignoring my calls for weeks—no months— he asks "What's up?"

Instantly I lose it!

"What the fuck do you think is up CJ? *Your fucking children!*" I scream.

"Fuck you cussin' at?"

"Who am I talking to!?" I snap.

"You need to ask yourself that question," he counters and I imagine a smug look is on his damn face.

"I want to know why haven't you called to check on Leron and Loran? They could be sick, kidnapped, anything! I bet you know where Tamika's at and how she is doing."

"You right; she's right here in my arms, and she's doing fine. You wanna holla at her?" the bastard has the nerve to ask. If I didn't have so much to get off of my mind I would hang up on his disrespectful ass.

I count to ten calming myself then I respond in a nice and sensible tone, "Listen CJ, I don't care if Tamika is in your mouth, let alone your arms. I need to know do you love Loran and Leron?"

"What kinda question is that, yo?"

"Just answer it."

"You know damn well I love my seeds," he replies.

"They aren't fuckin' seeds! They are real live children with real live feelings, and they need for you to show them some of the love that you claim to have for them on a consistent basis. Not whenever you find the time."

"They need me on a consistent basis or you need me?"

"The only thing *I* need from you is for you to either be a part of their lives or stay the hell away from us!"

"You don't want that."

"CJ, you can fucking die for all I care. This isn't about me; this is about the twins," I emphasize.

"You say I could die for all you care, right?"

"That's what I said." I refuse to back down.

"Well, pretend that I'm dead cracker bitch!"

A dial tone pounds in my ear like so many exclamation marks.

He called me a 'cracker bitch!'

I feel numb, which is why my eyes don't water and my heart does not shatter. CJ has just confirmed what I should've accepted a long time ago; he does not care about our children.

I want to catch a flight to New Jersey and go blow his brains out.

He'll get what's coming to him, sooner or later.

Needing to talk to someone, I call up Hakeem. We talk long into the night. The twins are asleep when I finally say goodnight to Hakeem. I take a shower then crawl in bed and fall asleep listening to Sparkle's CD, trying not to think about CJ's cold-hearted ass.

TWENTY-NINE

KAYUNDRA/SPARKLE

The lights in the hotel suite are dimmed. An old school slow jam *Turn off the Lights* by Teddy Pendergrass plays softly on the CD player. I step out of the shower, wrap a towel around me and walk into the bedroom to find him already undressed, laying across the bed, confident in his beautiful black nakedness.

It has been two weeks since the last time that we were together. I hadn't expected him to join me here in L.A., where I'll be performing this weekend because he had a prior engagement in D.C., but then he called earlier today and asked if I could send my limo to pick him up from LAX airport.

What a surprise!

"Unwrap the towel and let a nigga see your body." His voice sounds so thuggish and sexy.

I do as he asked and he sits up on the edge of the bed admiring my nudity, making me feel so beautiful.

"You're still as fine and sexy as the last time I saw you," he comments, licking his lips.

"It's only been two weeks," I remind him.

"Seems like two years—fa real shorty." He grabs me by the ass and pulls me to him. His face is pressed against my pussy. "Umm!" he interjects, kissing my coochie. "Lay down and let me taste you."

I lay across the bed and open my legs.

"Did you miss me?" he asks while sliding his tongue up the length of my tingling kitty cat.

"Oh—yes," I pant.

"Tell me!"

"I—missed—you, Scare," I moan when his tongue makes contact with my clit.

After an hour of fucking, we lay out some lines of coke and get nice. I feel the burn inside of my nose caused by the potent white devil. Within minutes a rush hits me like a sledgehammer. Then it feels like it's softly raining inside my head.

Butt naked, me and Scare snort coke and sip Remy. The high I get from snorting is much different from the paranoid desperate high that I felt when I used to smoke crack. Snorting has me crunk but it also has me depressed. The more coke I snort, the more depressed I feel—the more I snort—the more...

On and on until guilt hits me and I think, *I've already fucked up. Gettin' high and fucking another dude behind my man's back. Might as well smoke some crack. My life is spiraling out of control, anyway. I've allowed the fame to break my will to remain honest with and devoted to the one who loved me before any of this. I put a singing career over our love; murdered our unborn child, and hid it from Raheem. Now, maybe God is punishing me for it.*

First, I turned to smoking weed and a little drinking to help me deal with the demons that haunted me after the abortion. Then Preston kept on pressuring me to hook up with Scare, feeding false rumors to magazines about "the hottest couple in the music industry"! Every time the rumor appeared in print and I found out about it, I would call Raheem from wherever I was at and reassure him that the shit wasn't true.

"I trust you, baby. Just don't betray my trust," he would always state.

"I won't, sweetheart. I'll give all of this up before I allow it to destroy our love," I'd vowed.

I knew that the rumors had to bother Raheem. He just has too much pride to let it show.

Then Quida, my backup singer who pretended to be a true friend, let it "leak" to a slime ass magazine: THE TRUTH WHY SPARKLE FAINTED DURING A CONCERT IN CHARLOTTE.

For reportedly $25,000, Quida sold our friendship and my deepest secret.

I denied having an abortion but Raheem saw right through the lie.

"Just tell me the truth Kayundra. Was the baby mine?" he asked.

"Of course!" I cried. The tour was in Kansas City, Missouri at the time and Raheem had flown in to confront me after reading the story in the mag. Barged into my hotel suite, face twisted. "I'm sorry honey, I didn't know what to do. My CD was doing well; I'm on tour, and Preston and others were pressuring me to have the abortion, saying that it was the best thing in regards to my career."

Raheem had looked at me like—like—he had lost all respect for me. That crushed me. Then he turned and walked out and flew back to Atlanta.

The next day I was back in Atlanta myself. "Damn the tour!" I'd told Preston. "I'm not losing my man."

When I walked in the house, Raheem was at his desk in the study on the computer.

"Hi," I spoke timidly.

"Good morning," he'd replied kind of dryly.

"Raheem, baby, we need to talk."

"We can talk, Kayundra, but not about *that*. Not ever."

"Please, allow me to try to explain." Tears were streaking down my face.

Raheem put up his hand to silence me. "I thought about it all last night and I'm not gonna give up on our relationship; not unless you wish for it to end."

I shook my head indicating that I did not.

"I still love you, Kayundra, but what you did hurt a nigga real bad. I had a right to weigh in on your decision before you went forward with it. Before you did what you cannot *undo*."

"I'm sorry," I said again.

"I'm not promising you that I can forgive you and I'm not sure that I'll ever completely trust you again but I'm gonna try. But don't ever bring up the subject of what you did again. Ever!" Raheem's voice had been heavy with the hurt that my actions caused him. I had wanted to plead with him for us to talk about it because I knew that keeping our feelings inside would destroy us but I had been afraid to push the issue.

All I could say was, "I don't know how but I'll make this up to you."

"You can't so don't try. Let's just try to go on from here Kayundra."

I saw in his eyes that he may still love me but I am no longer his "Sparkle"; he has not referred to me by the pet name since.

I begged Raheem to travel on the road with me so that the whole world would see that he is my man but he said that he had business to attend to. A month ago when I was in New York to receive an award for a video, Raheem did join me for a weekend. However, he did not escort me to the award show.

"I prefer to remain anonymous," he said.

Not only that, I could feel the disdain that Raheem has for what I done. That weekend, in New York, he was not eager to make love to me. And when I wasn't able to seduce him. I could tell that his passion for me was all but gone.

"You don't love me anymore, do you?" I asked, crying after the lukewarm lovemaking ended that night.

"It's not like that. Just give me time to heal," he said.

"Baby, let's take a vacation together. We can go away somewhere and get away from all of this," I suggested. I was desperate to save the relationship which I felt was on shaky ground.

But Raheem had to go to Orlando to plan a party for some guy named Dwight Howard who balled for the Magic, and myself and my label mates had to do a three-day gig in Monaco so a vacation was ruled out.

It was in Monaco, two weeks ago, that my affair with Scare begun. That's also when I began using drugs again. The cocaine made me numb to the guilt I felt; Scare made me feel wanted again.

Mama told me, in regards to what had happened with me and Raheem, "He still loves you; he'll need time to forgive you though."

224

"No, mama, he'll never forgive me. I told you and Preston that I shouldn't have gotten an abortion without first talking to Raheem about it."

"What's done is done now," she'd replied like it was not a big thing.

I was so damn mad at her. If it hadn't been for mama and Preston pressuring me into aborting my pregnancy, my man would still love and trust me and I would've never gone back to using drugs. And I certainly wouldn't have started sleeping with Scare.

"You done with this?" Scare asks, indicating the remaining cocaine laid out in lines on a mirror.

I toot a few more lines then chase the coke with two fingers of Remy.

"You wanna try some of these?" asks Scare, holding a palm full of aqua blue pills.

"What are those?" I ask, already high as a cloud.

"These them blue dolphins, shawdy. X pills." Scare hands me a couple and sure enough, a tiny blue dolphin is imprinted on each pill.

I have never popped X but why not try it? I' m already snorting coke, creepin' and all. If Raheem was to find out about any of this, it would end our relationship for sure. Maybe in Raheem's heart, it is already over between us, ever since I deceived him. So what do I have to lose? *Nothing.*

I pop two blue dolphins and before long I am zoning. All of my senses are heightened. Now when I sip Remy it feels extra smooth going down my throat and tingles inside my chest. When Scare talks, it sounds like he's rapping; I never noticed that before. *He licks his lips a lot when he's high, and his teeth aren't as pretty as Raheem's.*

Scare stretches me out on the bed and caresses my breasts. His touch vibrates all over my body. I feel his neatly trimmed goatee tickling my chin as we kiss. When he enters me my whole body surrenders to his hardness.

This X is the shit!

Now Scare is sitting up with his back against the headboard, writing rap lyrics in a small leather bound notebook that he calls his "book of rhymes." I'm sitting up in bed next to him, snorting lines of coke off of my small compact mirror that I carry in my purse. I look at Scare and he turns into Raheem.

I squeeze my eyes shut. When I open them again; Scare is himself. He is so thuggishly fine; one of the hottest rappers in the industry, and chicks would kill to be in bed next to him. But he is not Raheem.

I know I'm fucking up. I really do love Raheem with all my heart and soul and I pray that I can regain his trust.

Not like this, you can't, my conscience says.

I've got to end this affair. And I've got to stop getting high, I tell myself after snorting two more lines.

The phone rings. I look at the digital clock on the nightstand; its 12:01 A.M., one minute past midnight. I wonder who's calling. I reach for the phone and accidently knock it off the nightstand. *Am I that high? How much coke have I snorted? A quarter of an ounce? How much Remy have I drank? Dayum! I'm fucked up.*

"Hello."

"Happy birthday!"

"Huh? Uh—who dis?" I babble.

"Raheem, baby. Happy b-day!"

"Oh, hi Raheem. Hap—Hap…Happy Birth…day…to you too." *What in the hell am I saying? Wow! I'm too damn high! Is it really my birthday?*

"Kayundra, are you drunk?"

"Uh—no—I was asleep." I quickly lie. I gotta stop lying. *"Why is he talking so loud?"* The question is a thought that slips out. *Oops!*

"Am I talking loud? My bad. Go on back to sleep baby. I just wanted to wish my Sparkle a happy b-day," says Raheem.

Did I hear him just call me his Sparkle?

Thank you, Jesus!

Thugs Cry

I'm about to tell Raheem that I love him when Scare starts rapping in the background:

"On that X havin' sex/ got a nigga feelin' like the matrix/scorin' big like the Patriots/is this shit fa real? What's next/a hood nigga starring at the Ciniplex?/ Out-dueling villains that wanna do me/who me? Wait back up/y'all niggaz lyrics don't move me/beats don't groove me/fake capers don't fool me/I'm from the streets you dudes yap about/over beats, rap about/but I'm on some other shit/so get yo' bitch off my dick."

"Who is that yo? Scare Me? I thought you said you was asleep?" Raheem asks accusatorily.

"I was; that was the radio, baby." I lie, yet again. I cover the phone, stare knives at Scare and motion for him to shut the hell up!

"My bad, shawdy," he mouths.

"Oh," says Raheem. "Well, go back to sleep, I didn't mean to awake you. Happy birthday again. I love you."

"Do you really?" I ask in a voice heavy with emotion.

"Yeah, I love you. A lot," he replies. And I miss you too."

"Will you come join me on tour? I'll be playing ten cities with Alicia Keys beginning next week. Please baby."

"Yeah, ma, I'll join you."

"When?" I ask excitedly.

"Real soon," the love of my life promises.

"Raheem, baby, I love you so much." I begin crying.

"I love you, too. We gon' be a'ight."

"Okay. Goodnight." I hang up, happy to know that my sweetheart still loves me.

Scare looks at me and shakes his head.

"Bitches ain't shit," he states.

I don't bother to comment. What difference does it make what he thinks of me? Tonight is the last time we'll do what we're doing. I swear.

"You might as well let a nigga hit dat one mo' time," he says as if reading my thoughts. He stands in front of me with his erection in my frace.

Ca$h

"I don't think so." I shut him down.

"Whatever, shawdy." He plops down on the bed, grabs the TV remote off the nightstand and channel surfs. Then he orders an adult movie, kicks back and starts masturbating.

I get up and go sleep on the couch.

In the morning, a light knock on the door awakens me. Probably room service, I guess as I go to the door in panties and bra, prepared to decline breakfast. When I crack the door mama is standing there smiling. *When did she fly in?*

Oh—my—god! Raheem is behind her. They come bounding right past me shouting "Happy birthday!" Raheem is carrying a large birthday cake.

"Girl, put on some clothes. Ain't you got any shame?" mama exclaims laughing. But I don't move, I'm paralyzed with fear.

All three of our heads snap around to the sound of Scare's loud voice as he walks out of the bedroom as naked as the original man saying, "You still trippin', Sparkle? Or are we gon' snort some more coke, pop a few more Blue Dolphins and sex each other some more?" He doesn't notice that we are not alone because his nose is buried in a glass bowl of coke.

"You want some of this? It's—" he looks up and says, "Oh, shit!" right before Raheem punches him in the grill.

I stand there wishing that I could click my heels together and disappear.

THIRTY

RAHEEM

It's been two months since I broke up with Kayundra after walking in on her and Scare Me apparently doing what they had been doing all along, creepin' and getting high.

All the time that the rumors were out there that they were more than label mates, Kayundra kept denying them. I never once accused her or doubted her devotion to me but man was I wrong. I would say that, just like that—at a snap of a finger!—our relationship was over with. Except, nothing ever falls apart just like that.

The beginning of the end probably was when Kayundra had an abortion and hid the shit from me. I had to find out about *my* woman aborting *my* baby, in a goddamn magazine article. Word, I tried to forgive her and I loved her enough to stick with her, though that shit tore-me-the-fuck up. It took a few months for my anger over Kayundra having an abortion to simmer down. Then my love for her kicked back in and I flew out to LA, where she was on tour, to surprise her for her birthday, me and her Mom Dukes both.

As you already know, the surprise was on me.

After I saw what I saw, I punched Scare Me in the mouth. Knocked the nigga the fuck out! Not because he was bangin' my girl, it takes two to tango. I knocked the nigga out because he had been getting her high.

While the nigga was ass-naked on the floor, Miss Freeda was crying, "Oh God! This is bad!" and wrapping a blanket around Kayundra as if it could cover up what her daughter was busted doing.

I searched the suite, found coke, X pills, liquor, weed, and used condoms. Flushed all the drugs down the toilet and said to Miss Freeda, "I'll ship all of her clothes and things to you." Then I bounced, without saying a word to a crying Kayundra.

Reflecting back on it all, it seems like once Kayundra became "Sparkle" to the world and her CD blazed the charts, our relationship was destined to fail. I had always heard it said that fame and money changes a person; and it changes those around them. I hadn't wanted to believe that Kayundra would go out like that. I knew for certain that I was not going to change; I was determined to love and trust in Kayundra even after all the rumors surfaced about her and Scare Me.

I guess I was naïve.

I haven't seen or talked to Kayundra since the incident. I shipped all of her belongings to her Mom Dukes in New Jersey, where I assume Kayundra is staying now that the tour has ended. The house here in ATL is in my name, and since me and Kayundra had maintained separate bank accounts, neither of our finances was complicated by our break up.

CJ and Tamika came in town a month ago. CJ came to check on the clubs, but really to make sure that my head was right, though he denied that that was part of the reason for his visit.

"I'm good," I'd assured him the first night that he was in town. We were on our way to Club Sparkle, ironically. I was behind the wheel of the Jeep I recently purchased; CJ was riding shotgun and Tamika was in the back.

The conversation carried over into the office of the club. We had left Tamika at a private table in the VIP area.

"I knew that crackhead ho was gon' let the limelight go to her head!" CJ continued on about Kayundra as he poured himself a drink from the bar in the office.

I sat behind the office desk and studied the video monitor which showed what was going on throughout the club.

"It wasn't really about the limelight," I'd begun, but realized that it was. "Well, I guess the limelight has a lot to do with her using drugs again, but it didn't have anything to do with her creepin'. Because when you're true to your convictions, you live by 'em," I said as I thought about all the pussy that was constantly thrown in my face at the clubs I owned.

I'd been tempted to hit something else a few times; I can't lie. I hadn't done it though. I'd expected the same faithfulness from Kayundra.

"You can clean up a fiend, fam, but you can't change 'em. Let that punk ho come back to Newark, I'ma get one of my goons to body that ungrateful bitch!" CJ said.

"Nah, fam, it's not *that* serious," I said.

Then my attention went to the video monitor. I was staring at a face that I could never forget; it belonged to a nigga that had caused me to get cased up.

Paco!

"Yo you see that fat muhfucka right there?" I said, pointing Paco out to CJ who was leaning over my sholder looking at the screen.

"Yeah. What about him?"

"That's the nigga who set me up!"

"With the feds?"

"Yep."

"I know we're bodying that ass tonight, right?" asked CJ.

I thought about it long and hard. *If I wet this nigga, that'll mean that I'm still on that street shit.*

Well, guess what? Apparently I'm still on it because I didn't stutter when I said to CJ, "Fam, you already know I'ma flat-line that snitch ass nigga tonight. Go post up where you can keep an eye on that fuck nigga; I'm 'bout to hit my nigga DaQuan, he wouldn't wanna miss out on this. You might wanna have Tamika call a cab to take her to my place."

CJ nodded as he accepted the door key to my crib that I offered to him to give to Tamika.

Two hours later, me and CJ eased out of the club behind Paco. We slid into DaQuan's whip which was idling at the door.

"Sup, my dude?" I spoke to DaQuan who was behind the wheel.

"Time to put a snitch nigga in the ground," he replied.

We pulled up on the side of Paco's silver '76 Monte Carlo about three miles away from the club. When he looked over and saw my face, his eyes bulged and his mouth dropped open. I stuck my arm out the passenger window and pointed my Glock .9 at his bitch ass.

"Snitch ass bitch!"

Boc! Boc! Boc! Boc! Boc!

I let loose. Then CJ's banger joined the deadly melody my Nine sang. DaQuan threw the whip in park, hopped out and got up close and personal on Paco, who had crashed into a nearby utility pole trying to accelerate away from death.

I jumped out of the whip, a step behind DaQuan. We could see Paco slumped over the steering wheel, head leaking.

"Fuck boy!" snarled DaQuan before pumping six from his fo-fo into Paco's twisted corpse.

THIRTY-ONE

SPARKLE

I've made a complete mess out of my life!

Right after Raheem broke up with me, Scare Me dumped me too. Preston, who was the one pressing me and Scare to hook up all along, now wants Scare to get with this new rap chick who's on our label. That is so damn ugly!

"You caused me to lose the man I love, now you're discarding me?" I challenged Scare the other day.

"Fall back, bitch!" he'd replied, mushing me in the face with one hand while holding hands with his new chick with the other. I'd wanted to act a donkey right there in the foyer of Platinum's office where I confronted the two.

But what the fuck!

With Raheem out of my life nothing matters anymore. Not even my music career. Snorting cocaine couldn't keep me high enough to run from the guilt and pain so I've started back smoking crack. Whatever city the tour was in, I would sneak off and go looking for the projects where I was sure to find as much crack as my broken heart desired. I'd dress plain, no make-up or jewelry, trying to be incognito.

"Yo, shorty, you look just like that singer Sparkle," a slanger or two had observed.

"I wish I had the ho's money," I replied, throwing them off.

Alicia, whom I was now touring with, could tell that I was getting high again; she straight up said so.

"Just sing, bang on your piano, and stay out of mine!" I checked her.

It's only been a little more than a month since I picked back up the pipe and already I'm smoking like a choo choo train gone wild. Sometimes I stay locked inside my hotel suite all day getting geeked; not even answering the door when Mama knocks to tell me that it's time to go do a concert. Since I'm opening for Alicia, the shows get delayed until I arrive hours late.

I don't even know what city we're in.

I take the stage so geeked up that I can't even remember the lyrics to my own songs.

The audience shows patience at first,\ but when I continue to mess up, a rumbling of boos fill the auditorium. This happens three consecutive nights. Alicia has no choice but to complain to the tour's organizers; my unprofessional behavior is hurting *her* reputation by association.

"I'm resigning as your manager unless you check yourself into a drug program," mama threatens.

My record label covers up my suspected drug use by issuing a press release that blames my erratic behavior on "…medication the singer has been prescribed for migraine headaches and low sugar levels."

All Peston cares about is continuing to milk the cash cow that is my music career at all cost.

No one can cover up my drug use anymore after police raid a crack house in Jackson, Mississippi where the tour has taken me and I'm caught with the glass dick in my mouth. I'm arrested, and my mug shot is splashed all across the television for the whole world to see.

R&B SONGSTRESS CAUGHT SMOKING CRACK.

Mama and Preston are trying to persuade me to seek help but what's the point? The one thing that matters most to me is lost forever: Raheem's love and respect.

Without my boo, what's left to live for? I might as well smoke myself to death. To hell with this thing called life. It is just too damn painful.

I'm going through pure hell inside, missing my man like crazy, and this muthafuckin' Preston, all he cares about is me going to rehab so I can clean up then release a new CD.

"You blood suckin' bastard!" I scream at him, crying.

Mama restrains me. I swear, I wanted that ass!

Even if my life depended on it, I can't write a song in my present state of being. I write from the heart and right now my heart is gone. I know that in reality I have no one to blame but my own dumb, weak self. Raheem was everything a girl could hope for in a man, and I messed up.

The past two weeks I've been fucking a different nigga every night: stage hands, security, groupie dudes, you name it, I fucked 'em.

I would wake up with a nigga lying next to me in bed that I didn't even recognize. All I do lately is get high and fuck. It's not about the sex either. Because when I'm smoking crack it kills my desire. I slept with those men to forget about Raheem.

But I cannot push Raheem out of my mind, I realize as it also hits me that I've been kicked off of tour, replaced by Keisha Cole.

Now I'm back up in Jersey, far away from the pressure of the spotlight, Preston, fans, and all of the shit that caused me to kill my baby and to lose the love of my life.

The cold winter wind whistles outside of the bungalow I've rented in The Hamptons to get away from everyone and everything except what's on the table in front of me: four ounces of crack, a half dozen crack pipes, and a box of lighters.

I place a chunk of crack on the pipe, wrap my lips around the opening at the end of the steam, and flick the lighter.

I smoke until my lungs threaten to collapse like punctured balloons. My head feels lighter than air; I'm about to float right up through the ceiling. Now my heartbeat increases at an alarming enough rate to make me panic. I get up from the table and lay across the bed until the beating inside my chest slows to a moderate rate.

Suddenly, I begin to cry.

I extract my cell phone from the pocket of the cashmere pants I'm wearing, and with trembling fingers I dial his number.

"Hello," he answers. *Oh—my—god! What can I say to justify what I've done?* Click. I chicken out and hang up.

Call back, gurl! I do as my inner voice urges me.

"Hello." Raheem's voice is as familiar to me as my own.

"Hi," I utter nervously then lick my parched lips.

"Who dis?" *Dang! Has he forgotten the sound of my voice already?* I take a deep breath to calm my nerves.

"This is the person who used to be your 'Sparkle' before she messed up; the woman who is so sorry for the heartache she caused you; the woman who still loves you and always will—until the day she dies," I reply, pouring my heart out.

"Hello, Kayundra. How you doing?"

"Not so good, baby. I want to come back home," I cry. No reply. "Please, Raheem," I beg. "I need you so bad. More than needing you—I love and miss you so much—it's killing me baby. Please find it in your heart to take me back."

Still he doesn't reply.

"We don't have to share the same bed; we don't even have to talk to each other right away. I just need to be near you baby. Please Raheem, I'm nothing without you," I sob.

"Kayundra! You gotta pull yaself together ma. You have a lot to live for; you have your mother, your career and your fans. But more importantly, you have *yourself.* Now stop crying and stand up and take responsibility for your choices. I accept your apology but there's no way we can get back together," says Raheem.

"Please, don't say that, baby. Allow me to try to earn back your trust," I plead.

"Na, it's about more than trust. A nigga has principles that he lives by. If I compromise those principles, I lose sight of who I am. If you hadda just relapsed, I would stand by your side. But what you did—fuckin' another nigga—lying 'bout it all the time—hell no, I'm not taking you back."

The tone of Raheem's voice tells me it's over. My high comes crashing down and I feel desperate. I cry, "I thought that you promised to be with me through thick and thin? Now you're turning your back on me just like everyone else. Nigga, you ain't shit but a fair weather muthafucka!"

Raheem remains calm despite my hysterics.

"Don't try to reverse the game to reflect away from what you did. Trust, I recognize."

"And crackheads got the best game, right?" I throw out there, trying to make him feel bad.

"I never called you a crackhead, not once! I never judged you; I never lied to you or cheated on you. I kept it one hunnid, from the bottom to the top! You played yaself ma. Now you need to accept that it's over. Bottom line!"

"Just answer one question."

"What's that?"

"Do you still love me, Raheem?"

"That don't matter, yo."

"It does, baby. Love conquers all."

"Goodbye Kayundra. I wish you all the best."

The dial tone screams out so loud, I cover my ears with both hands. Raheem's goodbye feels, to me, as irreversible as death. I look down at my cell phone which is now on the floor and silently pray for my baby to come back on the line. But when I retrieve the cell, the dead silence mocks me. Tears run down my face; I look over at the crack and the crack pipes on the table.

Come to meeee, Kayundra. Come to meeeee! The crack and the paraphernalia seem to call out.

"Shut the fuck up! I scream but the calling grows louder.

I rise as if I'm in a trance and go over and submit to the drug's call. "'Til death do us part," I pledge as I beam up.

Ca$h

THIRTY-TWO

STEPHANIE

"'Til death do us part."

That's the vow me and Doctor Hakeem Jordan will be making to one another in two weeks.

It has now been so long since the twins or I have heard from CJ, that I've lost count of the number of months. Not that I have been sitting around praying that he would call. Okay, I will admit that after CJ told me to pretend that he was dead, for a while I held out hope that he could not simply abandon me and the twins so easily. After months of not hearing from CJ, I realized that he had meant what he said. So I told my babies that their father is dead!

For all practical purposed, he *is* dead.

Me and the twins will be moving to Denver, Colorado after the wedding, where Hakim has accepted residency as an orthopedic surgeon at a prestigious hospital. Yes, the same pompous Hakeem from a few years back. Out of the blue, one day I received a call from him.

"Hi, Steph. This is Hakeem Jordan. I was just calling to see what's been going on in your life," he'd said.

Needless to say, Hakeem was not surprised to hear that CJ has abandoned me and the children. Hakeem had vociferously warned me not to get involved with CJ.

"Aren't you going to gloat?" I asked.

"Would I do something like that?" he'd replied and I could picture him smiling smugly.

"The Hakeem that I know would."

He laughed. "Well I've changed. I'd like to believe that I'm not as pompous as I was in the past."

"Hold up! Is this Hakeem Jordan or an imposter?" I kidded.

Two weeks later Hakeem and I went out on a dinner date. True to his claim, I found Hakeem to be less snobbish than I'd recalled. It was as if his becoming a surgeon had given him the security he'd needed to not look down his nose at people. Once we began dating, Hakeem quickly ingratiated himself to the twins. Although I had been a little reluctant to introduce another man into my children's lives so soon, especially after I'd told them that their father was dead. Hakeem assured me that he would not abandon us.

It's unfortunate, but I've had a serious falling out with Raheem; who did not approve of me telling Loran and Leron that CJ is dead.

"You're wrong for dat yo!" Raheem fumed.

"I'm only doing what your boy asked me to do," I'd reminded him.

"So you wanna stoop down to that level, huh?" he'd countered.

"I'm doing what I feel is best for my children," I maintained and the ensuing argument has led to me not even allowing "Uncle Raheem" to remain a part of the twins lives.

I'll be so happy when I become "Mrs. Hakeem Jordan" and move away with my husband, putting CJ and everyone associated with him behind me. The contrast between Hakeem and CJ is as great as the world divide. Where Hakeem is intelligent and confident, CJ was street-wise and arrogant. Hakeem values family and fidelity; CJ valued his "mans" and he was your typical male whore.

In retrospect, I can't imagine what I ever saw in CJ. It most certainly could not have been a future because CJ has no future. I guess that I was enticed by the proverbial "forbidden fruit."

There's something else that I must be honest about: okay, here it is: I am *not* in love with Hakeem. I'm marrying him, however, because I know that he is a good catch. In time, I will grow to love him. Hakeem's love and devotion to me will be something that I can bank on. With CJ, I could not bank on *anything*. Well, I could bank on his touch setting my whole soul on fire. But I could not count on receiving his touch when I craved it most.

So to hell with CJ.

Thugs Cry

It's been an adventure—that's all I can say.

Ca$h

THIRTY-THREE

CJ

I'm at the crib chillin' with Catabria, a chick I met in the 'A', the last time I was there kickin' it with Rah. Shorty like about five-nine, one-fiddy; chunked up in the back; real pretty, with a black skin tone, white teeth, and flat-ironed hair that flows down to her ass.

Catabria is twenty-four years old with pussy like kryptonite! That's why I've temporarily moved ma up to New Jersey with me. Yeah, I'm kinda whipped, nah mean?

It's a Saturday night; winter's about to break and step aside for spring. The unusually warm March temperature has melted the snow outside so, of course, shit is poppin' off in the streets. I've got traps to check and niggaz to body but that's on hold, at least for tonight, 'cause I'm about to freak Catabria so good, she'll think dat ass done died and went to heaven.

Yeah, I know I'm playing Tamika real close by playing house with Baby Girl but trust, Catabria knows what time it is; this is just temporary fun. I'm not about to wife ma.

I sit up on the edge of my bed and take a sip from the bottle of Cuervo Gold that's resting on the portable bar nearby. "Ahhh!" I exclaim with satisfaction as the smooth liquor coats the back of my throat.

I watch Catabria move around the spacious bedroom; her freshly showered body wrapped in nothing but a towel. Her chocolate thighs are like magnets to my eyes.

"Let a nigga peep up under that towel."

"Boo, you already know it's that wet wet up underneath this towel," she cooes with her back to me, preening in the full length wall mirror. "Now, if you wanna hit it, I'm game." She drops the towel and wiggles her booty.

Then she slowly turns to face me, cupping both perky breasts. Her dark chocolate nipples are tout and the size of an infant's pinky finger. Her waist is slim and her stomach is a washboard; her hips flare out wide; her pussy is deliciously bald.

I get up and walk over to Catabria, who takes my hand and places it on her bald pussy. "Is this what you want, baby?"

My joint stands up and pokes her in the belly.

"Ooooh, don't make me suck it, Daddy," she whines then slowly traces my mouth with her tongue.

I play along.

"Get down on your knees and put it in your mouth."

"Nooo! Daddy, please don't make me do that. It's too big, it'll stretch my mouth."

"Suck it!"

Catabria sinks down to her knees and slides my boxers down around my ankles. I feel her lips encircle the head of my dick.

"I don't wanna suck it, Daddy," she mumbles, then proceeds to give me slow neck that a nigga can't even describe.

Shorty has me bustin' all down her throat in just minutes. *This bitch oughta be banned from TV!* I think as my legs go weak.

I stumble back onto the bed.

"Crawl to me!" I command.

Catabria obeys. When she reaches the bed from her knees, she reaches up and strokes my still-hard dick.

"Are you gonna make me put this big ol' thing inside my tight little pussy? Please CJ, don't! It's going to hurt my little coochie!" she whines as she straddles me.

Life is never all sex, fun, and games.

Eventually, a nigga gotta put his dick inside his pants and get back to handlin' business. I've been chillin' for a minute 'cause Cujo hasn't hit me off with any work since a new mayor took office and after a special election last month appointed a new police chief.

I'm not privy to who was actually pulling the strings down at City Hall and inside the narcotics unit to make it possible for Cujo to break me off the way he had been doing, but I do know that the change of mayors and the appointing of the new police chief has put a huge dent in my operation. I haven't received any drugs from Cujo in more than two months.

While I wait on Cujo to holla, other niggaz are out here tryna break the chokehold I have on the game in Newark. Plus I got proof that it was Kareem not Flip who had been setting up Flips clientele for KD and Ghetto to jack awhile back. *Be careful of the dog that brought you the bone,* I recall Flip warning me when I confronted him. True enough it was Kareem who tried to convince me that Flip was the sour one when all the time he was the snake in the grass!

Kareem has since branched out on his own. KD is in the ground, remember? But Ghetto escaped the bullets I'd shot at him that night. Afterwards, he got ghost. Now the nigga has resurfaced as Kareem's right hand man. Those two niggaz got shit poppin' off nice over around Branch Brook Park. Niggaz must think I wear a skirt!

There are other niggaz in the city trying to make power moves while I'm shut down. That's to be expected though. As long as they fall back when I get back straight, I'll spare their mamas and girlfriends from having to bury 'em. But ain't a prayer ever been uttered that's gonna spare Ghetto and Kareem from the wrath of my choppa, especially Kareem, because that bitch ass nigga straight violated.

Cujo calls me up and tells me that we're back in the ball game. I meet with him and pick up a shipment of work, disperse it to my team, then call my nigga Rah back; he had called earlier but I was tied up. Rah tells me that Stephanie has gotten married and has moved the twins away.

"Like I gives a fuck," I say.

"Fam, them are your seeds."

"Not now, son." I stop his banter before he builds up steam. "I got too much shit going on to even sweat that."

We chop it up about other things for a minute then I say, "Fam, I'ma fuck witchu later."

"A'ight, one."

"One."

I hang up from Rah and answer a call from Eric, who wants to know if I'ma be ready to ride on Ghetto and Kareem tonight.

"I got them bitch niggaz scoped out," says Eric.

"That's what's poppin'. Hit me after it gets dark."

No sooner than I disconnect from Eric, I get a call from Mom Duke. She presses me for money. Now, Catabria is on hold, the other line, tryna persuade me to come home and dip in her honey pot.

All this drama, plus I'm missing Tamika like crazy. That's just being real yo. Tamika has been wifey since I was a peon in the game; back when all I had was a dollar and a dream. So damn right, I miss my shorty even though I got Catabria playing her position and mad other hos on my dick. Still, I gotta wonder about these come-lately bitches. It's easy for a ho to love a nigga when he's on top. But where was all of these dimed up hos when a nigga was no more than a block hustla?

Tamika proved her love way before I became *that* nigga.

I put Jay Z's *The Blue Print* CD in deck as I climb into the black Maybach I recently copped. The CD is one of his old joints, but it's classic.

Leaving Mom Duke's crib, where I've just dropped her off a coupla stacks, I listen nostalgically as Jay Z spits some real shit.

I can understand why you want a divorce now/though I can't let you know it/pride won't let me show it/pretend to be heroic/that's just one to grow with/but deep inside a nigga so sick...

I'm thinking about Tamika. I done took shorty through mad drama with other bitches, outside seeds, lies and all. I'm understanding now, that money and hood fame has attracted flocks of females and I've allowed it all to tear down the bond between me and my boo. That's why she has bounced, and now she's fuckin' with another nigga.

...a face of stone/was shocked on the other end of the phone/word back home is that you have a special friend/so, what was oh so special then?/You have given away without getting at me/that's your fault, how many times have you forgiven

me?/How was I to know that you was plain sick of me?/I know,
the way a nigga was livin' was wack/but you don't get a nigga
back like that!
Jiggaz lyrics land like a punch to the heart.
I rewind the CD and listen to "Song Cry" over and over
again until I'm pulling up in Tamika's driveway. I wipe my eyes
before getting out of my whip and going up to Tamika's door.
Tamika's mother lets me in.
"Tamika! Somebody's here to see you!" she calls upstairs.
Somebody? I see how it is!
"Who is it, ma? If it's Nard, send him up."
I try not to blow.
"Come downstairs and see for yourself," her Mom Dukes
replies as if my name tastes too bitter to speak.
"Miss Jerkins, you mad at me or something? 'Cause you
sho' acting all salty. I thought I was your son-in-law?" I say,
reaching out to hug her but she quickly steps back.
"I don't approve of the way you've been treating my
daughter!"
"Aww Mother-in-law, what man you know of who hasn't
ever messed up? Dat don't mean I don't love her."
Tamika bounds down the stairs, looking mouthwatering in a
pair of tight capris and a form-fitting wife beater.
"What doesn't mean you don't love me?" asks Tamika,
overhearing CJ's comment.
"Trust and believe, you don't wanna know," replies her
Mom Duke with a snake of her neck.
Me and Tamika take a seat on the living room sofa; Tamika's mom saunters off to the kitchen.
It's been three weeks since the last time I saw Tamika. That
was when I had heard about her and some young nigga named
Nard. I snatched that ass up and took her to a tattoo parlor, and
made her get a tattoo covering each place where my name had
been tatted on her body.
Fuck you gon' rock my name on your mafuckin' body, while
kickin' it with the next nigga!" I'd spat.

"Sup, baby girl? Long time, no see," I say now.

"Hi, CJ."

I take her hands in mine. "You ready to come back home to me?" Looking into her brown eyes.

"Don't ask me that." She lowers her head to hide the fact that her eyes are watering up.

"Why not?"

"Because yo' ass ain't gonna do right; you want me and every other chick you can stick yo' dirty ass dick in."

"Nah, boo, I'm through fuckin' around."

"How many times have I heard that?"

"Too many," I admit. "But this time I'ma keep my word," I promise.

"No, CJ, I cannot trust you. I'm so tired of all of your lies and other women."

Fa real, Mika, a nigga ain't the same without you. Boo, those other chicks can't compare to you," I state with pure honesty. Then I lean in to kiss her but Tamika turns her head.

"Apparently, you thought they could!"

I get down on my knees holding her hands in mine, looking into her eyes with a sincerity that can't be faked.

"Please, baby girl, just give a nigga one last chance. I promise to never, ever fuck up again. Boo, you're the only girl I've ever loved or wanted. When I hear about you being out with that nigga—it be damn near about to kill me. Why you gotta chump my name in the streets like that?"

Tamika snatches her hands out of my clasp.

"That's all you're worried about, your rep. Yo ass wasn't worried about *my* reputation when you was running up in my own cousin! Worse, when you stuck yo dick up in that nasty bitch who gave you herpes, then you brought that triflin' ass shit home to *me*. Besides muthafucka, you have a lot of nerve coming over here, asking me to come back to you and you already got the next bitch sleeping in *our* bed."

"What you talkin' 'bout," I stutter.

"See!" Tamika grills me. "You can't tell the truth when you're caught in your shit nigga. I drove out to your house, two or three times, and saw you and a bitch carrying groceries inside once; holding hands on the porch another time and kissing in the driveway a third time. Same bitch each time! Just today, I called your home number and the bitch answered the phone. So nigga, stop playing games and be a man about it."

"A'ight. Tell me you'll come back to me and I'll go home and put her ass out."

"No, CJ, you're too much of a ho. You only want me back because you can't stand knowing that someone else wants me."

"It's not like *that* boo. I may have creeped but I love you and I never mistreated you."

"Creepin' *is* mistreating me!" Tamika's mom yells from the kitchen.

"Damn! Is these walls made of paper?" I huff.

"Mama, quit eavesdropping!" yells Tamika.

"Don't fall for any bullshit baby!"

"It ain't bullshit, boo," I say to Tamika, trying to counter her mother's salt. I kiss Tamika's fingers and whisper pleadingly, "I miss you, baby. Come back home to me; you got a nigga sick."

"When you realize that love brings your ass home at night, and not with an STD, that's when I'll think about coming back to you."

Tamika gets up, walks to the front door and opens it. "Goodbye, CJ, I'm expecting company shortly," she says, crushing a nigga'z heart.

Like a niggaz' heart, winter is gone.

Spring is in full bloom. The Bricks are alive, with muhfuckaz out in hordes on every block. The evening sun is closing its eyes, allowing the night to spread its darkness over the city. Me, Eric, Flip, and Snoop are strappin' up, ready to welcome in the warm weather with some fresh warm blood on the streets of Newark.

This shit is long overdue but tonight Kareem and Ghetto are about to get it.

I park down the street from where Kareem and Ghetto are posted up on the hood of Kareem's Turbo Porsche, holdin' the block's attention with the fly new whip; both of them rockin' enough shine to light up the night. A crowd of about two dozen stand around them soaking up jewels about how to become hood supastars.

Them niggaz on stage stunnin'. Right down here in Little Bricks, where I made my name and helped Kareem to make his! I think to myself as my top lip curls down in anger. *Niggaz must think I've gone soft.*

Me and my niggaz fan out, hoodies pulled low and tight as we creep like cat burglars. Nobody notices us until we are in murdering range of our targets. My choppa lets loose first, cutting niggaz up like paper confetti. Eric's Mac II spits its ominous rhythm seconds later, followed by the thunderous clap of Snoop's pistol-grip pump. Flip's twin Nines join the blood bath late. He's the *clean-up* man.

The unexpected ambush clears the block of all on-lookers and bystanders fortunate enough not to get caught up in the deadly assault. Only eight mafuckaz, besides me and my goons, are left out on the block after the initial gunfire.

Three unlucky bystanders are sprawled out on the ground, victims of bad timing. Two others are hit but not down; they stagger like drunks until Snoop blows a hole the size of a dinner plate in one of them and Eric wets the other.

That's five.

The sixth one is a chick named Shanika; a seventeen year old who I can tell recognizes my face. *No witnesses!* I chop shorty down like a paper target.

That leaves Kareem and Ghetto. Well, only Kareem actually, because Ghetto is sprawled crookedly across the hood of his boy's Porsche; half of his head is missing.

Kareem is shot up on the ground crawling. I kick him over onto his side. Blood covers the jacket he's rockin. I look down into his pleading face and smile menacingly.

"I own The Bricks, nigga!" I spit then turn out his mu-hfuckin' lights.

Ca$h

THIRTY-FOUR

TAMIKA

I have the top down on the peach-colored Saleen Mustang that Nard copped for me just a week ago. My hair is tinted gold and worn in crinkles that cascade down to my bare shoulders. The dark Jackie Onassis shades I'm rocking blocks out the glint of the sun.

I pull up behind Nard's truck, where he's standing talking to his brother Man Dog and his man Big Nasty. Nard and Man Dog, who are both about five-foot-ten and medium build, look like midgets next to Big Nasty, who is six foot nine, about three zillion pounds of muscle.

Big Nasty is as black as freshly poured tar with a huge bald head, and a quiet demeanor that makes a bitch's skin crawl. His pit bull, Lil' Nasty, is on a chain leash at his side. So of course I don't dare get out of the car.

"Y'all hol' up," I hear Nard say, then he strides up to my car, leans inside and kisses me.

"Sup, baby?"

"You told me to come by and pick up the money to pay for your birthday party, remember?

"Oh yeah. Damn, I'm slippin' yo. Big Nasty, bring me five stacks—nah make that ten or fifteen."

Big Nasty chains Lil' Nasty to a light pole and dips inside the house. He returns with a shoe bag.

"Fifteen," he announces, handing the bag to Nard then going back over to where Man Dog is posted.

Nard passes the bag inside the car to me.

"Use whatever you need boo," he suggests.

I remove my shades and wrinkle my brow.

"What if someone is watching? You're getting careless Nard," I admonish.

"Check."

"Stay on point, baby."

"I will," he promises as his eyes follow three half-naked little hos that walk by and stop to talk with Man Dog and Big Nasty.

"Is one of them here to see you?" I question Nard after doing the math.

"Nah. You know I don't get down like that. I don't have but two. You and the one you're carrying." He leans over inside the car and affectionately rubs my belly.

Yes, I'm pregnant with Nard's child.

"Don't let me find out Nard," I threaten.

"Yo, Big Nasty! Bring those three hos over here," Nard commands.

Big Nasty leads the girls over to us, followed by Man Dog and two other trap boys of Nards, who have just emerged from inside the house.

Nard addresses the three chicks who are popping gum simultaneously. "Y'all tell my lady who each one of you are and who you came over here to holla at. Don't lie, either, or I'ma make Big Nasty choke y'all out."

A little, freckled face redbone says, "I'm Contoure, Man Dog's girl." Rolling her eyes.

A thick red chick with big titties and hardly no ass says, "My name is Tropicana, and I s'pose to be kickin' it with Quentin's crazy ass," pointing at one of the two trap boys.

The third chick sucks her teeth in protest. She's eye candy, so I guess she feels that she doesn't have to explain shit to me.

"And who might you be, bitch?" I ask.

She fixes her mouth to say something breezy but thinks better of it when Nard reaches for the burner on his waist.

"I'm nobody," she pouts. "Zakee, don't call me no more!" she says to the second trap dude then she storms down the street.

Nard chuckles. "See Tamika, it's all about you."

Talk about whupped!

I got Nard so sprung. It scares me at times. Truth be told though, I'm still in love with CJ. But I might as well accept that it's really over between us. Because even if CJ does get the ho out of him, he'll never accept me back with another man's child. How did that happen? All I can tell you is that Nard must've skeeted right through the contraceptives. Last week, my mouth hit the floor when my GYN told me that I was five weeks pregnant. I've thought about aborting but decided not to. This baby means everything to Nard and it doesn't look like CJ is in a rush to have me back; he hasn't called or come around in a month.

Nard loves me whole-heartedly.

"I want a pretty baby girl who looks just like her mama," he's always telling me. And I don't have to worry about him creeping around, bringing a diseased dick home to me.

Oh wow! Speaking of diseases; my girl Star has HIV! Three weeks ago, she called from LA crying so hard on the phone, I could hardly understand her. When I was finally able to figure out what she was crying about, all I could do was gasp, "Oh—my—god!"

What do you say to your best friend after she tells you such terrible news?

I didn't know what to say. But I was thinking, *see what letting all those different niggaz run up in you led to.* Of course I didn't verbalize the thought.

"Gurl, I'm sorry to hear that. I really don't know what to say and I don't wanna say anything that might upset you more. Just know that I'm here for you," I managed to reply.

One Month Later

I'm waiting on mama to finish applying her make-up; I swear, her old school butt is slower than a turtle. Nard and his mother is outside in the chauffer-driven Escalade stretch-limo, just chillin', waiting for us so we can make our grand entrance at Nard's birthday party which is being held at The Atmosphere. The party has been broadcasted on the radio and the ghetto gossip airwaves for the past month so I expect a packed club to be awaiting our arrival.

Mama comes downstairs looking damn near younger than me. The short, strapless dress that she's rockin' exposes her smooth thighs. "Mommie, you might mess around and catch you a young nigga tonight," I tease.

"I know, right?" she giggles.

Star, who has moved back home from LA, is next to me on the couch, applying gloss to her lips. She winks at mama as if to say, "You're killing 'em, gurl!" mama winks back.

Star is dressed to kill, oops! Bad choice of words, considering that she is infected with a deadly disease. She is glamourous though. The honey mustard jumpsuit that she's wearing fits every contour of her lean but shapely body like it was air-brushed onto her. Her hair is cut into a sharp bob and the bitch is bejeweled something serious. If I wasn't equally as glamorous myself I might be a little jealous.

I'm wearing a soft cotton Chanel dress that leaves one shoulder bare, shows a lot of cleavage and stops mid-thigh. The back is cut out to show the sexy curve of my back. My sharkskin stilettos match perfectly with my purse. Of course, I'm icy. Smelling so delicious is the new Paris Hilton perfume that I wear lightly.

When we get to the club, the parking lot is packed. The whips in the lot tell the story. Newark hustlaz and hustla-seeking chicks are out in abundance. We step through the door and Nard is greeted with a chorus of "Happy birthday nigga!"

Nard gives everybody the middle finger while a smirk is on his thuggishly handsome face.

The club is packed. Bouncers whisk us straight into the glass-enclosed VIP area where Nard's team and their chicks are partying like rock stars. Bitches are on the small dance floor, in VIP, grinding ass on nigga'z dicks like crazy.

"They might as well be fuckin'," mama whispers in my ear.

"I know, right?" I laugh.

Our entourage is seated in a booth. Nard quickly excuses himself to go holla at his brother, Man Dog, and his other mans.

"Hey, gurl! That dress is definitely you!" Tropicana slides in next to me like we're girls.

"Thanks. I like your little outfit, too."

"Oh, this ain't nothing. It's what's underneath it boo," she replies discreetly, rubbing my thigh.

"I'm sure Quentin likes what's underneath it," I say and remove her hand from off my thigh where it had crept too damn close to my coochie.

"I bet you would like it too, slide me your number, we can hook up without our niggaz knowing a thing. I got a tongue so long; it'll reach your uterus."

"Holla at me when you grow a dick," I shut her down.

The club is poppin'. Mad young people are present so I know no one has been carded. The young niggaz are wildin' out, smoking spliffs, pouring bubbly, talking loud over the music, and showering money down on half naked chicks. VIP is a little more laid back, but it's poppin' off in here too as Nard's team flaunt their growing stature.

Mad dudes are trying to push up on Star, especially after the DJ announced her presence. What they don't know is that the pussy they're scheming to get will set that ass on fire.

Hol' up! I think I see my cousin Nee Nee. Yep that's her. Why is this trick bitch at my man's party? My nose flares out at the sight of her.

Bitch, you're lucky I'm looking too cute tonight or I would kick that ass, I think to myself.

Nard's voice interrupts my thoughts.

"Yo, everybody, listen up!" He stands front and center, speaking to the whole VIP room. A bottle of Remy XO in his hand; a blunt in the other. "I wanna make a toast. First, to my Mom Dukes. Ma, thank you for bringing me into the world and for raising a knucklehead into a man. I love you baby!"

Nard takes a gulp of Remy to the head then hits the blunt.

"I love you too, honey. But I'ma whup that ass if you get drunk!" his mama replies, causing us all to laugh.

When the laughter quiets down, Nard continues.

"To my big bruh, Man Dog. Nigga, you paved the way for a beast. To Big Nasty, Quent', my whole team here tonight and even to those we lost along the way, we came from the bottom, now we're headed to the top!

Nard raises the bottle of Remy in salute and his team of about twenty niggaz go wild. He lets them hoot and holla for a few minutes before raising his arms to quiet them down.

"Last but definitely not *least*, to my lady, Tamika. Baby, thanks for understanding the game; for seeing the potential in a young nigga; and for being that quiet force behind my come up." Nard motions for me to join him in the center of VIP. I proudly stride up to his side.

Nard announces to everyone that I am carrying his child. My eyes find mama's, her mouth is hanging open, so is Star's.

Nard goes down onto one knee and motions Man Dog over to us. Man Dog walks up and hands Nard a small velvet box.

On bended knee, Nard takes my left hand into his.

"Tamika, I love you. I promise to always love you and place no one or nothing before you. I swear to you that I'll never desire any other woman but you—if you will marry me?" He releases my hand to open the small velvet box. An engagement ring sparkles from inside.

Faces from outside in the main area of the club are pressed against the glassed encloser. I hear the VIP room take a collective gasp at the glint on the flawless diamond when Nard slides it onto my finger.

I looked over and noticed Nee Nee and wonder, *Why is your damn face pressed against the glass wearing a look of pure envy? Why?*

A jumble of emotions run through my heart at once: *Am I in love with Nard? Or does my heart still belond to CJ?*

I look toward mama for direction, but she just looks tipsy. So I hug Nard and say, "Thank you, baby. Of course I'll marry you."

Nard's mans cheer!

When I get back to the booth, Star says, "I'm happy for you gurl." Tears run down her face. "Nard really loves you; I can see it in his eyes."

Mama and my future mother-in-law hug each other. Mama's eyes meet mine. *Do you love Nard?* Her eyes question me. She knows that in my heart of hearts, I'll always love CJ.

The DJ must be a mind reader because the record that he plays sums up my thoughts *In my heart I'll always be his lady—and in my mind I'll always be his gurl,* bellows from the club's speakers. Tears slide down my face and stain the table.

Later, I'm sitting on Nard's lap, lost in my own thoughts, when Star taps me on the arm and mouths, "Oh shit!"

My eyes follow hers; coming through the VIP door is CJ, Eric, and about thirty more niggaz from Little Bricks. CJ approaches our booth, flanked by Eric, Snoop and Flip. His other mans post up around the room like the Ghetto Marines.

I immediately understand what this is all about: CJ has come to reclaim what he considers "his." His team is with him as a show of power; CJ is letting it be known that he's still *that* nigga.

Oh—my—god! This could get ugly.

I glance at CJ's waist as he approaches. Yep, he's strapped. His whole team is probably strapped as well because CJ has the clout that allows him and his people to enter clubs without having to be searched. Nard is strapped too. I can feel his burner pressing against my hip. But Nard's clout is not as strong as CJ's so he's lucky if two or three of his people were able to bring their burners into the club.

"Mika, I need to holla at you," CJ grits.

"She don't wanna holla," Nard replies for me.

"Let her answer for herself unless you're just itching for some beef you can't handle, fam."

259

"I'm not ya, fam," Nard shoots back.

"CJ," I speak up before something sparks, "I'll come and talk to you in a minute." My eyes beg, *please don't start anything.*

"Make it quick or I'ma make it sad," CJ turns and leads Eric and 'em to the bar area of VIP.

I go to work on Nard pleadingly. Respectful of his male pride. "Baby," I whisper, "ain't no sense in there being a whole lot of drama over nothing."

"Fuck that nigga! I go hard for mine!"

"I know you do baby. But please, just let me run over and talk to him real fast; I'll come right back."

"Hell no! Dat nigaa don't regulate shit! Unless you still wanna be with him."

"No Nard, I am with who I wanna be with. Baby, don't let your ego play you out of pocket; that's how most niggaz blow their rise."

While I'm trying to talk some sense into Nard, mama scoots out of the booth and storms over to where CJ is posted up. I can tell by the roll of her neck that she is giving CJ the business.

I tenderly stroke Nard's face, "Boo, I'm your girl. Just allow me to handle this. Please."

Nard huffs.

"Go handle ya business. If you don't come back I'll know that you'sa fake bitch." Steam is coming from his head.

"I *will* be back," I promise.

Sitting across from CJ in a private booth, arms folded across my chest, out of the corner of my eye I can still see Nard and his peeps.

"Why did you show up here, CJ?"

"I came to reclaim my lady."

"It's too late for that."

"Mika, this *me*. It's never too late for us. You told me to get all of the hos outta me before I stepped back to you again. Well, I handled that. I haven't been with anyone in more than a month;

I wanted to test my own self. I'm ready to play square with you, baby. That's my word."

"What about the jump off you had living with you?" My eyes turn into slits at the thought of her.

"That wasn't about shit, boo. I been kicked her to the curb." CJ says convincingly.

"You should've called before now CJ. I told you I'd come back to you; now it's too late." I show him my engagement ring.

"That ain't shit! Take that mafucka off and give it back to that nigga. I'ma buy you a diamond so big I'll have to hire mafuckaz to lift your arm up for you."

"You so silly." I laugh.

CJ takes my hands into his own. Looking into the windows of my soul he asks, "Do you love that nigga?"

I swear, I see water in CJ's eyes.

I shake my head, "No CJ. I don't love any nigga but you." Tears spill from my soul's windows. "Still, it's too late. I'm pregnant by Nard." I break down in a sob.

CJ's head drops. Our foreheads rest against one another's, and I feel my tears wet his face.

"Don't cry, baby doll. We can fix things," CJ says.

"How?" I utter.

He raises his head and looks me in the eyes.

"Mika, I love you like no other but I can't take you back with another nigga'z seed. You gotta have an abortion or it's a wrap for us."

The line in the sand has been drawn.

"Can I think about it?"

"No. Answer me now," he demands.

I don't have to think it over too long; it's well documented that I love this nigga more than life itself.

"If I have an abortion and come back to you, do you promise not to ever throw it up in my face?"

"Yes, baby, I promise."

"CJ, if you ever cheat on me again I'm going to cut off your dick."

"I won't creep, ma."

"And since I'm aborting my baby for you, you have to give up your half-bred children; no more visiting them or anything." I demand.

"That's already done," he says. "True story."

"CJ, don't let me find out," I warn.

"Trust, boo, it's a wrap. Now, go give that nigga back that bootleg diamond ring and all those other jewels you're rockin'. That crab mafucka can't lace *my* woman."

"CJ, don't make me disrespect him in front of all of his people. Tonight is his birthday. I owe him more respect than that."

"You don't owe that nigga shit! Fuck you sayin'?"

Big Nasty's voice interrupts us as he approaches.

"Nard wants you," he says in monotone.

"Tell him I'll be there in a minute."

Before Big Nasty walks away, he grills CJ.

"The bigger they are, the more the casket cost," CJ grills him back.

Once Big Nasty is gone, I say to CJ, "This is getting crazy. Somebody is going to get killed if you turn this into a battle of foolish pride." You can't tell a street nigga nothing though, when he's drunk on his own reputation.

So, no matter how I try to put it to CJ he insists that I "clown that nigga or clown me! You had no bidness getting wit' dat nigga no way!"

This mafucka knows he's my weakness.

"CJ, I have other things of Nards, besides this ring, to give back to him. I have other jewelry and clothes, at the house, that he bought me, plus I have two hundred thousand dollars of his inside a safe deposit box," I try to explain.

"That ain't shit! We can give that pussy ass nigga all of that shit back *tonight*. No problem. I got that shit just laying around at the house," boast CJ, with the type of arrogance that makes my pussy pulsate.

CJ waves Eric, Flip, Snoop, and Premo over to where we're seated. "Premo, you and Flip go out to Tamika's house and collect every stitch of clothing in her closet, shoes and all. Grab all of her jewels too. And get that punk ass Mustang that's parked in her driveway and bring all of that shit back to the club. Eric, you and Snoop go to that stash house we got out in East Orange and bring me two hundred stacks. Oh Premo, be sure to bring back one of Tamika's mother's gowns out of her closet."

"A'ight, fam, wassup?" asks Premo.

"Just do it, homie," replies CJ.

Eric asks CJ, "You gon' be a'ight, bruh?"

"If not, a lot of mamas gon' bury sons." His crew is still twenty-something deep up in the club after Eric and 'em leave to carry out CJ's order.

CJ instructs me to go back over to Nard and play things on the DL until Eric and 'em return.

"I apologize for staying away so long," I say to Nard. "Mommie, will y'all let me and Nard have a little privacy, please?"

Mama, Nard's mother and Nard's mans slide out of the booth.

"Why is your face all twisted up?" I ask Nard nervously.

"Why you clown a nigga?" I hear pain in his voice.

Remember, I made Nard into the nigga that he's become. So I know how to pull his strings. I wouldn't be the boss bitch that I am if I couldn't. It takes a half hour for me to erase the frown off of Nard's face.

CJ and his team has left the VIP room to go mingle throughout the club, so the tension inside VIP has withered away like a mean, toothless old man. I go and let the club's manager know that I'm ready to present the birthday boy with his cake.

The huge cake is wheeled into VIP on a rolling table. A ten inch replica of a king sitting atop his thrown, made out of candy, adorns the single layer chocolate cake. The Bricks R Urs is scrawled underneath the throne in lemon icing.

We all watch as Nard makes a private wish, inhales then blows out the nineteen candles that surround the king and his throne. Nard's mother and Man Dog give him their presents first. Then I hand him the icy platinum bracelet that I bought for him.

"Happy birthday!" I say and quickly peck lips with him.

The party is poppin' again. I'm faking the festive mood as best I can while cringing inside at what I know will soon go down.

I wish CJ wouldn't make me do it this way. But I have to, or I'll lose CJ. Please Lord, I don't call on you often, but I need you now. Do not let CJ and Nard kill each other up in here tonight.

"What's wrong?" Nard's voice interrupts my prayer. "That nigga ain't on your mind is he?"

"No." I lie through my teeth as we sit alone in the booth holding hands. "Nard, do you love me?"

"To da grave!"

"Don't say that." I shiver. "Don't ever love *me* or anyone more than you love yourself. Don't allow no one, including me, to stop your rise." I swallow back a few tears. I do care for him.

"Say what's on your mind Tamika."

"Okay. Baby, always remember that most people and most things are replaceable. If you truly love me, promise me that you'll remember that." A single tear drips down from my eye.

Nard looks at me quizzically.

"Promise me Nard," I plead.

"A'ight."

Nard leads me to the dance floor, where we slow grind through three songs. I wonder whether or not CJ is looking. *Is he somewhere up in Nee Nee's face? What is Nard thinking about?* He hasn't uttered a word since we started dancing.

The DJ is playing one of Sparkle's—umm…Kayundra's songs. The song is nice, but none of her records are on the charts anymore. The bitch was hot for a minute then she got back on the pipe and fell off the map.

I'm thinking that maybe I should just tell Nard now that I'm going back to CJ. He'll be hurt, but at least it won't catch him by surprise when Eric and 'em return with all of the things Nard has bought me including the Mustang. Perhaps Nard will choose to leave, to avoid the drama; I hope as we return to our booth.

Hours later, the DJ spins a Lil Wayne song and the VIP room gets crunk. Nard has his arm around my shoulder. I lean so that I can whisper to Nard. "Nard, I need to tell you some—"

I stop in mid-sentence. CJ, Eric, Snoop, Premo, Flip, and the other Little Bricks niggaz has just returned!

Nard hops up in a hurry when they approach our booth. His hand goes to his waist, Eric and 'em reach for their waists too.

CJ says to Nard, "It don't have to go there, my dude. I just came to claim mine."

By now, Man Dog, Big Nasty, Quentine, and a few others on Nard's team are pushing through the bodies that surround the booth.

"I just came for my woman. Trust, y'all niggaz don't wanna take it there," says CJ, unflinchingly.

"She ain't your woman no more," retorts Nard with confidence.

"Ask her. Maddafact, c'mere, Mika," CJ opens his arms. I stand up and walk right into them.

"Oh, it's like dat?" Nard stares at me with pure hate.

"Tell that nigga what the deal is, boo," prods CJ.

"Nard, I'm sorry. I'm going back to CJ."

"What's up with my seed you're carrying?" Nard growls.

I don't reply.

"Answer the nigga," says CJ.

"I'm not going to have the baby," I mutter, with my head down.

"Mika, look that nigga in the face and tell him. Fuck you scared of?"

"Nothing," I say. Then I repeat, "I'm not going to have the baby," looking into Nard's eyes. They are two balls of fire.

"Go get the bags," CJ instructs his mans without speaking to anyone in particular.

"They right by the door," says Eric, and he nods to several other members of the clique who are posted outside the VIP room door. They drag a dozen or so plastic bags over to the booth and dump all of the contents out on the floor in one big pile. One huge mound of designer clothes, shoes, and bags. A small pile of jewelry.

"I bought some of that stuff before I met Nard," I whisper to CJ, holding on to his arm.

"Fuck dat! I'ma buy you all brand new shit."

"CJ, a lot of that stuff you bought."

"I said fuck it! Didn't I?"

I nod meekly.

CJ sneers at Nard, "Nigga, that's all the shit you bought her; she's givin' it all back so she don't owe you shit."

Eric dumps the $200,000.00 at Nard's feet.

"And the whip you bought her is outside in the lot," intones Flip, tossing the keys to the Mustang on top of the pile of money.

No music is playing; mad faces are pressed against the glass, peering in at us.

"Take off that ring; the necklace and the earrings too!" barks CJ.

"Baby, mama bought me—"

"I said *take it off,* Mika," he repeats sternly.

I do as he instructed, dropping the jewelry onto the growing pile of things.

"Did he buy that dress you rockin' and the shoes?"

I nod reluctantly.

"Take that shit off, too!"

Eric hands me a robe that belongs to mama then he and four others make a circle around me. I slither out of the dress after kicking off the stilettos. Now I'm barefoot in only a robe and thong.

Nard and his people stare at me with pure hate.

"I'm sorry," I mouth but I don't think he catches it.

"Now, she don't owe you shit so don't let me catch you in her space!" CJ threatens Nard. "Mika, tell this wannabe *me* ass nigga goodbye."

"Goodbye, Nard," I utter softly yet my words seem to boom out in the silence.

"Whud up, Nard? Tell me something dawg." That's Big Nasty speaking, bouncing from foot to foot.

"Fuck you want to be up? We can spark this bitch up; all you gotta do is get stupid, and I'll get *stupider*!" Eric exclaims, pulling out a burner.

"Bitch, you're the cause of all this!" Nard's mother says to me.

Mama butts in on my behalf, "Don't call my daughter out of her name!" Taking off her earrings.

Nard steps between both of our mothers.

"Everybody, just chill! We ain't gotta kill each other. Tamika chose who she wants. Now, they can get the fuck on, and I can finish enjoying my birthday party. DJ! Pump the music back up!"

Whew!

On the way out of the club I pass by Nee Nee. She looks at me and shakes her head in disgust.

"Fuck you! You're just a hater; you would sell your soul to be me, bitch!" I clown her.

"Ya ugly ass mama a bitch!" she replies, and it takes two burly bouncers to hold Mama off that ass.

I take one last look over my shoulder as our entourage leaves the club, Nard is staring death threats at me.

Ca$h

THIRTY-FIVE

SPARKLE

I've tried so very hard to leave drugs alone and get my life back together after hitting rock bottom again. Forget the singing career; it's hell just to make it through a normal day without all the pressures of being in the spotlight. Nobody around me seem to understand that the success or the music didn't mean a thing to me once I lost the person whom I wanted to share it with most. Without Raheem in my life, what good is a hit song?

When Raheem broke up with me, I lost my will to write; my desire to perform in concert. Raheem was my inspiration; the wind beneath my wings. Without him in my life, when I sit down and attempt to write a song, my pen holds no magic, only ink. In the studio, my voice could still carry a note but it was lifeless. So I didn't want to record. All I wanted to do was hide out from the world and smoke crack. I loathed myself.

I skipped one studio session after the next. I ignored every obligation associated with my record label. Preston and mama would try their best to track me down but I was hid out well. My only company was crack.

After my third arrest for attempting to purchase crack, Preston released me from my contract with Platinum. Now he's suing me for everything under the sun. Mama went to court and got a judge to put her in charge of my finances because obviously I was not responsible enough to look out for my own welfare. I had pawned everything of value that I owned to crack dealers.

I fell so low. I ended up serving sixty days in jail for shoplifting. That's when I began to bounce back. The president of Universal Records visited me in jail and promised to help me, if I was willing to help myself.

I had sunk as low as I could go so I made him that promise. He made all of my pending drug charges disappear. After my jail stint, I checked into a world-renowned drug rehab center and got myself together. After rehab, I went straight into the studio to work on a new album on the Universal label.

Now I'm in New York backstage at the Apollo, preparing to perform the first single from my new CD, which is titled "Back Where I Belong."

I'm alone inside my plush dressing room. I'm thinking of all that I've gone through in my life; the years before this singing thing, and the years since: My relationship with my mother which remains strained at best. My lost relationship with Raheem.

I love and miss him so much!

It's very hard to go on without him.

I flip through a photo album full of wonderful moments with my honey. My tears stain the pages as I weep. The makeup technician has to hurry and work wonders when I'm called to the stage.

My performance is aired live on BET.

"Hello, New York!" I say into the mic "It's so good to be joined by you tonight. I guess most of you know my story; it's not a pretty one, but—"

"That's okay, girl, we still love you!" A voice from the audience shouts.

I hear other shouts of endearment joined by loud applause.

"I'm supposed to sing a new song of mine tonight New York!" I say. But I don't want to sing that song."

"Sing *anything* Sparkle!" someone yells enthusiastically.

"Oh, I'm going to sing *something.* How many of you ladies out there know what it is to lose the man you love?"

Women scream and raise their arms in the air.

"I imagine a few of you fellas know what it is to love and lose and can't get back," I continue.

"That's right, ma!"

"I'll take you, Sparkle!"

"Sing for us, baby!"

I smile to the crowd. "I'm going to try to sing a classic of the late great Ms. Minnie Riperton. Some of y'all might be too young to recognize this song but that's okay. See, I got to sing it to Raheem, the one I love but lost because it's his favorite song. So, if you're somewhere listening Raheem—baby this is for you."

I begin acapella, since the band is caught off guard.

I stumbled on this photograph—it kinda made me laugh—it took me way back—back down memory lane.

The band joins in.

...why did I have to find this photograph—I thought I had forgot the past—now I'm slippin' fast—back down memory lane.

The audience rears its approval as if they collectively feel my pain. I sing on from the depths of my very soul, tears flowing with each line.

...the way you hold me— no one could tell me—that love would dieeeee!!!!!

I collapse to my knees in heartache and can't even finish the song.

I don't remember how I got off stage; all I know is that I'm again alone inside my dressing room, dripping tears on the photos in my album.

"Raheem, baby, I need you," I sob.

Ca$h

THIRTY-SIX

RAHEEM

I'm at the crib working on my manuscript. I'm taking some time off from managing the night clubs; in fact, I'm thinking about selling my interest in them. That type of business seems to be in conflict with the principles of Islam, causing me to fall off my Deen.

My cell phone rings.

"Hello?"

"Hey, you busy?" ask LaKeesha.

"Not really sis. Sup?" I shut off my laptop.

"Turn to BET, your girl is about to perform."

"A'ight." I hang up and go turn on the television in the den.

By the time I turn the television back off, tears wet my shirt. I'm not soft, by no means, but that shit touched me. The pain in Kayundra's voice, and the way that she broke down on stage, in front of the whole world, has me hurting for her. Real talk.

LaKeesha calls back to ask if I saw it.

"Yeah," I say solemnly.

"Rah, she really misses you. That was so sad, I cried."

"Yeah, I know."

"You should give her another chance."

"I don't know, LaKeesha. It would be hard to trust her," I say.

"You could try."

"Maybe," I allow.

It's not easy to see the woman you love hurting so bad. I stay up all night thinking about my Sparkle. When I do fall asleep at the break of dawn, I'm awakened by the ringing of my cell phone.

"Hello?"

"Rah, do you have the radio on?" It's LaKeesha once again. Why is she calling me so early?

"No, wassup?"

"Well, I'm in Jersey but I'm sure it's on all the stations in ATL too," she says, as if I don't know where she is.

"LaKeesha, what are you talking about?"

"I better let you hear it for yourself bruh. Turn on the radio."

I sat my cell phone down and lean over to turn on the radio on my nightstand just in time to hear; *"Once again, I have some sad news from the music industry. R&B singer Sparkle is dead."*

My head drops and the tears began to fall.

THIRTY-SEVEN

TAMIKA

I'm at the house chillin' with Mama and Danyelle. We're at the kitchen table drinking spiked smoothies and discussing Sparkle's death.

"I still can't believe she slashed her wrists," says Danyelle.

"That's a shame. But you could tell that she was in so much pain over breaking up with Raheem; the way she sobbed about it on BET last night. I feel so bad for her mother," mama adds.

"It is sad," I agree.

"I know Raheem is probably tore up," guesses mama.

"Mmmhmm." That's Danyelle.

"Isn't it kinda *his* fault?" I wonder out loud.

"Don't say that!" Mama admonishes me.

A loud crash interrupts our conversation. I hear footsteps run through the house. *Police raid!* I think.

Danyelle screams. I do too when I see Nard and Big Nasty walk into the kitchen, burners pointed at us.

"Everybody shut the fuck up! Scream again and I'm bodying all three of y'all bitches!" Nard barks, smiling at me menacingly.

"Please, Nard!" I cry. My plea is met with a slap across the face. I fall out of the chair and onto the floor.

"Don't cry now, bitch!"

Mama tries to help me up but Big Nasty kicks her so violently in the side, she collapses to the floor next to me.

"Move again, you die!"

My head is still spinning from the vicious slap; my ears are ringing, too. My heart is trying to jump right out of my chest. I know we're in trouble. Mama is holding her side, moaning in pain while Danyelle is frightened stiff.

Man Dog, Quentin, and Zakee come into the kitchen, all three of them holding assault rifles. *Lord, have mercy!*

"We checked the whole house; that bitch nigga ain't here," says Man Dog.

"Quent, go watch the front of the house," Nard instructs his young goon.

"Tamika, you know you gotta pay for clowning a nigga and for killin' my seed, right?" Nard cocks one in the chamber.

"I haven't gotten the abortion yet." I lie for my life and probably mama's and Danyelle as well.

"What? You lyin', fake ass bitch!" Nard grits but I can tell that he's unsure so I play on instinct.

"Oh, so now I'm a bitch, huh? What happened to the respect you used to have for me?" A scrowl etches across Nard's face. *I fucked up!*

He points the gun at my head. "Don't talk to me 'bout respect, bitch! Not after the way you disrespected me for that nigga. I oughta shoot you in ya mafuckin' mouth, just for uttering the word *respect*!"

"Nod that punk ho!" says Man Dog.

"Nard, baby, please let me explain," I cry, and when he doesn't shut me up, I lie for all I'm worth. "CJ made me clown you baby. He was going to kill me if I didn't. Nard he's crazy. I swear I don't want CJ. I love you. Take me away from here, please."

"So, you saying you chose that nigga over me that night because he was gon' kill you?"

"Yes, baby. I swear," I sob.

"She's not lying, Nard," co-signs mama. *If we can just play our way out of this, I'ma make sure that CJ buries each one of these niggaz.*

"Why haven't you called?" Nard asks.

"I was waiting for CJ to go out of town then I was gonna pack my things and come back to you baby."

"What do you know or care about a *baby*?" Nard snaps. "I'ma ask you only one time and you bet' not lie. Did you kill my seed?" His eyes study my face for the slightest sign of dishonesty.

276

"No, I haven't gotten no abortion. I swear on everything that I love." Nard's face goes expressionless.

He says to Man Dog, "Bruh, see how easily lying comes to this bitch."

"I'm not lying, baby."

"Is your daughter lying?" he questions mama.

"No," mama lies to protect me.

"Danyelle, keep it one hunnid—is she lying?"

"I don't know Nard; we haven't talked about it," she answers truthfully. Then she pleads to Man Dog who has always been cool with her. "Man Dog, I know y'all can find a better way to handle this."

Man Dog ignores her.

"You and yo mama some lyin', deceitful-ass hos!" Nard angrily intones. "I've been watching you every day since the party. I saw CJ take you to the abortion clinic Tamika. Fuck you gon' lie? You lie 'bout dat, yo ass lyin' 'bout everything else." He points the gun down at me.

"Wait!" I scream.

"Tell the truth, bitch! I already know it; if you keep denying that you killed my seed, I'ma do all three of y'all!"

I break down and admit that I've had the abortion since he already knows.

"I don't know why I lied about it," I conclude in tears.

"You lied because you're fake. Yo mama is fake too. Plus you a dumb ass ho! Ain't nobody been following yo ass. See how I played ya stupid ass into admitting the truth? Big Nasty, go get Lil' Nasty out the car."

"Nard, what are you about to do?" I ask in a quivering voice. "Baby, remember it was *me* who saw potential in you and helped you to come up. Whatever disrespect I've shown toward you, don't all of the good things I've done balance it out?"

"Man Dog, shoot that bitch in the face if she says another word, fam!"

I'm on mute.

When Big Nasty returns with his pit, a feeling of terror envelopes me. I wanna plead for mercy but I don't want Man Dog to shoot me.

They take us into the living room, where Quentin is watching the street from the window.

"Get naked, ho!" Nard commands me. "Since you a dog bitch, I'ma let a dog fuck you. You get naked too!" he says to mama.

"No! Go ahead and kill me," says mama bravely.

"Man Dog, go in the kitchen and bring me a knife."

Man Dog heads to the kitchen, returning with a butcher knife. He hands it to Nard with a sinister smile.

"I'ma cutt off your daughter's fingers one at a time until you get naked, bitch," Nard snarls at Mama.

"Wait!" mama cries and gets undressed.

I close my eyes and turn my head away when Big Nasty forces mama onto her hands and knees and positions Lil' Nasty behind her.

I can hear mama crying. Danyelle too.

"Peep that shit yo! Lil' Nasty tearing that old beat up pussy up!" Nard laughs sadistically.

"He can fuck all night. Gave him some crushed up Viagra," I hear Big Nasty say.

They all laugh.

Nard allows the dog to violate Mama for what seems like a half hour. *I'm so sorry, Mama,* I cry silently.

"Lil' Nasty you want some slow neck? Tamika is good at that shit."

Hell no! This nigga gon' just have to kill me.

"Bitch, give Lil' Nasty some neck!" Nard says, grabbing me by the hair and slinging me down. I wonder where CJ's at.

"No, Nard. I'm not doing it!"

Boc! Boc! Boc!

Mama's head explodes from the sudden eruption of Nard's gun. Danyelle and I both scream. Big Nasty shoots Danyelle right between the eyes! I cower up against the base of my entertainment center.

"Please don't Nard!"

"I don't have no pity for you bitch!" he snarls over the dog's barking. He rips open his shirt and I see that he has gotten a tat' across his chest. It reads: LOYALTY OR DEATH.

The bullet rips through my face as I try to scurry up onto my feet. A second shot rips into my side. I stumble over an ottoman as a third shot brings darkness…

To Be Continued…
Thugs Cry 2
Available Now!

Coming Soon From Lock Down Publications

RESTRAINING ORDER

By **CA$H & COFFEE**

GANGSTA CITY **II**

By **Teddy Duke**

A DANGEROUS LOVE **VII**

By **J Peach**

BLOOD OF A BOSS **III**

By **Askari**

THE KING CARTEL **III**

By **Frank Gresham**

NEVER TRUST A RATCHET BITCH

SILVER PLATTER HOE **III**

By **Reds Johnson**

THESE NIGGAS AIN'T LOYAL **III**

By **Nikki Tee**

BROOKLYN ON LOCK **III**

By **Sonovia Alexander**

THE STREETS BLEED MURDER **II**

By **Jerry Jackson**

CONFESSIONS OF A DOPEMAN'S DAUGHTER **II**

By **Rasstrina**

WHAT ABOUT US **II**

NEVER LOVE AGAIN

By **Kim Kaye**

A GANGSTER'S REVENGE

Thugs Cry

By **Aryanna**

Available Now

LOVE KNOWS NO BOUNDARIES **I II & III**

By **Coffee**

SILVER PLATTER HOE **I & II**

HONEY DIPP **I & II**

CLOSED LEGS DON'T GET FED **I & II**

A BITCH NAMED KARMA

By **Reds Johnson**

A DANGEROUS LOVE **I, II, III, IV, V, VI**

By **J Peach**

CUM FOR ME

An **LDP Erotica Collaboration**

THE KING CARTEL **I & II**

By **Frank Gresham**

BLOOD OF A BOSS **I & II**

By **Askari**

THE DEVIL WEARS TIMBS

BURY ME A G **I II & III**

By **Tranay Adams**

THESE NIGGAS AIN'T LOYAL **I & II**

By **Nikki Tee**

THE STREETS BLEED MURDER

By **Jerry Jackson**

DIRTY LICKS

Ca$h

By **Peter Mack**

THE ULTIMATE BETRAYAL

By **Phoenix**

BROOKLYN ON LOCK

By **Sonovia Alexander**

SLEEPING IN HEAVEN, WAKING IN HELL **I, II & III**

By **Forever Redd**

THE DEVIL WEARS TIMBS **I, II & III**

By **Tranay Adams**

DON'T FU#K WITH MY HEART **I & II**

By **Linnea**

BOSS'N UP **I & II**

By **Royal Nicole**

LOYALTY IS BLIND

By **Kenneth Chisholm**

BOOKS BY LDP'S CEO, CA$H

TRUST NO MAN

TRUST NO MAN 2

TRUST NO MAN 3

BONDED BY BLOOD

SHORTY GOT A THUG

A DIRTY SOUTH LOVE

THUGS CRY

THUGS CRY 2

TRUST NO BITCH

TRUST NO BITCH 2

TRUST NO BITCH 3

TIL MY CASKET DROPS

Coming Soon

TRUST NO BITCH (KIAM EYEZ' STORY)

THUGS CRY 3

BONDED BY BLOOD 2

RESTRANING ORDER

Ca$h

In-depth interview of Cash by Nene Capri (author of The Pussy Trap)

NC: Tell us, who is Cash the Author?

CASH: I'm like all people. I'm complex and multi-dimensional. I'm a father, a brother and a friend. As an individual, I'm a man who is conscious of my origin and my own god power. I have, above all, a fierce determination to atone for the harm I've caused before I elevated to this level of understanding.

NC: Where did you get the inspiration to write your books?

CASH: I've always been a writer at heart but the streets had me in its unrelenting clutches for a long time. On lock, I've been able to put my energy into writing and my inspiration comes from within. I did not want my crime to be the final chapter to my story.

NC: What sets your books apart from other books in the same genre?

CASH: My books will never border on make-believe. Of course there are some other authors who rock the same way. There's nothing new in the hoods that we write about, I just strive to tell my story more profoundly and with a strong message.

NC: As an author, what is your writing process? How long does it take you from start to finish?

CASH: Well, for me it all begins with a message that I want to send. Then a title comes to mind. I can't proceed without either. And my pen won't flow fluidly if I don't have an ending in mind. It's like life, if you don't know where you're headed how can you know which direction to take? Now, a book can take a few months to write or a few years. It depends on how the story grows on me. Once I become the characters, it's no stopping my pen.

NC: As an African American author do you see your work as being relatable to a general public?

CASH: I consider the general public to mean mainstream. There are morals in my stories that anyone from any walk of life can relate to because loyalty, deception, love, betrayal, greed, heart break and perseverance is not limited to urban life. However, mainstream might not like the grittiness with which I write. But that doesn't fade me, I write for my people, which is anyone who feels me. I'll never sugarcoat my pen for sales. I tell it like it is so nobody is left disillusioned. You wanna thug it? Well, thugs cry too. Your gun ain't the only one that will pop off. And prison ain't no picnic. They get you in here and snatch away your life. A few get away but they got scars on their souls. That's how I write it because that's the truth.

NC: Urban fiction has a lot of negative press as being a "so-called" bad influence on the youth and perpetuating black stereotypes. What are your thoughts on that?

CASH: People always criticize what they don't like or agree with. Street-lit ain't nothing but telling it like it is. You can't hide the truth and you shouldn't try. In the hood people look out of their front doors and see the very thing that street-lit portrays. And anybody that follows the genre but is not caught up in that life is not going to go change their stripes because of a book. They read it for entertainment and to learn about a life they want no part of. Speaking for myself only, there's the glitz and glitter in my books along with the consequences. I put it all out there and let the reader see that it's not a fairytale. When a book misrepresents the game, and portrays it to be all peaches and cream, that's when I trash it.

NC: What do you want the readers to get out of your work?

CASH: I want readers to always gain a better understanding of the hood through my stories. I want them to understand that all misbehavior is not a flaw in the person's soul. Circumstances matter too. Don't try to tell me that if your plate runs over with food, what you won't do for a meal is the same as what you wouldn't do if you were starving. On the other hand, there's always consequences for your actions, and there's really no right way to do a wrong thing.

NC: What type of literature does Cash read?

CASH: I'm an insatiable reader. I read everything but science fiction and fantasy. If it can't happen, I'm not wasting my time.

NC: What can we expect from you in the future?

CASH: In the future, you can expect more classics from my pen, and a few collaborations with other authors. But writing is a platform for me to ultimately be in a position to positively affect the lives of my urban brethren, so look for me to do that. That is my duty.

NC: There is a lot of passion in you and it is refreshing. Are there any thoughts you would like to leave us with?

CASH: Yes, indeed. As a man who's been in prison for 22 years I urge you not to forget about your family members and friends on lock. Brothers and sisters behind bars have nothing if they don't have family support. Peace.

NC: Thank you Cash for taking the time to do this interview with us, we wish you continued success.